A housemaster in a Girls' School

Paula Mann

Published by Paula Mann, 2023.

A Housemaster in a Girls' School

Charles and Sarah work as Housemaster and Matron in a Girls
boarding school where spanking is required
By Paula Mann
Published by Mann Publishing
https://www.spankingbooks.com/

Copyright © 2023 Paula Mann

Table of Contents

A Housemaster in a Girls School - Autumn Term

Charles is the new housemaster and spanks the older girls and teachers

By Paula Mann

❦

I ntroduction
In this books, you will find a middle-aged man and his wife who both love to spank naughty girls and their teachers on their bare bottoms with a hand, leather slipper and cane. There's also lesbian spanking and orgasms and if this is not your thing don't read any further.

Charles Nicholas is appointed as a housemaster of Saint Samantha's school for girls in Norfolk, England. He is the only male teacher in the girls' school and is asked to be the disciplinarian for the senior girls and the teachers where necessary. His wife Sarah gets the job of the Matron at the school and they have a lovely apartment to live in on the school grounds. In the first few months in his new position, he has to spank a few of the naughty girls but also the headmistress and her friend. His wife Sarah also enjoys spanking the girls and other things as well, so they are delightfully happy in the new school. This story is set in 1970 when spanking in private schools was common practice.

Chapter 1 - His first spanking at the school

"What a beautiful sight," Charles said to his wife as he stared out the window at the girls playing hockey. "All those nubile young ladies running around in their short dresses and long legs, displaying their green sports knickers when they fall over, which they seem to do rather often."

"Oh stop it, Charles, you know it only gets you worked up," Sarah Nicholson said as she sat behind her desk in the sanatorium.

"And there's Miss Pritchard, dressed similarly, I'm sure that dress is too short, you should measure it sometime."

"My mandate is to measure the skirts of the students when they look too short, not the teachers," Sarah said.

"Maybe I should speak to the headmistress then, see if we can change that mandate."

"Stop it, Charles, you'll get me excited soon and I have to get on with this report." Charles Nicholson laughed as he left his wife to her work in the sanatorium and walked back to his office. He was a tall man and very distinguished, with prematurely grey hair and a military walk that he had developed as a young man. He had never been in the army, but he liked to look as if he had. He always took a slight detour past the shower block when he made the trip from the sanatorium to his office, sometimes he was lucky and saw one or other of the senior girls running back to the dormitories wearing just a towel, and occasionally not even that. Then he would call out one of the school rules: "No running in the corridors," and watch with delight as the young lady had to slow to a fast walk to get to the dorms.

Charles Nicholas decided that he was the luckiest teacher in the world and cast his mind back to his interview with the headmistress of Saint Samantha's school for girls. He remembered it well because it was his fiftieth birthday. He had travelled from London by train with his wife and stayed over in the little village of Trumpton about ten miles from Norwich. His interview for the job of Housemaster in an all-girls boarding school had surprised him, but he needed a job and they had approached him with the offer of an interview. "It's a formality of course," Miss Brandon, the Headmistress, had said on the phone. "You have been recommended and have excellent references."

It seemed that she was right. The interview was really just a tour of the school, a look at the very nice accommodation that came with the job, and a discussion about the duties of being a Housemaster in a girls' boarding school. Charles had saved the most important question until the end of the interview. "Why are you appointing a male into a senior position in a girls' school?" he asked the Headmistress. "Isn't that rather unusual?"

"That's a very good question and I was asked the same by the board of governors." Miss Brandon replied. "We are a modern school and the year is 1970, not 1920. We have to embrace the fact that there are men in the world, much as we like to deny it here at Saint Sam's. I think one good male teacher will reinforce that. Now if only I could find a good Matron we will be complete for the start of the Autumn term."

"I think I might be able to help you with that Miss Brandon," Charles said.

"Oh, please call me Amelia," she said. "And how can you help with the appointment of a new matron?"

"My wife was the Matron at the school where I taught in South Africa. That's where I met and married her twenty years ago. She was well thought of and also comes with excellent references."

"Oh really?" Amelia seemed excited. "Is she with you?"

"Oh yes, she's in the hotel in the village."

"Fantastic, I will send a car for her, then you can both join me for lunch."

"I will call her if you like, can I use your phone?"

An hour later after another tour of the grounds including the sanatorium this time, the three of them were sitting in the headmistress's private dining room eating an excellent meal of roast beef with all the trimmings. "That was an excellent meal headmistress," Sarah Nicholson said.

"Oh please, call me Amelia, I can see we will be close friends in no time at all."

Charles wondered about that, he was used to the head of a school, being a little aloof. At his last school in Johannesburg, the new head was almost unapproachable, and he really only had a decent conversation with him just before he was fired. He had been accused of spanking the senior girls in the mixed school for not doing their homework. He had worked at that school for twenty years and had often spanked the girls, but when the new head took over he made it very clear that spanking the girls was not appropriate, even if they were over eighteen.

This didn't stop Charles of course and eventually, he was asked to leave, which he agreed to do, but only with a glowing reference. Sarah Nicholson was well aware of her husband's penchant for spanking naughty senior girls and liked to watch as well. She would even participate sometimes, and the intercourse with her husband afterwards was always excellent.

Even with glowing references, he knew that the word would spread in South Africa so he came back to his home country,

England, and applied to an agency in London, which is where he heard about the vacancy in Norfolk.

After a very nice lunch, Amelia Brandon asked when they would like to move into the housemaster's accommodation.

Charles said. "We don't have a house in London, we are staying at a hotel at the moment."

"Oh good Lord," Amelia said. "We don't want to waste all that money, the accommodation is available here right now, but you will not need to start until the beginning of September. If you move in now it will give you a chance to settle in and for us to get to know each other.

Charles looked at his wife and then said. "Well, that will be very nice. We will send for our belongings and move in tomorrow if that works for you?"

"Capital," she said. "I will get a few of the senior girls to give it a good clean this evening before light's out.

Back in the Village Hotel, Sarah Nicholson said to her husband that they seemed to have landed the best job in the country. "Did you see Amelia pat the girl's bottoms when they came in to clear the table or to serve the meal?"

"Yes I did," Charles replied. "Just a love tap, but I wonder what would be said if I did the same thing?"

"Let me try it first," Sarah said. "I'll let you know how it goes."

After lunch in the headmistress's office, Miss Pritchard, the sport's mistress, was chatting to Amelia Brandon, "What do you think Amelia?"

"I like Charles Nicholson, he seems the sort of man any woman would bend over backwards for."

"And bend over forwards?" Jasmine Pritchard said and giggled.

"Don't be a silly girl, he's old enough to be your father."

"So maybe I need a father figure in my life, someone to call Daddy." They both laughed now.

Jasmine Pritchard was the sports mistress at the school and at twenty-four, she was the youngest member of the staff. Jasmin and the headmistress had formed a close relationship almost as soon as Jasmine joined the staff the previous year, and they share a great deal, even Ameilia's bed from time to time. Of course, that was a closely guarded secret that every member of staff knew about.

"Did you pat the girls' bottoms as they served you lunch?" Jasmine asked

"Oh yes," Amelia replied. "And they both noticed, and smiled, I'm sure they will not get in the way of the fun we have here, maybe even join in, who knows."

That was all a few months ago now and Charles and Sarah had settled in as the housemaster and matron of St Samantha's school for girls. The school had one hundred girls with ages ranging from thirteen to eighteen. There were sixty borders and forty day girls in three houses named after famous British writers. Agatha Christie, Mary Shelley and Jane Austen. Charles was the housemaster of Christie house and their accommodation was on the ground floor of the largest of the houses. The three floors above accommodate thirty girls in dormitories and smaller rooms for the senior girls with the house captain in her own small apartment on the top floor. The housemaster's flat on the ground floor had two bedrooms, a large lounge that doubled as the housemaster's office, a dining room and a kitchen, with a bathroom next to the bedrooms and an additional guest toilet off the entrance hall. The secluded garden at the back was maintained by the ground staff. Although they had their own kitchen Sarah and Charles usually ate in the main dining room with the girls and some of the live-in teachers.

That was all a few months ago and Charles and Sarah had settled in now. Charles was sitting in his office when there was a knock at the door. "Come," he said loudly. He had a deep voice and Mary

Becker shivered as she opened the door and walked in. "Hello Mary," Charles said. "What can I do for you?"

"I'm sorry to bother you, Sir," Mary started uncertainly, "But Miss Brandon said I should report to you, she said that it was a matter for the housemaster, not the headmistress."

"Oh dear Mary, what have you been up to?"

"I was smoking behind the bicycle sheds Sir,"

"Oh Mary, you know that you're not allowed to smoke on the school grounds," Charles said. "What punishment did Miss Brandon suggest?"

"She said I needed a spanking Sir, but I understand if you don't want to give me a spanking, being as you're a man."

"Well, I think we had better do as the headmistress says, don't you?"

"I could just say that you spanked me, Sir."

"Yes you could, and then we would have to punish you for lying as well wouldn't we?"

"I suppose so, Sir."

"Who spanked you the last time you were caught smoking?"

"Oh, that was Miss Brandon, but she said that now I'm eighteen you should be spanking me."

"So this is a regular thing is it?"

"Oh no Sir, I don't usually get caught," Mary said and then instantly regretted it.

"So now I have to spank you for being caught smoking and for all the other times that you were not caught. That will definitely be a hard spanking, won't it?"

"Oh Sir, please."

Until now Charles had not spanked any of the girls at the school. His wife Sarah had caught two girls skiving instead of doing homework and she had given them a sharp whack with a ruler on their knickers, but that was it. They had discussed this and decided not to push their luck until they were settled in the school. Being sent by the headmistress to Charles to be spanked, however, was not an opportunity to be missed.

Charles pushed his chair away from his desk and called Mary Becker over to him. He directed her to stand on his right-hand side and proceed to tell her about the horrors of smoking. As he was doing that he had his hand on her bare leg and he was rubbing under her skirt, getting higher and higher until he had his hand on her bottom. "Over you go then," he said as he guided her across his lap. She fell forward and had her hands on the floor, but her feet came up as she bent her legs. When Charles flipped up her skirt, Mary gasped. She was used to her boyfriend seeing her knickers and a lot more but this was an old man who had his hand on her bottom.

"When Miss Brandon spanks you for smoking, does she let you keep your knickers on Mary?"

"Oh no Sir," she said. "She always spanks on the bare bottom."

"In that case," he said as he took the elastic of Mary's green knickers and started to pull them down."

"Oh no Sir," Mary said. "Please don't take my knickers down."

Charles stopped with her knickers half down so that he could see her lovely bottom. "Well, if Miss Brandon spanks you on your bare bottom and she sent you to me for a spanking, then I am sure she would expect me to do the same, don't you think?"

"I suppose so Sir," Mary said

"So lift up then so that I can push your knickers to the floor."

Mary had to put her feet back on the floor to lift her bottom and that made it easy for Charles to finish the disrobing. As Mary's bottom came into view, Charles marvelled at the beautiful sight he had before him. Mary had a large bottom and with her knickers right off her legs fell apart a little and her cheeks separated delightfully. He would have liked to take his time as he had done with the girls in his previous school, but he decided that it would be better to just spank Mary and see if there are any repercussions before he explored his deeper desires.

He started to spank Mary's bottom hard and fast. Over and over again his hand came down on the unprotected bottom and Mary was crying almost immediately. "Oh please Sir, not so hard," she said. "It was only one ciggy, Sir."

Charles didn't spank her for too long, he didn't want to leave any bruises, just a red glow. When he had finished he patted her bottom. "Up you get Mary and pull up your knickers. I think you had better go and tell the headmistress that I have just spanked you."

"Yes Sir," Mary said as she left the housemaster's office.

Chapter 2 - Charles spanks the teachers as well

Mary came back about thirty minutes later. "I'm sorry to bother you again but Miss Brandon has asked if you could pop into her office when you get a chance."

"Of course, Mary, I will go now. Thank you." As Charles walked towards the headmistress's office he wondered if he had gone too far. Maybe he should have left her knickers on or maybe spanked her over her skirt. He realised that there was no point in worrying about it, he would either talk his way out of it or lose his job.

Charles walked into the reception area and said hello to Miss Brandon's secretary. "Ah, there you are," she said. "Miss Brandon said to go straight in." He was surprised to see Miss Pritchard with Miss Brandon. He had heard the rumours of course, but he had never seen them together in her office.

A little earlier the headmistress and the sports mistress had been colluding to see if Charles Nicholas was a spanker. "He looks like someone who would take the senior girls over his knee and spank them," Amelia said.

"I hope so, Amelia," Jasmine said. "I need a good spanking."

"We are talking about the girls to start with," Amelia said. "We don't want to frighten him off. I had a word with the headmaster at his old school and he didn't say anything bad about Charles Nicholson, but I got the impression that there was something. I have no idea what."

"Maybe he spanked one of the girls there?" Jasmine said. "Maybe he spanked them all."

"Maybe," Amelia said looking at her watch. "But now is the time to find out. Mary Becker usually has her lunchtime cigarette just about now, you go to the bike sheds and catch her and then send her to me. I will send her to her housemaster to be spanked and we will see what he does."

"Okay," Jasmine said giggling.

Now Charles walked into Miss Brandon's office expecting the worst. "Hello Charles, Jasmine was just leaving."

"Oh, was I?" she said and then left and winked at Charles on the way out.

"Do sit down Charles," Amelia said. "You look so important standing up and towering over me, I almost feel the need to curtsey."

"I'm sorry, Amelia."

"Oh don't be, Charles. You have created quite an impact in the few weeks you have been here and everybody looks up to you."

"Well thank you," Charles said, but what he was thinking was that he was going to keep his job, which would be nice.

"Oh, yes," Amelia said. "Mary Becker came and told me you spanked her on her bare bottom."

"Ah yes, well I can explain..." Charles didn't finish his sentence.

"No need to explain, I'm delighted that you have done that. Now the other girls will respect you more, and the teachers perhaps."

"The teachers?" Charles asked.

"Oh yes, they need discipline, and I'm hoping I can persuade you to attend to that as well. I know it's an extra chore and is not exactly on your job description, but I just can't manage it sometimes."

"Oh, I see. You want me to spank the younger teachers as well?"

"Not just the younger ones, the older ones need just as much discipline. Of course, you do not need to spank your wife if that's awkward.

"On the contrary, I spank her sometimes when she's naughty and if I'm spanking the teachers from time to time she will expect to be spanked."

Miss Brendon patted her legs. "Good that's settled then. You will be responsible for the spanking discipline of the older girls and the teachers when necessary. I will spread the word. Now, there is just one last thing. I have to be sure you know what you're doing so I want you to spank me."

Charles looked up, "Pardon?"

"I want you to spank me. I have to make sure you're a competent spanker and I know of no other way than for you to spank me as if I was a naughty senior girl at the school. And I want a proper spanking, not just pretend. Imagine I had done something really bad." The headmistress thought for a while. "Imagine that I had been caught with a boy, or another girl, in the gym after lights-out. How would you spank me then?"

"Well," Charles had to think quickly, "It would depend upon what you were doing with this fictitious boy or girl?"

"Maybe I had my bra off and he, or she, was playing with my boobs," Amelia said.

Charles had to get rid of the picture and concentrate on what the headmistress was saying. "Well, why not go out and I will take your chair and when you come back in you will be an eighteen-year-old girl and I will be... well, I will be me."

"Okay," Amelia said as she opened the door and walked out, closing it behind her. The school secretary looked up and wondered what was going on. When she saw Amelia knocking at her own door she shook her head and went back to her books.

"Come," Charles called and Amelia walked into her own office as if she was a schoolgirl. "Ah Amelia, I'm very disappointed with you."

"I'm sorry Sir," Amelia said.

"Sorry for what? Sorry, you were with that boy from the village after lights-out, or sorry you were caught."

Amelia smiled. "A bit of both I guess."

"So you think this is funny girl, do you?"

"No Sir, sorry Sir."

"You will be my girl," Charles said. "And this is not the first time is it?"

Amelia had to think for a second. "No Sir."

"And last time it was with that sports mistress Jasmine Pritchard, wasn't it?"

Amelia did not like where this was going, she had nearly been caught in the gym with Jasmine but she thought she had gotten away with it. Apparently, she had not. "How did you know about that Sir?" Amelia asked.

"I know everything Amelia and you will be getting six with the cane to make sure you don't do it again."

"The cane?" Amelia said. "I have never had the cane before."

"Well there's a cane in this office I'm sure, and I think you deserve it, don't you?"

"I guess," Amelia said, but she was no longer playacting.

"You're a senior person at this school and you should be setting an example for the others."

Amelia plonked herself down on the chair in front of the desk. "I'm sorry Sir, I knew it was wrong but I just couldn't help it, Jasmine is so... so lovely. And her boobs, have you seen them? They are perfect."

"No I haven't, Amelia," Charles said. "But there's a time and a place for everything, and in the gym, after lights-out is not the time nor the place."

"I know, I'm so sorry Sir." Amelia was crying now.

"There's no need for tears, Amelia. But there is a need for punishment, so I want you to get up and bring the cane to me. The adult cane, not the junior one."

How does he know I have two canes? Amelia thought as she stood up and went to the big grandfather clock in the far corner of the room. The clock hasn't worked for years, but the front opens and it's a good place to hide a couple of canes, amongst other things. Bringing back the cane she handed it to Charles and then started to bend over the desk.

"It's not that simple, I'm afraid Amelia. I never cane a bottom unless I have warmed it first with a spanking, and I would never spank you over that thick skirt." Amelia was wearing a formal black pencil skirt and a white blouse, under the blouse her large boobs were pushing at the material. Underneath she was wearing a matching white lace bra and knickers with hold-up stockings and black shoes.

"Oh, I could pull it up, Sir," Amelia said hopefully.

"You could take it off," Charles said and she knew she was beaten. Undoing the clip and the zip on the side of the skirt she let it fall to the floor and stepped out of it. Bending to pick it up Charles admired her stockings and knickers and especially the bare skin in between them. Pushing back the chair he was sitting on, he patted his lap. "Over you go then and I'll give you your spanking."

Amelia was not used to this at all. She had played spanking games with Jasmine but she was usually the spanker and they were usually just foreplay. This was different. This was punishment and she hadn't been punished like this since her father had caught her with that boy when she was eighteen, and he really laid into her. Charles didn't waste any time. Just like spanking Mary an hour or so earlier, he decided not to explore his innermost desires and just get down to the spanking. He raised his hand and lowered it with some speed onto Amelia's thin knickers. He did this a few times and Amelia knew she was in for a real spanking, just like her Dad gave her all those years ago.

He took the elastic of her knickers and started to lower them. "Not on my bare bottom Daddy, please." Amelia said and she didn't realise that she had called Charles, "Daddy".

"Spankings are always on your bare bottom, you know that Amelia," Charles said as he finished lowering her knickers, leaving them crumpled at her ankles.

"I know Daddy, but it hurts so much."

Charles continued to spank his boss for another five minutes and she was sobbing when he had finished. "Stand up now Amelia, just six strokes with the cane and it will all be over."

"Oh no Daddy, please," Amelia said but she was standing up at the same time and she positioned herself on the other side of her desk. Charles suspected that it was there that Amelia caned her students, so she associated that position with spanking. Her blouse had fallen over her bottom so when Charles stood up and walked around his desk, he flicked up her blouse to bare her bottom completely.

Aiming at her bottom he said, "Just spread your legs a little Amelia so that you're balanced. If you stand up or fall over we will have to start again."

"Yes Sir," Amelia said and did as she was told, holding onto the far side of the desk to make sure she didn't stand up.

Charles didn't want to do too much damage or even leave marks that would bruise, so he quickly gave Amelia six strokes with a short swing and a little flick of the wrist. Even though it wasn't a hard caning, Amelia was sobbing when Charles put down the cane and sat back on the guest chair, leaving the chair behind the desk for Amilia to take up her rightful position.

Pulling up her knickers, she didn't bother with her skirt as she gingerly sat at her desk and wiped her eyes. "Well," she said. "It seems that you're well versed in the art of spanking bottoms and using the cane as well. You're perfect for the job of disciplinarian for the older girls and the teachers. And," Amelia took a breath. "You have acquainted yourself with the goings-on at the school at the same time. Well done Charles. I deserved that caning, whether you know it or not, and if I deserve another, I will let you know."

Charles nodded and realised that he had been dismissed, so he stood up. As he was leaving, Amelia said. "Thank you, Charles." and he left without saying another word.

Later that evening he told Sarah all about his spanking and caning encounters, and the fact that he had been offered the position of disciplinarian.

"Did you take it?" Sarah said and they both laughed.

Chapter 3 - Charles spanks another schoolgirl.

The word spread very quickly and by the following morning, the staff room was buzzing with the news that Charles would be taking on the spanking duties of the older girls. The news was well-received.

"Thank God for that," Daisy Andrews said. Daisy was older than the others at forty-eight, and she was a small lady who always dressed as if she was attending the Queen's garden party, without the hat, of course. "Some of those girls are taller than I am and I know they need a spanking but I'm afraid that they would turn around and spank me instead. They need a good strong hand. Well done Charles."

"Thank you Daisy," Charles said. "And if you ever need a hand with discipline, I'm your man." Daisy giggled as she walked away with the coffee she had just made.

"What about if I want to spank a girl, can I still do that?" It was Jasmine who was talking now. "If they are naughty in the gym, a sharp smack on their bottom and they are well behaved again. Can I still do that?"

"Of course you can Jasmine," Amelia had walked into the staff room and was answering Jasmine's question. "This is just for more serious naughtiness. If you just don't want to spank or cane the girl, send her to Charles." Amelia was rubbing her bottom absentmindedly, "I can assure you that he is very good at it. He tells me that he has also started a punishment book where he will record all the punishments and what they were for. We should have been

19

doing that before of course, but now it will happen." Amelia clapped her hands. "Nine o'clock, everybody to their classrooms."

On their way out Jasmine stopped Charles, "Can I have a word with you, Charles?"

"Of course," Charles said.

"No, not here. Can I come to your flat this evening?"

"By all means," Charles said. "Seven o'clock?"

"Yes, right," she said and then she was gone.

Apart from being the housemaster, Charles was also the senior maths teacher and at nine he had the upper sixth for applied mathematics. He loved this course and some of the girls were very bright, some, not so much. All of the girls have to be over sixteen to do the A Level course and most of the girls in the upper sixth were over eighteen. All were doing their A Levels before looking for a position at University. The girls that were not so bright would have already left at the end of the fifth form with a few O levels. Charles enjoyed this two-hour lesson with his favourite subject and the cleverest girls.

As he walked into the classroom, the girls went silent. It usually takes a little while before they settle, but not today. It was Nicole Asher who raised the question that everybody wanted to ask. "Is it true, Sir, that you're now the disciplinarian for the school?"

"Yes, it is, well, for the older girls anyway," Charles said.

"Like us, Sir?" Nicole said.

"Yes, like you, Nicole," Charles said. "Now, can we get on with the class, please?"

Nicole continued. "And will you be spanking us on the bare bottom, like you did with Mary Becker?"

"If you continue asking silly questions, Nicole, you will find out first-hand before the end of the lesson."

"But we need to know, Sir," Nicole said, but she quickly realised that she had gone too far when Charles helped her up from her front-row desk and, as he sat down on her desk, pulled her over his knee. Lifting up her skirt, he pulled down her green school knickers and spanked her six times on her bare bottom. Then he pulled her up and placed her back at her desk with her knickers around her ankles. "Leave them there," he said as she tried to pull them up.

"Anybody else want to know about spanking?" he asked the horrified class.

Nicole had to sit on her bare bottom through the full two-hour lesson, with her knickers around her ankles, and only when the class was dismissed was she allowed to pull them up. On the way out Nicole went up to Mr Nicholson and said, "Sorry, Sir."

Charles just looked up and smiled at her, "Dinner detention tonight, Nicole." He said and then she nodded and left. Nicole Asher was one of the girls that Charles had identified as one that he would like to spank. She was a small girl with short blond hair and a small bottom. He had watched her running around the playing field playing hockey and he had also seen her wrapped in a towel after her shower, so he was delighted that she was one of the girls who was outspoken. He thought that he might get an opportunity to spank her lovely little bottom again in the future, and he was right.

Chapter 4 - Jasmine asks for a spanking

The word spread around the school very quickly and each class he taught for the rest of the day were perfectly well-behaved.

That evening Charles and Sarah had just finished their evening meal when there was a knock at the door. "Come in," Charles shouted from the dining room. The Nicholsons had gotten into the habit of getting one or other of the girls to bring their dinner at six-thirty on a Monday, rather than eating in the main dining room. It was a chance for them to chat and they would usually invite one or other of the senior girls in the house to join them. This was to get to know the girls in a more personal way. So when Charles heard the knock he presumed that it was Nicole Asher, who was doing dinner detention, and therefore it was her job to serve their food and clear away afterwards. It turned out that It was Jasmine at the door.

"Hello Jasmine," Charles said. "You're a little early, just go through to the lounge and I will be with you in a second." Then he turned to Sarah. "Can you finish here and see that Nicole clears away properly while I see what Jasmine wants?"

"Of course darling," Sarah said.

Walking into the lounge he saw Jasmine standing at the ornate fireplace looking at the clock on the mantelpiece which startled her as it chimed for seven o'clock. "That's my favourite clock," Charles said as he came up behind her. "Made in Germany before the war, has three different chimes, that's the Westminster chime we're listening to at the moment."

"Yes, it's lovely," Jasmine couldn't think of anything else to say.

23

"Let's sit down Jasmine, you sit over there," Charles said pointing to a comfortable chair next to the settee. He considered sitting behind his large dark oak desk in the bay window, but discarded that idea and sat on the settee. "What can I do for you?"

"Thank you for seeing me, Mr Nicholson." Jasmine started.

"Oh please, call me Charles, after all, we are colleagues," Charles said.

"Yes of course," Jasmine said. "Only my Daddy taught me to be respectful and you're like my Daddy in many ways. Anyway... um Charles, Mr Nicholson, Amelia told me about her spanking and the fact that you knew what we had done in the gym after lights-out. I have no idea how you know but you did."

"Actually, I didn't know," Charles said. "Well, I had heard the rumours about you and the headmistress, these things get around, and I'm not someone who would interfere in someone's personal life. But I was making it up when she wanted to test my spanking skills, and only then did I realise that I had stumbled upon something that did actually happen."

"Oh, I see," Jasmine said. "Amelia thought it was common knowledge."

"Not at all, and it never will be if you're careful. You're both adults and what happens behind closed doors is none of my business, nor anybody else's for that matter. But." Charles took a breath. "If that did actually happen in the gym after lights out, that was very naughty, and that's what I eventually caned the headmistress for."

"Well, I guess that's why I'm here," Jasmine said. "You're right, it was naughty and we will never do it again, but it was my fault as much as Amelia's and I think I deserve the same punishment."

"You want me to spank you?"

"Yes please Sir," Jasmine said as she looked down at her fingers clasped on her lap.

"And cane you?" Jasmine nodded.

"Well you certainly deserve to be punished, I will call Sarah in and she can observe to make sure nothing inappropriate happens."

"Oh," Jasmine was shocked. "Is that necessary?"

"Well, I'm a man and you're a very attractive lady. It's better to have a witness."

"Yes Sir, I guess."

Charles got up and walked back to the dining room where Nicole had just finished clearing away the dishes. "Good girl," Sarah said and spanked Nicole's bottom to send her on her way.

When they were on their own, Charles said to Sarah, "I have Jasmine next door and I'm about to spank and cane her, I thought you might like to watch?"

Sarah rubbed her hands together, "Oh yes please." she said in response.

Back in the lounge, Charles said. "Matron has agreed to be the witness, so we better get started." Charles moved a dining chair that had been placed in the lounge specifically for this purpose, into the centre of the room and sat down. Jasmine was wearing her usual outfit of a short (actually too short) sports skirt and a short-sleeve shirt with an open collar, long socks and plimsolls. "Right, Jasmine, over my knee for a spanking to warm your bottom before you get six strokes with the cane."

"Yes, Sir," she said as she stood up and bent over Charles's lap. Sarah was sitting to the right of Charles so she had a very good view and she was smiling as Charles lifted up Jasmine's skirt and lowered her knickers. Jasmine had a lovely bottom to spank. Not small, but not too large, she had a long bottom which you will often see in athletes with a lovely long crack in between. She was very fit and that showed on her bottom and upper legs which Charles was determined to spank as well sometime. That was not today's task however, today it was just a spanking on her bottom, but he knew that she would need a harder spanking than Amelia. Once

Jasmine's bottom was bare Charles started spanking hard and fast. He had told Jasmine that he was just warming her bottom for the cane but he wanted her to be crying before he had finished. Jasmine was surprised by the spanking. Her father had spanked her hard, just like Charles, but she hadn't been spanked like that for many years, and she started to cry with the memory of her father as well as the pain of the spanking.

Sarah was enjoying the spectacle and she was pressing her hand between her legs over her dress to enhance the excitement she felt, watching Jasmine's lovely bottom being spanked.

Eventually, Charles decided that was enough and he lifted Jasmine and then turned her so that she was sitting on his lap. Patting her bare bottom he said, "There you go Jasmine, just cry it out." Charles loved to hear girls cry when he spanked them, it added to the pleasure he felt from actually spanking their bottoms. Five minutes later, when the crying had finished, Charles patted her bottom and then said, "Just the cane to go now Jasmine."

"Oh no," Jasmine said. "I had forgotten about the cane. Do you have to, Sir?" Charles nodded and helped Jasmine up. "But Sir, I'm already very sore, and the cane will hurt terribly."

"What would you have felt if you had been caught in the gym and then reported?" How would you have felt if the governors had heard about it and Amelia lost her job?"

"I know Sir, I'm sorry," Jasmine said as she bent over and placed her hands on the floor. Charles was impressed that she could get that low and was focused on her bottom as Sarah passed him the cane and kissed him on his cheek.

"Six strokes then Jasmine," Charles said and then landed all six in quick succession not giving Jasmine any time to complain. When he finished Jasmine stood up sharply and held her bottom pushing her pussy forward in the action of rubbing away the pain. Tears were running down her face, spoiling her makeup and she was sobbing.

"Come with me Jasmine," Sarah said, "And I will put some cream on that for you." Without giving Jasmine a chance to argue, Sarah took Jasmine's arm and led her to the bathroom. Holding onto the bath Jasmine stuck out her bottom to make it easy for Sarah to apply some soothing cream. "Charles can be a bit hard with that cane sometimes," she said "I know that from experience."

"Does he spank you as well Matron?"

"Only when I'm naughty, Jasmine. That's why he is perfect for this job."

"He spanks hard like my Daddy used to. I miss him since he passed away. I was thinking that maybe I could come to Mr Nicholson to ask for advice sometimes, just like I used to do with Daddy."

"I'm sure he would be delighted, we don't have any children of our own, and our students have always been our children. And the young teachers as well of course."

Jasmine was making soft moaning noises now. "That cream is lovely on my bottom Matron," she said as her legs eased apart. Sarah was not slow to catch on and she rubbed the cream between Jasmine's long cheeks and over her anus getting a much louder moan. As she was doing this Charles called. "I have to go and do my rounds now Sarah." which broke the spell a little and so she said. "I have to do the same, Jasmine. You better run along now, and don't be so naughty in the future."

"Yes, Matron," Jasmine said as she felt a sharp smack on her sore bottom.

Later that evening Charles was lying in bed with his wife recounting the day. He told her about spanking Nicole's small bottom and hitting him gently on his arm, she said. "Oh you rascal, I wanted to spank that one first, is she as cute as she looks on the sports field?"

"More," Charles said and he got another hit on his arm. "Do that one more time and you will be over my knee for a spanking," he said as she hit him again. "Right," he said and pulled her body over his lap in bed without any complaint from her. Lifting her long nightie and lowering her knickers, Charles spanked his wife gently to start and then built up a little pressure until her legs drifted apart. Charles knew the signs so he stopped spanking her and ran his hand up her inner thigh until he found her pussy. She was very wet. "You enjoyed watching me spank Jasmine didn't you?"

"Yes Sir," she said moaning at the same time.

"And was she wet when you took her to the bathroom and applied the cream?"

"Oh yes sir, wet and ready."

"Next time maybe," Charles said as he easily lifted his wife up and placed her on her back then climbed on top of her and made love.

Chapter 5 - Jasmine and Amelia are Spanked again

There were no more spankings for the rest of that week. The whole school had heard about Charles spanking both Nicole and Mary on their bare bottoms and that seemed to have changed the atmosphere. Everybody seemed to be well behaved.

"Don't worry," Amelia said at the staff meeting on Friday, "They will be back to their naughty selves next week, and she was right.

The weekend at St Samantha's was always festive. There were sports on a Saturday morning during the term, hockey, rounders, or cross country depending on the term. St Samantha's also had a good tennis team because Jasmine was an Olympic tennis player and all the girls and staff were encouraged to be there to support the girl's team. Charles and Sarah always enjoyed watching the girls running around in their sports skirts, showing off their knickers whenever there was a fall. After the sports, Matron was often called into the showers to fix a sprain or graze, so that was an additional attraction for Sarah on a Saturday.

After they all went to the school church on Sunday the boarders were encouraged to run around the grounds or walk off to the village as long as they were back by dinner at six. Charles had invited both Jasmine and Amelia to join him and Sarah for dinner on Sunday evening. The school dinner on Sunday was not a big meal as the girls would usually have spent their pocket money on sweets or cakes from the village. There was always enough food but it would be sandwiches or something similar, so Sarah decided that she would prepare bobotie, a dish that she had learnt while she was in South Africa.

After dinner, they all went to the lounge to chat, and the subject of the conversation turned to spanking. "I don't think you have had anybody to spank since Monday, Charles," Amelia said.

"No, If your intention was to create perfect children in your school, the plan has worked," Charles said and they all laughed.

"Never mind," Jasmine responded, "If you're looking for someone to spank Charles, you will always find Mary Becker behind the bike sheds after lunch." Amelia glared at her friend, realising what she had said.

"Oh really?" Charles was thoughtful for a while. "So let me get this clear. You know that Mary likes to have a cigarette behind the bike sheds after lunch, so when you needed someone to get a spanking to test me, you chose Mary Becker. Is that right?"

Amelia was quick to respond. "Of course not Charles."

"So you just happened to walk past the bike sheds on Monday did you, Jasmine?"

"Yes of course," Jasmine said.

"Where were you going?" Charles asked. "The bike sheds are at the end of the grounds, there's nowhere to go after that."

"Oh, I was just walking," Amelia said.

"No, you weren't, Jasmine. You knew she would be there smoking, and you wanted to catch her."

"Why would I do that?"

"Because you wanted to find someone to send to me to see if I would spank them properly."

Amelia was silent for a while, and then Jasmine was about to say something, and Amelia held her back. "Okay," she said. "We had to know if you would spank her. I had thought about offering you the discipline job before but I wasn't sure if you were able to spank a girl, so I had to know."

"And were both of you in on this?" Charles asked looking at Jasmine, but she just nodded guiltily.

"So you tricked me, you could have just asked, you know."

"I know," Amelia said. "But we thought a practical example would be better."

"Well, I think another practical example is called for, what do you think Matron?"

Sarah leaned forward in her chair, "Yes definitely." she said.

"Right," Charles said as he turned the two dining chairs that were in the lounge to face each other in the centre of the room.

"What are you doing?" Amelia asked, well aware of what Charles was planning.

"I think you know what I'm doing Amelia, you two are going to have your bottoms spanked. I will be spanking you, and Matron will be spanking Jasmine, on your bare bottoms."

"Oh please, you can't do that," Amelia said.

"I think you will find that I can. I'm the school disciplinarian for the senior girls and the teachers. That's the position that you put on the notice board. So I decide upon the punishments, and if you don't want me to enter these punishments into the punishment book I suggest that you get your bottoms bared and present yourselves for a spanking."

Jasmine looked at her friend and Amelia nodded. Then they both stood up and started to pull up their skirts. "Oh no, I think we will have those skirts right off, and the knickers as well, we don't want them to get in the way do we?"

"Charles, please," Amelia said, but Charles just looked at her so she pulled her dress over her head as Jasmine undid the button on her skirt and let it drop to the floor. Amelia was now standing in her bra and knickers feeling very silly, but Charles said, "I can always ask Matron to get the hairbrush that's on her dressing table, I understand that hurts quite a bit."

"No," Amelia said and pushed her knickers down cupping her hands over her hairy mound. Jasmine did the same and Sarah said. "Hands on your head girls, you have nothing we haven't seen before. There were some groans but the two teachers did as they were told.

Charles was organising again and he pointed to one of the dining chairs. "You sit there Matron, and I will sit opposite you. Come on girls, you know how to do this. Jasmine, you're over Matron's lap."

Once Amelia and Jasmine had placed themselves over the appropriate laps, Charles nodded to his wife and they started to spank the bare bottoms together. They had done this many times in their last school but after that incident, they didn't think they would have the chance to do it again. It seems they were wrong.

The spanking lasted a while but after twenty spanks they both stopped and rubbed the bottom over their lap. Then the spanking started again. There was complaining during the spanking and moans of pleasure during the rubbing. Charles had seen this before and recognised that all four of the participants were getting turned on by the spanking.

Sarah was really enjoying spanking Jasmine's long thin bottom. This was the first teacher's bottom she had had a chance to spank since joining the school although she never missed an opportunity to spank the schoolgirls to send them on their way when she got a chance. Now she was enjoying a proper spanking and she made up her mind not to leave it so long next time.

After about ten minutes spanking and rubbing, Charles indicated to Sarah that it was time for the next stage of their practised performance, and they rubbed the bottoms a little bit longer this time, slipping their fingers between the cheeks and down towards their pussies. The moans of pleasure were obvious from both Amelia and Jasmine and both pairs of legs opened to encourage easy access. "Right girls, time to swap over," Charles said with groans from the participants, but they swapped anyway so that Sarah had Amelia's larger, older bottom to spank and Charles had Jasmine's.

The spanking started again but it didn't last that long this time. After twenty spanks both the girls receiving their spanking had spread their legs so the rubbing of the bottoms progressed to massaging of their hairy pussies. Had either of them been told this would happen after Sunday dinner with the Nicholsons, they would not have believed it, but here they were approaching their orgasms together after a hard spanking. Jasmine came first, loudly as usual and the sound of Jasmine coming pushed Amelia close to the edge. Charles still had his hand between Jasmine's legs but he was watching Amilia pumping her bottom up and down to reach her conclusion, and then she orgasmed, clamping her legs together like a vice with Sarah's fingers holding her clitoris. Eventually, Amelia relaxed and stood up quickly. "We must go," she said irrationally. "Come on Jasmine."

"You will do nothing of the sort, Amelia," Charles said. "I know you're embarrassed but we have experienced something beautiful and you will not leave until you're relaxed and properly dressed. What do you think the girls would say if they saw you leaving my apartment looking like that?"

"Yes, sorry Charles, you're right. I'm just so embarrassed."

"No need to be, come here and I will hug you." Amelia hesitated and then walked over to Charles and sat on his lap for a hug. Jasmine did the same when Sarah opened her arms and they were both crying.

Later, after Sarah had made them all a cup of coffee, Amelia said. "Thank you Charles for not letting me go when I wanted to. It would have been too awkward at school tomorrow. I have had a wonderful evening, but I think it's time to go now."

Charles and Sarah walked them both to the door and there were hugs and kisses all around before they left. "Phew," Charles said. "That was intense."

"Intense?" Sarah said. "I'm flooding, quick, take me to bed."

Chapter 6 - Katie is Spanked with a slipper

Monday morning and the school gets back to normal. The girls had had a weekend off and now they are hyped up and have to be controlled. The first thing on Monday is the school assembly, where they sing the school song and teachers watch for girls singing the rude words instead of the right words. If they are not careful the rude words are the only thing that can be heard, especially on the last day of term. "In God, we trust" becomes "Bob feels our bust." and "In church and steeple" becomes "and squeezed our nipples." I expect you can work out the rest.

After the school assembly, they all went back to their classes. Charles had a free period and was in the staff room marking when Amelia came in. "I thought you might be here Charles, I just wanted to have a word about last night."

"What about last night, it was lovely wasn't it?"

"Yes, it was, Charles," Amelia said. "But I'm not sure it should happen again. I have a position of authority to maintain here and if the other teachers knew what we got up to last night. Well, you can imagine what would happen."

"The others would want to join in?"

"Be serious Charles," Amelia said. "I'm worried, that's all."

"Okay, I get it. Nothing is lost yet, The rest of the staff don't know anything and they will not find out from me. There are rumours about you and Jasmine but it's just speculation at the moment."

"Oh God, Charles, what am I going to do?"

"Do you want my advice?"

"Yes I do," Amelia said as she sat down on one of the old overstuffed chairs in the staff room.

"It would not be good if the rumours about you and Jasmine were more than rumours, so you need to be more careful. You shouldn't be seen with her all the time. Spread your time with the other teachers. Spend time with me and then they will think you like men and not women."

"I'm not a Lesbian." Amelia was indignant.

"Okay, so don't act like one. The rumours will soon die down if you're careful." Charles said.

"Okay, I will do that," Amelia said as she lent forward and kissed Charles on his lips. "I'm not a lesbian and I will prove that to you one day."

Charles laughed, "You will probably get another spanking for that."

Amelia giggled, "Oh, I hope so," she said as she left the staff room.

Charles was laughing to himself when Daisy Andrews raised her head from the settee with its back to the position Charles was sitting in. "I wasn't eavesdropping Charles, I was just dozing, I didn't hear a thing, and if I did, it would stay a secret," Daisy said as she got up and walked to the door. Only, next time you want a bottom to spank, don't forget me." She laughed as she left the staff room.

It was later that same day that Katie Owen was knocking at Charles's office door. The lounge in his apartment is used as his office during the day and their front door is always open, so students could walk in and knock on the lounge door without any announcement. "Come," Charles called in his usual gruff voice. "Hello Katie, what can I do for you?" Katie Owen was a bright young lady with a nice figure and curly blond hair. She was very chatty but quick to anger which got her into trouble sometimes. Strangely Katie was carrying a leather slipper and a note. She didn't say anything, just gave the note to Charles. Opening it he read the following:

Dear Mr Nicholson.

Katie was very rude to me this afternoon and I think she deserves to be punished. Now that you're the school disciplinarian, I thought you might like to keep a leather slipper that has been in my family for a while, and apply it to Katie's bottom twelve times for her rudeness."

Yours

Daisy Andrews

Charles looked up. "Did you read this letter?" he asked.

"Oh no, Sir," Katie said.

"Did you read this letter, Katie?" Charles repeated.

Katie looked down at her feet. "I may have glanced at it, Sir," she said.

"So you know what it said. Were you rude to Miss Andrews?"

"I may have been." Katie was evasive. "But she started it."

"What do you mean?"

"Miss Andrews said that I probably didn't study for the test, and that's why I got low marks."

"And did you study for the test?"

"I did a little, Sir," Katie said. "But I got low marks because she's strict with her marking."

"Yes, she is, but she is strict with everybody isn't she?"

"I guess."

"And where do you come in class?"

"I was in the lower half," Katie said.

"Where exactly Katie."

"I came last, Sir."

"I see. And what did you say to her that made her angry? And be honest now, I will ask her."

"I called her a silly old bat."

Charles thought for a while. "I expect you know what's going to happen, don't you?"

"You're going to spank me with that silly old slipper?" Charles nodded. "But please Sir, not on my bare bottom."

"What have you heard about me, Katie?"

"That you always spank the girls on their bare bottoms."

"Right, so what do you think you should do next?" Katie didn't say a word, she just reached under her school skirt and pulled down her knickers, putting them on Charles's desk, then she bent over the desk and looked up at Charles who was only a few inches away now. He nodded and got up, picking up the slipper on the way.

"Twelve with this nice leather slipper is going to sting Katie. You had better hold onto the other side of the desk, if you stand up we will start all over again, so hold tight."

"Yes Sir," Katie said as she felt the sting of the first stroke. Charles had used a leather belt in his last school but the slipper was nicer. He thought that he must remember to thank Daisy for it, maybe give her a few with the slipper as well. The second spank landed centrally on Katie's bottom just like the first but she didn't say a word. By the time Charles had landed ten spanks on Katie's bare bottom, he thought he must be losing his touch. Katie was stoically keeping quiet. He put extra effort into his eleventh stroke with the slipper and Katie let out a grunt, on the twelfth stroke she let it all go and burst into tears.

"Up you get Katie," Charles said, and as soon as she stood up she turned and hugged Charles while she cried herself out, all the while Charles was gently patting her sore bottom.

"Thank you Sir," Katie said. "My father does that when he spanks me, it helps. I know I was wrong to call Miss Andrews names."

"Well, you pull up your knickers and go and apologise to Miss Andrews, and tell her I say thank you for the slipper, and I will give it to her if she needs it."

"Yes Sir, I will." with that Katie was gone.

Chapter 7 - Nicole is spanked by Matron

"You are not going to send me to Mr Nicholson are you, Matron?" Nicole Asher said. "He will probably cane me."

"Don't you think you deserve it?" Sarah said to the distraught girl. "Stealing is not only against the school rules, but it's also against the law."

"But I just wanted to see what it tasted like. I have never had communion wine before, I've not been confirmed."

"I don't think I have a choice, Nicole," Sarah said. "I'll have to give you a full physical first of course so that I can determine if the wine has any physical effects on you, and then it will be off to your housemaster for the cane I expect."

"Oh please Matron, can't you spank me instead?" Mary said that you spanked her.

Sarah recalled that she had spanked Mary Becker a month or so ago. She had enjoyed spanking Mary's big bottom but it was Nicole's bottom that she really wanted to have a go at. She pretended to be thinking. "Okay, Nicole. I'll spank you myself after the physical as long as you give me the names of the other two girls that were with you stealing from the vestry."

"Oh I can't do that, they are my friends," Nicole said.

"Well I think that probably answers the question, doesn't it? That will be Katie and Lucy then."

"Oh no, please don't tell them I told you. They will hate me forever."

39

"Don't be a silly girl, I'll tell them that you were all seen coming out of the vestry. Now let's take those clothes off for your physical."

Nicole is a short girl at just five-foot-one with short blond hair and a cute figure. Sarah Nicholson had wanted to spank Nicole for a while and while her husband had spanked her for being rude to Daisy Andrews, Sarah had not had an opportunity until now. Watching Nicole take off her school skirt and white blouse was a pleasure. Nicole was wearing a sports bra but she didn't really need it. Her small boobs didn't shift at all when the bra was removed, then she looked at Matron with a question in her eyes. "Yes, everything Nicole, and then lie on the examination table."

Nicole slipped off her knickers and climbed onto the table and lay there nervously as Matron pulled on her medical gloves. "Don't worry Nicole, nothing bad is going to happen, well, not until you're spanked anyway."

Matron listened to Nicole's chest with the stethoscope and massaged her small breasts, paying particular attention to her erect nipples. After checking her eyes, mouth and throat, she turned her attention to Nicole's pussy. She was almost hairless between her legs and Matron noted that she was no longer a virgin, which was not unusual in school where they played a lot of sports and that did not mean that she was necessarily sexually active, however, in Nicole's case she thought she probably was with her friends Katie and Lucy. "Roll over Nicole, I just need to take your temperature."

"In my bottom Matron?"

"Yes, of course, it's the most accurate," Sarah said, and the most fun, she thought.

Rolling over, Nicole was told to get on her knees and pull her cheeks apart, then Sarah used some vaseline to lubricate her finger and then Nicole's anus. Pushing her finger inside Nicole she heard a groan as she felt around a little and then replaced her finger with the thermometer. Nicole hadn't complained when she had Matron's finger inside her bottom and Sarah stored that information for later. With her bottom in the air and her head on the table Nicole felt very exposed and then she thought she heard a click, but the music in the clinic was so loud she couldn't be sure.

Eventually, she felt the thermometer being pulled from her bottom and Matron said that her temperature was normal. "I think you can stay in that position for your spanking Nicole."

"Yes Matron," Nicole said and she felt even more exposed waiting for her spanking, then she felt the flat side of a wooden spoon landing on her bottom.

"You are a very naughty girl stealing from the church," Matron said as she continued to spank Nicole with the large wooden spoon she had brought from South Africa. Each cheek was spanked in turn but in that position with her bottom in the air, Nicole's cheeks were wide apart as well so they also felt the sting of the spoon. The tops of Nicole's Legs were not left out either and Sarah enjoyed watching Nicole's anus pull in and out in anticipation of the spanks. Sarah knew that this spanking mustn't be too hard or the other two girls would not fall into her trap, so she stopped spanking Nicole. "There you are, Nicole. Not so bad really, was it?"

"No Matron," Nicole said.

As she was about to get up Sarah said. "Would you like me to put some cream on your bottom Nicole?"

"Oh, thank you, Matron, that would be nice."

"Stay where you are and I'll get the cream," Sarah said and she went to the cupboard and pulled out a tub of cold cream. Putting a generous amount of cream on Nicole's bottom and legs she rubbed in letting her fingers graze over Nicole's anus and pussy by 'accident'. Nicole was obviously enjoying the extra attention to her secret places and she was moaning slightly. Sarah decided to see what would happen if she paid more attention to Nicole's anus and she was rewarded with louder moans, then Nicole pushed back slightly so Sarah's finger slipped inside.

"Oh Sorry Nicole," Matron said, but Nicole pushed back even more. "I think that's enough for now Nicole. Sarah said but she knew that Nicole wanted more. Patting Nicole's bottom Sarah said. "Get dressed now and don't say a word to the others until I call them to come and see me. We don't want them to think you have told me their names."

"No Matron," Nicole said, and then stood up on her tiptoes and kissed Sarah on her cheek, "And thank you for... well, you know."

After Nicole had left, Sarah Nicholson looked at the Polaroid instant pictures she had taken with her hand in her knickers. The rest of the staff wondered why she would have pop music playing in the sanatorium, she said that the girls liked it but it was to hide the noise of her instant camera.

Chapter 8 - Charles spanks a mature teacher

Later that same day Charles was in his office when Daisy Andrews knocked at the door. At forty-eight, Daisy was the oldest of the teachers apart from Charles Nicholson, but she looked a lot older. Her slight body was topped with prematurely grey hair tied up in a bun and she always dressed as if she was going to visit the queen. She only had one passion, geography, and she was happiest when she was walking the hills with a group of school girls describing the terrain and how it was formulated.

"Hello Charles," Daisy said. "Got a minute?"

Charles was just catching up with some marking in his office, he had another class to teach in an hour, but that would be it for the day. "Always have time for you Daisy, you know that."

"You say the nicest things to an old lady Charles, makes me want to give up my life of celibacy."

"Just let me know when, Daisy," Charles said.

Charles and Daisy had flirted with each other for the last few months. It was harmless fun and Sarah encouraged it. "Maybe we can have a threesome one day," she said to her husband in bed one night.

"Wouldn't be the first time," Charles said. "Remember that girl in Johannesburg, what was her name?"

"Sandy," Sarah said. "She was fun."

So now Daisy had appeared in Charles's office for no apparent reason. "What can I do for you, Daisy?" Charles said.

"You know you spanked Nicole for being rude to me and you told her to tell me that I could have the leather slipper if ever I need it?" Charles nodded. "Well, I think I need it now."

"Are you going to spank someone?"

"Oh no, I need you to use it on my bottom. I need you to spank me." Daisy said.

"Oh, I see," Charles said, but he didn't see at all. "Have you been naughty?"

"No, I don't think so."

"So why do you want me to spank you?"

"Remember when I was eavesdropping, and Amelia thanked you for spanking her and Jasmine, that Sunday night?"

"Yes, of course," Charles said. "And I also remember you promised you would forget it."

"Yes, I have tried, but I can't." Daisy sat on the chair in front of Charles's desk in the bay window of his lounge. "Since then I can't get out of my mind that Amelia enjoyed the spanking, and by the sound of it, so did you, am I right?"

"A gentleman never tells," Charles said.

"Of course," Daisy said. "But I'll take that as a yes." Daisy thought for a while. "Remember that slipper I gave you? It belonged to my father, and he spanked me with it until I left home when I joined the ATS. When my father died in the bombing there wasn't much left of his belongings but the slipper had survived unscathed so I kept it. You're quite like my father, Charles, and I would love you to spank me again with that slipper if you wouldn't mind?"

"Mind?" Charles said. "It would be my pleasure, is there any particular naughtiness you want to be punished for?"

"Yes," Daisy was serious now. "I was due to be with him that night when the house was bombed but I went out with the girls and missed the train home, I feel guilty that I wasn't with him in his last moments."

"Oh that's silly Daisy, and you know it," Charles said.

"I know in my logical brain how silly that is, but if I could just have that spanking he would have given me because I was drinking with the girls and missed the train. I know I'll feel better about it."

"Okay," Charles said. He had been looking forward to spanking Daisy ever since they had started flirting, but he had never had the opportunity until now. "How did your father spank you?"

"He always had me over his knee, bare bottom of course," she said.

"Of course," Charles said as he moved the spanking chair into the centre of the lounge. He knew that Sarah would be home soon but she wouldn't disturb him if she heard a spanking going on. Sitting down on the chair he instructed Daisy to stand and pull up her skirt. When the skirt was around her waist Charles noticed that she wasn't wearing any knickers. "No knickers, naughty girl," he said.

"I didn't think I would need them for this spanking."

"No, of course not," Charles said as he pulled Daisy over his lap. Resting his hand on her bottom he felt Daisy shiver and then relax. She was where she wanted to be. "Daisy, I'm disappointed in you," Charles said before he started to spank her. "I expected you home, I even prepared dinner for you and you know how challenging that is while we have rationing, and you stayed out drinking with your friends. You deserve this spanking, don't you?"

"Yes Daddy," Daisy said and Charles could hear that she was already crying, so he picked up the slipper and started to spank her bare bottom. Over and over again the leather-soled slipper landed on Daisy's bottom. This was the third time he had used the slipper since she had given it to him to spank Katie Owen, and he liked the feel of it in his hand as he spanked a naughty girl. Now he was spanking Daisy with her father's slipper. It seemed to have a greater meaning.

Daisy was sobbing now but she didn't ask Charles to stop, she just asked to be forgiven. Eventually, Charles stopped spanking her bottom and held her over his knee. Patting her bottom he told her that he wanted her to go and stand in the corner and think about what she had done. Climbing off Charles's lap he could see that she had been crying hard, and when she got to the corner he said. "Hold up your dress so that the world can see how naughty you have been. "Yes Daddy," she said and started to cry again.

Charles left Daisy in the corner for ten minutes and then said. "Come here Daisy," so she walked over to Charles and he had his arms open so she sat on his lap and he hugged her. "All forgiven now," he said, holding her until she stopped crying.

It took a while for Daisy to pull herself together and then she asked if she could use his bathroom. When she came out she seemed a lot better and her makeup was repaired. "Thank you, Charles," she said and left.

Sarah had been hiding in the bedroom while all this was going on and she came out when she heard Daisy had left. "What was that all about?" she asked.

"Just a little therapy, darling," Charles said and Sarah knew not to push for more information. He would tell her sometime if there was anything to tell.

Later that evening Sarah told Charles about the spanking she gave Nicole and showed him the pictures. "Such a lovely bottom to spank," Charles said. "And you say you took her to stage two?"

"Yes," Sarah said. "And she seemed to like the attention."

Chapter 9 - Sarah spanks Katie and Lucy

The following day Sarah asked Katie Owen and Lucy Smith to come to the sanatorium during the break. Nicole had obviously kept her word and not told the other two that they would be in trouble for breaking into the church vestry and drinking the communion wine.

Sarah was sitting behind her desk writing something when the girls walked in and she told them to wait. When she had finished she looked up. "Now Girls, what have you got to say for yourselves?"

"About what Matron?" Katie asked.

"About breaking into the church vestry and drinking the wine?"

"But we didn't," Katie said.

"That's six extra strokes with the cane for lying, Katie," Sarah said.

"But Matron," Lucy said.

"Do you also want the extra strokes, Lucy?"

She looked at her shoes, "No Matron."

"How did you know?" Katie asked.

"One of the teachers saw you coming out of the church with Nicole and she investigated and found the vestry door open and the bottle of communion wine left empty next to the candles. It was obvious that it was you three. Nicole has already been punished so it's just you two. I'll give you a medical to make sure there are no ill effects from drinking that much wine, and then send you to Mr Nicholson for your punishment."

"Oh please Matron, Mr Nicholson spanks hard," Katie said, "Especially if I have to get the cane as well."

"You should have thought of that before you lied to me, Katie."

"I'm sorry Matron, but can't you spank us yourself?"

Sarah pretended to think about it. "Okay, but I don't have time for both of you now. Lucy, you stay and I'll give you your medical and the spanking, Katie, you will have to come back after school."

"Yes Matron," Katie said and left Lucy with Sarah.

"Okay Lucy, Medical first, strip off and get on the examination table."

"Do I have to, Matron?" Lucy said. Lucy was a big girl for her eighteen years and at five foot eight inches she was the tallest in her class. She didn't mind that but she also had the biggest boobs and a bottom that stuck out, and she didn't like that at all. She was shy about her body and didn't even like showering with the other girls.

"Yes you do Lucy," Sarah said. She enjoyed watching shy girls disrobe, there was something about the way they tried to hide their bodies as they were taking off their clothes that made the whole process exciting. Eventually, Lucy was lying on her back on the examination table with her left arm across her boobs and her right hand cupping her hairy mound. "Hands by your side, Lucy," Sarah said. "I can't examine you like that." Lucy did as she was told but she kept her eyes tight shut as Sarah examined her.

"On your tummy Lucy, so that I can take your temperature," Sarah said.

"But my Mum always takes my temperature in my mouth," Lucy said as she turned over.

"Well this thermometer always goes up girls' bottoms, you can have it in your mouth if you like."

"No, that's okay," Lucy said and Sarah smiled.

After the medical, Sarah spanked Lucy with the wooden spoon again and she cried from the start of the spanking to the finish. Sarah offered to put cream on Lucy's bottom but she just wanted to get out of there.

When Katie Owen arrived for her punishment after school, the process was entirely different. It seemed that she didn't mind taking off her clothes for the examination, and welcomed the thermometer up her bottom. "My Mum always takes my temperature up my Bum," Katie said. "She's a nurse and she says it can be as much as a degree different."

"Your mother is right, Katie. Up on your knees now with your head down on the table. Katie also had nice boobs and they hung down when she was on all fours, but with her head on the table, they were squashed flat. Sarah put some vaseline on her finger and eased it into Katie's bottom without a word of complaint.

"That's nice Matron," Katie said as she pushed back a little.

"Yes, some girls find that very exciting, Katie," Sarah said. "But just be careful if you try this on your own or with your friends."

"Yes Matron, I'm always careful."

Taking her finger out Sarah replaced it with the thermometer. "Just hold that there for me Katie," Sarah said. As Katie reached behind her to hold the thermometer in place, Sarah turned on the bright light so that it pointed to Katie's bottom and took a couple of polaroid photos. Katie held it inside for perhaps a little longer than necessary, but eventually, Sarah took over and pulled it out. "Your temperature is just a little higher than usual Katie, but that's nothing to worry about. Come back in a couple of days and I'll take it again to see if it has improved."

"Yes Matron," Katie said. "Maybe I'm feeling a little hot being in this position."

"Maybe, Katie. But you can stay in that position for your spanking."

"Do I have to, Matron?" Katie said.

"No, of course not, Katie. I can send you straight to Mr Nicholson for the cane if you like."

"No," Katie said as she shook her head.

"Right then, I spanked the others with my wooden spoon, so I'll do the same for you and then the cane for lying."

"Yes, Matron," Katie said as she felt the first spank of the wooden spoon on her upturned bottom. The spanking wasn't a long one but the wooden spoon hurts. It's a little longer than normal wooden spoons and the spoon shape at the end is a little wider. The first few spanks leave an oval ring on the receiver's bottom and that stays visible until there are so many rings that they all seem to merge. Katie was crying when Sarah put the spoon down and picked up the cane. She didn't want to delay the cane so she gave Katie six strokes on top of her deep red bottom and Katie was howling when Sarah put the cane down.

Katie moved to get up. "You stay in position Katie and I'll put some cream on your bottom for you. Matron said as she pulled the medical gloves over her fingers

"Thank you, Matron," Katie said through the tears as she felt the cooling cream being applied to her bottom cheeks, and then between her cheeks. Katie moaned as Sarah's creamy finger slid over her anus, towards her pussy and then back towards her anus again. "Maybe you should take my temperature again now Matron," Katie said, and taking the hint Sarah slipped her finger into Katie's bottom. Katie pushed back and felt Sarah's finger go deeper. Sarah pulled her finger out and let her right hand fall towards Katie's pussy while the index finger of her left hand slipped back inside Katie's bottom. Pulling it out again and then back in. At the same time, Sarah had found Katie's clitoris at the top of her wet pussy and was massaging it for her.

"Ooh Matron, what are you doing?" Katie said.

"Don't worry Katie," Sarah said. "Just relax and I'll teach you a thing or two." There was no way that Katie was going to be able to relax in this position with Sarah manipulating her bottom and pussy and it didn't take her long to have a wonderful orgasm. This was not her first orgasm, but it was the first that had been orchestrated by an older experienced woman. When she came she cried out, and Sarah wondered if the whole school had heard her, but when nobody came she relaxed.

Five minutes later Katie was pulling on her knickers and smiling from ear to ear. "That was wonderful Matron," she said.

"I'm sure it was Katie, but I think we had better keep that between ourselves, don't you?"

"Yes of course Matron, I won't tell anybody, I promise."

Chapter 10 - Charles spanks the Upper Sixth.

It was two weeks later when all hell broke loose in the upper sixth classroom. Katie and Lucy were on the floor of the classroom fighting. They were both big girls so the fight was quite fierce. All the other girls in the class were crowding around cheering except little Amy Wilson who was sitting in the corner reading quietly.

"What the hell is going on in here?" Charles said as he walked into the classroom. The room went quiet and the two girls stood up.

"Sorry Sir, we were just discussing something," Katie said.

"It looked more like fighting to me, and the rest of you should be ashamed of yourselves. You will all stay behind after we finish this class and I'll be spanking every one of you.

"That's not fair, we were not all fighting." Ella Hall said.

"You will be getting three extra for arguing Ella," Charles said.

"What?" Ella said

"Six," Charles said. "Anybody else want extra?" The girls all moved to their seats and sat quietly.

At the end of the class, the bell rang and the girls started to shuffle. "Right," Charles said as he put his foot up on a small stool in the front of the class. "You will come up here one at a time, lift up your skirt and bend over my knee. I'll pull your knickers down and spank you. After that, you may leave the class to go to the hall for the break. It's raining outside and you don't want to get wet. You first Jade." Charles pointed to the first desk in the front row.

Jade was normally a good girl and Charles had not spanked her before. She was just five foot three with short curly blond hair. Jade had tears in her eyes as she pulled up her skirt and bent over Charles's knee. Putting his left arm around Jade's body he pulled her up off her feet and pushed down her knickers and they fell to her ankles. She received six hard spanks on her bare bottom and her knickers had fallen right off as Charles put her back on her feet. Bending, she picked up her knickers and ran out of the classroom crying.

One at a time he called the girls up and they got six spanks on their bare bottom before they went off to the hall. When Ella arrived she defiantly reached under her skirt, pulled down her own knickers and picked them up before raising her skirt and bending over Charles's knee. She got twelve spanks and then Charles held her in place and gave her three more. "Those last three were for not doing what I told you to do."

"Yes Sir," she said and she was still crying when she left the room.

The last person to be spanked was Amy Wilson. Amy was a short girl at just five feet with a slim, almost boyish body. Charles liked Amy and would have liked to spank her bottom but he knew she had been the only girl who was sitting quietly reading when the rest of the girls were making such a fuss. The class was empty now, apart from Charles and Amy as she walked up to her teacher and pulled up her skirt. "No need for you to get a spanking Amy, you were a good girl. I'll just clap my hands six times and the others will think I spanked you."

"Better not Sir," Amy said. "They will all be comparing bottoms in the hall, and if mine is not red they will not be talking to me for a week. Please spank me as hard as the others," she said as she bent over Charles's knee.

"Alright Amy," Charles said as he pulled down her knickers and spanked her small bottom hard and fast six times.

Amy was crying when she stood up but she was smiling as well. "Thank you, Sir," she said. "That's one spanking I'll never forget."

When Amy left, the headmistress Amelia Brandon walked into the classroom laughing. "Hello Charles, I hear you've been busy this morning."

"Just a little minor disruption to handle Amelia."

"Minor disruption?" she said. "You spanked the whole class."

Charles was laughing now. "Yes I did, it was fun."

Amelia turned to look at the door to make sure nobody was listening. "I think I need a little fun like that Charles, can I come and see you later? Just you and me?"

"Of course Amelia, shall we say seven o'clock in my office?"

Amelia nodded and walked away smiling.

Chapter 11 - Charles spanks the headmistress

ater that afternoon Sarah walked into Charles's classroom. "I hear you've been having some fun here this morning?"

"Hello darling," Charles said and kissed her. "Yes, I spanked the whole class, including little Amy."

Sarah was laughing. "So I heard. Was Amy naughty?"

"No, but she wanted to be spanked so the others wouldn't pick on her."

"Clever girl that Amy," Sarah said.

Then Charles leant closer to his wife and spoke in a soft voice. Amelia came in afterwards and asked me if I could spank her on her own this evening. She will be over at seven."

"Oh, will you fuck her?" Sarah asked matter-of-factly.

"I don't think so, maybe, we will see."

"Okay, I'll have things to do in the Sanatorium. One of the junior girls is quite sick so maybe I'll stay with her all night, just in case."

"Just in case?" Charles said.

"Just in case you want to use our bed for Amelia's visit," Sarah said laughing.

Charles kissed his wife passionately. "I love you, Sarah Nicholson," he said.

"I love you too," she replied as she left the classroom.

At seven on the dot, there was a knock at the housemaster's office door. "Come," he called out, knowing who it would be, but it was little Amy Wilson who walked into the room.

"I'm sorry to bother you, Sir," Amy said.

"It's no bother Amy, it's always a pleasure to see you. What can I do for you?"

"I just wanted to thank you for spanking me with the others this morning. I am never spanked but I am not always a good girl, so I was pleased to get spanked even though it hurt."

"That is a very mature thing to say, Amy," Charles said.

"Thank you, Sir," Amy had tears in her eyes. "It's just that you spanked me as my father used to, and I miss him. Would you mind if I come here sometime and ask for advice and things?"

"Of course Amy, that's the job of a housemaster."

"And maybe you will have to spank me sometimes," Amy said hopefully.

"Sometimes maybe, when you're naughty," Charles said. "But not today, you have already had one spanking today for something you didn't do, and that's quite enough for one day."

"Thank you, Sir," Amy said as she walked behind Charles's desk and kissed his cheek. Then she left. As she walked out of the door, the headmistress was just about to knock. "Hello Miss Brandon, have you come for a spanking?" Amy said and then giggled as she left.

"Cheeky little minx," Amelia said.

"Hello Amelia, I hear you've been a naughty girl again," Charles said.

"Oh no Sir," Amelia said. "I did what you told me and Jasmine and I have been very discrete. I'm also spending more time with the other teachers so I expect the rumours have died down."

"They have indeed, Amelia," Charles said. "So what can I help you with now?"

"Is Sarah here?"

"No, unfortunately, she has a sick child in the sanatorium so she has to be there tonight."

Amelia smiled, "Oh God Charles, I just need you to spank me again, like you did last time."

"You had better lock the door and come here then Amelia," Charles said from behind his desk. Amelia locked the door and then came over and stood beside him and he started to rub the back of her leg. "I'll need something to spank you for Amelia," Charles said as his hand went under her dress and discovered that she was wearing stockings. "Have you been naughty?"

"I think so Charles," Amelia said. "I've been having naughty dreams about a married man."

"Yes, that's naughty, what sort of dreams?"

"All sorts of dreams, Sir. I dream of being tied up and spanked, of being bent over and fucked up my ass, of having to kneel down and take that man's large erection into my mouth and swallow his sperm. All sorts of terrible dreams Sir." Amelia shivered as she felt Charles's hand slip under her knickers and squeeze her bottom.

"You're right Amelia, those are very naughty dreams, and you should be punished. Take off that dress and show me what you look like underneath."

"Yes Sir," Amelia shivered as she pulled her dress over her head and stood there for his inspection. Amelia had her hair pulled back in a ponytail and she kept her glasses on as she was standing there in a white lace bra holding up her large boobs. The best description for Amelia's body shape was tubby and she was wearing large knickers to support her tummy. Her suspender belt held up her stockings and the whole picture was finished with flat black shoes.

Charles thought she looked delightful and he told her so, she just blushed with embarrassment but said nothing. "Turn around," Charles said and she turned slowly all the way around. "Now take off that bra and suspender belt, and let your stockings fall to the floor. Again Amelia did as she was told, getting more and more excited as the evening progressed. Standing there in her knickers with her stockings around her ankles was rather humiliating. Her large boobs were hanging free and she held them gently. "Turn around and stop with your back to me, Amelia." She did as she was told and then lowered her knickers as Charles told her to. Her knickers had joined her stockings around her ankles and she was naked apart from that.

Charles was enjoying giving his boss orders. "Bend over and show me your bottom," he said and Amelia bent at the waist. "Now reach behind you and pull your cheeks apart, I want to see everything."

"Oh Charles please," Amelia said and this was the first time she had spoken since she started to strip for Charles. He did not reply and Amelia knew that she had to do as she was told. As she reached behind herself to pull her cheeks apart she thought that this was the most embarrassing position she could ever be in.

Charles had been sitting behind his desk the whole time but now he stood up and walked around his desk to where Amelia was bent over. "You can let your bottom go now Amelia, I'm going to spank you."

Amelia was relieved to be able to let her bottom cheeks fall back into place but then the spanking started. Over and over again Charles's hand fell on Amelia's bare bottom and the sting built up causing her to cry after just five minutes. In the past, he would have rubbed her bottom better after every twenty spanks but this time he wanted to see how much she could take, so he just continued spanking her bottom until his hand was sore. Then he picked up the leather slipper that had found a permanent position on his desk and he started to spank her again.

"Charles please, you are hurting me," Amelia said.

"Yes," said Charles, "This is a spanking. It's meant to hurt."

After fifty spanks with the leather slipper, Amelia was sobbing and her bottom was glowing red. Charles suspected that Amelia would have a bruised bottom in the morning and he was right.

Helping Amelia to get up he guided her to a comfortable chair where he sat and then pulled her onto his lap. Her bottom stung like that so she turned sideways and continued to cry on his shoulder getting his shirt wet. Charles held her there for a while and then lifted up her chin and kissed her passionately. "You're a naughty girl to have all those dreams about a married man, but who was the married man?"

"It was you, of course," Amelia said. "And now I want you to fuck me."

"I can't fuck you in your vagina, that's a pleasure I have promised to keep exclusively for Sarah, but anywhere else..." Charles left the sentence unfinished.

Slipping off his knee, Amelia knelt between his legs and reached for the clip of his trousers and pulled down the zip. Pulling his pants and underwear off, his erection bounced into view causing Amelia to gasp. Charles was still seated when Amelia leaned forward and took his erection into her mouth and sucked. With one hand on his balls and the other working his erection, Amelia went to work pumping up and down giving Charles a great deal of pleasure.

After a while, Amelia stopped and pulled Charles from the chair and knelt there herself pointing her bottom at him. Pulling her cheeks apart again she said. "Put it in there."

Charles pulled off the rest of his clothes. His erection was already wet with Amelia's saliva and he thought that may be enough as he held it against her anus and eased it past her sphincter. He was slow and deliberate as Amelia screamed when it slipped inside her. "Wait, wait, wait," Amelia said in desperation. "Let me get used to it before you go any further." Charles held it in place and when Amelia pushed back he pushed forward. It took a while before Amelia was comfortable with something that size inside her bottom, but eventually, he was able to pull out and then back in again to the delight of both participants.

Building up a little speed Charles was fucking Amelia in her ass just like in her dream, only she thought the real thing was much better. In her dream, Charles came too quickly but now he was able to keep it going for longer until he grunted and she felt him squirt inside her.

Charles stayed in place for a few minutes as he shrank and slipped out. Then, standing up he pulled his clothes back on and sat behind his desk.

Amelia was slow to turn around and sit on the chair, when she did Charles said formally. "Was there anything else?"

Amelia laughed. "Oh no Charles, that was exactly what I wanted."

Later that evening Sarah came back into their apartment. "I saw Amelia walking back to her flat so I guessed it was safe to come home," she said.

"Yes, all finished now."

"Well?"

"Well, what?"

"You know," Sarah said. "Did you fuck her?"

"Sort off," Charles said. "I didn't break our agreement though,"

"So you fucked her in the ass?" Sarah asked and Charles nodded. "Oh good. Have you had a shower, I could do with the same?"

Chapter 12 - Birthday spankings

One day Amelia Brandon asked Charles to come and see her in her office. When he arrived at reception, Emily Bell, the school secretary, looked up and said. "Hello Charles, you can go straight in, Amelia has got another project." Rolling her eyes she went back to her books.

Charles walked into the headmistress's office without knocking and was confronted with Amelia kneeling on the floor with her large bottom in the air pointing at him. Charles resisted the temptation to spank the bottom with the door open and the school secretary sitting outside, but he said. "What on earth are you doing?"

Amelia turned around. "Oh hello, Charles, I found all these papers in the basement along with the old punishment books and account books," she said, holding up a piece of paper. "Apparently they used to have birthday spankings in the old days. I wonder when that tradition changed?"

"Really?" Charles was interested and he got down on the floor beside her to look through the papers. "This is the old school rules," he said, picking up a document, "And the punishments that happened when the rules were broken." He carried on reading. "Good lord, these punishments were a little excessive. Do we have dates on these papers?"

"They seem to be around the end of last century, 1890 maybe," Amelia said.

Charles continues reading. "It seems that all the girls were spanked on their birthday to make up for all the times they were naughty the previous year but weren't caught. The spankings were held during the Monday morning assembly in front of the whole school. Bare bottom over the spanking trestle. I wonder where that trestle went?" Charles was thinking that he might have a use for it. "Look," he showed the second page to Amelia, "There is a drawing of it here with the headmistress spanking a girl."

They were both silent in their own thoughts for a while. "I wonder if we can start the birthday spankings again," Amelia said. "Not a hard spanking, just a bit of fun to celebrate the girl's birthday."

"Not the whole school, Amelia," Charles said, "and certainly not at assembly like they used to do eighty years ago. But maybe for the Upper Sixth girls and in the classroom, that will be okay." Charles was thinking that he would be able to spank the girls who are never naughty.

"Okay," Amelia said. "Our new tradition will be a spanking when any girl reaches the age of eighteen. In the classroom in front of the class but not the school at assembly. What about the teachers?"

"Oh, that would be different," Charles said. "Maybe in the staff room? Do we have any birthdays coming up?"

"Laura Taylor is coming to her thirtieth next week. Maybe we can start with her." Amelia said.

"They won't like it," Charles said. "Especially in front of the other teachers."

"Oh, I don't know," Amelia said. "Bending over the lap of a distinguished older gentleman may be one of their fantasies, I know it has always been one of mine." They both laughed.

"So you want me to do the spanking?" Charles asked. "It was the headmistress in 1890."

"Of course," Amelia said. "I'll tell Laura it will happen on her birthday so it's not a surprise. She may want to wear her best knickers or no knickers at all."

"So bare bottom then?" Charles asked.

"Spankings are always on the bare bottom, you know that."

The following Tuesday the staff were all told to meet in the staffroom early, and they were all in by quarter past eight. "I have an announcement to make," Amelia started formally. "Charles and I have been going through some of the old paperwork that was found in the basement last week. As you know we are a progressive school, but I think it's also important to have some traditions. Apparently, at the end of the last century, there was a tradition that the girls would get a spanking on their birthday to make up for punishments that they may have missed in the previous year. We are going to start that tradition again, but just for girls who reach the age of eighteen. In the past, these spankings were held at assembly in front of the whole school, but we think that would not be fair so in the future, the spankings will be just in front of their classmates. The spankings will be largely ceremonial and not designed to punish, but they will be on the bare bottom."

There was a great deal of chatter when Amelia finished. "In addition," she tried to get the staff to stop talking. "In addition, there will be a similar ceremonial spanking for any member of staff who has a birthday."

"What?" Alexandra Dixon, the biology teacher, exclaimed. "In front of the girls?"

"Oh no Alex, in the staff room," Amelia said.

"I'm not sure that's a good idea," Alex said. "What if the girls find out?"

"Oh, they will probably find out," Daisy Andrews said. "And I think it's a good thing, come on Alex, it's only once a year."

"Yes," Alex said. "But I'll get forty-eight spanks next month."

Charles had said nothing up until this point, but he thought he should say something. "It will be largely ceremonial, so no stinging spanks."

"Will you be doing the spanking Charles," Alex said.

"So I'm told."

"Well, in that case, I'm all for it," Alexandra said with a smile, and everybody laughed.

"Good," Amelia said. "Are there any more questions?" There was silence in the room. "Good, well we are gathered here today to wish Laura Taylor for her thirtieth birthday. As she said that the door opened and the cook walked in with a birthday cake burning thirty candles, and everybody burst into song. The cake was cut but before it was distributed, the chant went out, "Spanking, Spanking."

Daisy was standing next to Charles and she said above the noise. "Well if the girls didn't know there would be birthday spankings for the teachers, they certainly do now." Charles looked at her nodding as he smiled.

Amelia moved a dining chair into the centre of the room and said. "Come on then Charles, it's your turn to spank a teacher." Charles sat in the chair and Laura walked toward him. Amelia had spoken to her the day before so she knew it was coming but she was still nervous. Laura had never been spanked before. Her parents didn't believe in spanking the children which meant that they had three very naughty girls to bring up. Laura was not married but she did have a boyfriend who wanted to spank her, but she just refused to let him. When she heard about the birthday spankings she thought that this was an opportunity to see what a spanking would be like without giving in to her boyfriend.

Charles helped Laura across his lap and immediately lifted up her skirt, and she gasped. "You're not going to spank me on my knickers are you?" she asked.

"Of course not Laura," Charles said as he whisked down her thin cotton knickers, "I'll be spanking you on your bare bottom."

"Oh!" Laura said but Charles didn't give her a chance to complain because he started to spank her straight away. With the first smack, the room counted out loud, "One", then "Two." Laura was wriggling but Charles had his left arm around her body to stop her from wriggling away. At twenty-eight, he slowed down the spanking and for the last one he left a few seconds before he brought his hand down quite hard on Laura's bare bottom. "Ouch!" she said and rolled off his lap onto the floor amid clapping and laughter.

"Well done Laura, happy birthday," they were all saying and then she cut the cake and everybody had a piece.

Later that afternoon Laura stopped Charles in the corridor. "Thank you for my birthday spanking this morning, Charles, I'm sorry that I made such a fuss, I didn't know what to expect, but it was okay."

Charles smiled, "It's okay," he said. "You haven't been spanked before have you?"

"How did you know?"

"Oh, it was just a feeling," Charles said, "How do you feel about spanking now?"

Laura was absentmindedly rubbing her bottom as they were chatting in the corridor. " I don't know, I guess I quite like it."

As she said that a couple of younger girls walked past them and said. "Happy Birthday Miss Taylor."

"Funny thing," Laura said. "Straight after the spanking everybody in the school seemed to know it was my birthday and I have had girls coming up to me all day wishing me well for the day. That has never happened before."

"It's hard to keep a secret in this school." Charles laughed. "Anytime you need another spanking just let me know."

"Thank you, Charles, but I think my boyfriend might like to spank my bottom from time to time," Laura said and then walked off down the corridor, still rubbing her bottom.

The following week it was Leah Robson's eighteenth birthday. There was no formal notice about the change in traditions with regard to birthday spankings, and nobody had made any comment about there being birthday spankings for the girls, but when he arrived at the Upper Sixth classroom at nine o'clock it was Nicole Asher who raised the subject.

After everybody had stood up and said good morning to Charles as he entered the room (another tradition that he had re-introduced), Nicole remained standing as she said. "Excuse me, Sir," she was much more polite now since she was spanked for being rude.

"Yes Nicole," Charles said as he sat down at his desk and sorted out his papers. "It's Leah Robson's eighteenth birthday today."

"Yes," Charles said again, wondering where this was going.

"And we have heard that the teachers are getting a spanking on their birthdays, so we think that the girls shouldn't be left out."

"Teachers getting a spanking on their birthday?" Charles said.

"Yes Sir," Nicole said. "Didn't you spank Laura Taylor last week?"

"That's Miss Taylor to you, Nicole."

"Yes Sir, sorry Sir. Only she likes us to call her Laura. And didn't you spank her on her birthday?"

"A gentleman never tells," he said to Nicole, smiling.

"Well, we think that the girls shouldn't be left out, especially when they get to eighteen."

"Really?" Charles said. "And do you all think like that?"

"Oh yes Sir," they said.

"Not a hard spanking Mr Nicholson," Nicole said, "Just something to celebrate her birthday."

Charles stood up again and directed his attention to Leah Robson. "And how do you feel about that Leah?"

"Well, as long as it's not a hard spanking," she said.

"Have you been naughty?"

"No Sir,"

"Then it will not be a hard spanking, come here and I'll give you your birthday spanking."

Leah stood up nervously and walked to the front of the class. Charles had pulled the spanking chair in front of his desk so that everybody had a good view and then sat down guiding Leah across his lap. Lifting her checked school skirt he put his hand on her bottom. Leah was a small girl with short straight blond hair and small boobs, but she had a lovely bubble-shaped bottom and Charles was looking forward to spanking it. Taking the elastic of her green school knickers he pulled them down over her bottom and turned them inside out delighting in the traditional white material of the gusset.

Charles took his time with Leah's birthday spanking to the delight of the audience. He looked up at the girls and said, "You had better count the spanks, we don't want to give Leah here too many do we." The girls started counting at number one and when Charles got to seventeen the last spank was harder than the others. Jumping up from her position over Charles's lap, Leah was rubbing her bare bottom as everybody was clapping and wishing her happy birthday. As that was going on the cook opened the door to the classroom and brought in a cake with eighteen candles.

Nicole was standing next to Charles as Leah was cutting and distributing the cake and she said in a soft voice, "You knew didn't you," Charles just smiled. "She was going to get a spanking for her birthday anyway?" he didn't say a word, but just nodded slightly.

Charles clapped his hands, "Come on girls, the fun is over, we have to get back to the maths lesson," As Nicole was walking back to her place at the back of the class she was smiling.

Chapter 13 - Spanking for a midnight snack.

That night Sarah set out to catch four of the girls in the upper sixth. There was a rumour that the girls have a midnight snack when one of them turns eighteen. It seems that there were other traditions that the teachers were not certain about. Charles had done most of the spanking since they had started work at the school and so she was determined to balance the books a little.

Dressed in her nightie and dressing gown she was waiting outside the small dormitory where Leah and her friends slept. At ten to midnight, she heard them stir and she watched as they came out of the dorm and ran down the stairs not making a noise. Sarah followed them to the main hall, and into the storeroom at the back. This is where the props for the school play were kept. Sarah knew it was dusty and disorganised so a perfect place to hide for an hour or so. After waiting for ten minutes until the girls settled she burst into the storeroom and said. "What's all this then?" Like a policeman in amateur dramatics.

"Oh, God!" Leah said. Dropping her paper plate and some cake. I'm sorry Matron, but it's my birthday and, well, my friends thought this would be fun."

"All I can see you doing is dropping crumbs on the floor for the mice."

"Mice!" one of the other girls stood up and squealed.

"Shush now," Sarah said. "I'll just be giving you all a spanking for being naughty and then you can finish your party."

71

"Yes Matron," Leah said, then turning to the others she said. "It's better than being sent to the old man."

"And who is the 'Old Man'?" Sarah said.

"Oh yes, sorry, I forgot, he's your husband." Leah was embarrassed. "Only he's older than the other teachers, and that's what they call him."

"The teachers call Mr Nicholson "The Old Man?" she said smiling. "I didn't know that. Anyway, you will all get a spanking. Pyjamas down and bend over that desk." Sarah was pointing to an old desk that had found its way into the props room.

The girls were quick to obey and Sarah was looking at four beautifully pristine bottoms to spank. It wasn't a hard spanking, just a bit of fun really. She spanked each bottom, in turn six times, just to turn the bottoms a little pink. "There you go girls," Sarah said. "Can I have a piece of cake now?"

They all settled themselves down again and then Leah said. "Matron, If you are going to join us for our midnight feast, shouldn't you have a spanking as well?"

"Oh no girls," Sarah said, "I'm old enough to be your mother."

"You're right Leah," another girl said, "Matron should be spanked as well, and then they all pounced on Sarah pulling her to her feet and bending her over the desk.

"Now girls, you are going too far, you will get the cane for this."

"If we're going to get punished anyway," Leah said. "I think we should get the most out of it. You two, hold her arms while I bare her bottom.

"No girls please," Sarah said but very soon she was bent over the desk getting a spanking on her bare bottom. Sarah was used to getting a spanking but it was usually foreplay, so she didn't mind the spanking at all, it was just getting a spanking from four eighteen-year-olds that she wasn't sure off. The spanking didn't last long and eventually, they let her up, and then there was silence for a while. Finally, Sarah broke the silence by saying, "Well, as I have paid for my cake, I had better eat it," so she sat down and started on her piece of cake. The other girls followed suit and they were all laughing after a while.

Half an hour later Sarah said. "Bedtime I think girls, or I'll get into trouble and get the cane from the Old Man."

"Does Mr Nicholson spank you as well Matron?" Leah asked.

"If I'm naughty," Sarah said. "But you tell a soul I said that and you will be in trouble. Just between you all and me, okay?"

"Of course Matron," Leah said. "You're part of our group now, "Sam's Girls," and we will never split on another member."

That night Sarah tucked each of the girls back into their beds and kissed them on their foreheads. "Goodnight girls, and thank you," she said as she left, but all she could hear was deep breathing.

Chapter 14 - Amy is spanked three times in a day

A my Wilson is a good girl, everybody says that. A month or so ago, when all the girls in the Upper Sixth class were caught causing a riot in the class, Amy was the only girl sitting quietly at her desk reading. All the girls in her class were spanked and even though her housemaster, Charles Nicholson, offered to let her off the spanking she said that she wanted the spanking in case the others found out. At five foot nothing, Amy was the smallest in the class and she was also slim with a boyish figure, but Amy was clever. She was not at the top of her class but she could have been, she just didn't want to stand out in that way.

In the staffroom, Charles had said to Daisy Andrews, the geography teacher, that Amy could go on to get a Master's Degree in Mathematics at University. "Nonsense," Daisy said. "She should be studying B.Sc. Environmental Geography, she has such a talent in that area."

The fact was that each of the teachers wanted Amy to study their chosen subject because Amy had a natural talent in their field, apparently. Amy, against all the advice from her teachers, had set her heart on going to RADA to study Dramatic Arts.

So Amy was a good multi-talented girl who never got into trouble, until one day...

It all started when she got up late. Matron was doing her rounds to make sure all the girls were up and dressed ready for breakfast but when she walked into Amy's dormitory, she was still in bed. Sarah

Nicholson, the matron, clapped her hands. "Up you get now, Amy. It's time to get up." Amy nodded as Matron walked to the next dorm to check there as well.

Amy had been reading in bed that night with a torch under her covers, and she had lost track of time, only going to sleep at two in the morning, so when she had to wake up four hours later she was still tired. The rest of the girls in the dorm were already going down to breakfast when Matron walked back into the dormitory to discover that Amy had fallen back to sleep.

"Amy?" Sarah said. "Are you sick?"

"No Matron, sorry, I must be tired," Amy said.

"Well, you will be sitting at breakfast with a sore bottom. Get up, and bend over the back of your bed."

"Yes Matron," Amy said, and she clambered out of bed and bent over the end of the bed in her flannel pyjamas. Sarah's husband, Charles Nicholson was the housemaster in the girls' school and he had spanked Amy's little bottom, but Sarah hadn't and she was looking forward to doing just that. Sarah and Charles both loved to spank naughty girls and they always shared their spanking stories in bed at night. It excited both of them. When Charles had told Sarah how nice it was to be spanking Amy's little bottom she decided that she wouldn't miss an opportunity if it presented itself.

As Amy was bent over, still yawning, Sarah reached around her waist and pulled the cord that loosened her pyjamas, and then fell to the floor, followed by her knickers, and Sarah was faced with Amy's pristine bottom to spank. Sarah ran her hand over Amy's bottom but she didn't want to delay too long so she started to spank her. Six times Sarah's hand descended on Amy's little bottom. It was not a hard spanking but Amy was in tears when she stood up. "Let that be a lesson to you Amy, now get dressed or you'll be late for breakfast."

"Yes, Matron," Amy said as she pulled on her uniform.

Amy rushed down for breakfast just as the girls were finishing. It would have been bacon and eggs for breakfast which was Amy's favourite, but the bacon was finished and there was only one dried-up egg left. "This day can't get any worse," Amy said to herself, but she was wrong.

The first lesson of the day was history with Miss Dobson. Amy liked history and Molly Dobson liked Amy so it was a favourite class for her. As soon as Amy sat down, she noticed that the others were placing their homework on Miss Dobson's desk and she remembered her homework was still next to her bed. She had been studying for this class last night under the blankets after lights-out because it was her favourite subject, but after getting up late and getting a spanking she had forgotten the homework. She put her hand up to get Molly Dobson's attention.

"Not now Amy," Miss Dobson said as she was paging through the pile of homework on her desk, and then she went on to say. "Remember last week I said that if you don't hand in your homework on time there will be a spanking? Well, I notice that I'm two short. Rebbeca Scott, and..." Miss Dobson ran her finger down the list but she couldn't believe what she found. "And Amy Wilson. Is that right Amy? Have you not handed in your homework?"

"Well, no Miss but..."

"I told you that there would be no excuses. You will both get a spanking for not handing in your homework."

"But Miss," Amy said. "I left it in the dormitory."

"And I suppose, Rebecca, you left yours at home as well?" Molly Dobson said.

"Oh yes Miss," Rebecca thought she might get away with it this time. Rebbeca Scott was a weekly boarder. She lived in Norwich and she would go home on a Friday and return on Monday. She was also one of the naughtiest girls in the school, but she would often get away with it so Molly Dobson was not going to let her get away with it this time, which meant that she would have to spank little Amy as well.

At thirty-five Molly Dobson looked like an academic. She was a skinny lady with long hair that was always tied up on the back of her head and wireframe glasses permanently perched on the end of her nose. When she looked up at the class she was always looking over her glasses and she did not look like the sort of teacher who could deliver enough wallop to sting a bottom, however, looks can be deceiving.

"You first Rebecca," Molly said as she sat on the chair permanently placed in front of her desk for just such an occasion. Rebecca was used to this so she got up boldly and lifted her skirt as she bent over Molly's lap. Rebecca was of average height but skinny. She was a natural athlete and could take a hard spanking without blinking an eye, she was used to the pain and longed for the endorphins kicking in when she was spanked. Molly had spanked Rebecca many times over the years and she knew that she would have to be spanked hard if it was to have any effect, so after she lowered Rebecca's knickers, she picked up the hairbrush that was permanently on her desk and started to spank Rebecca hard. It was just twelve spanks but Molly Dobson had put some effort into it. Rebecca was not crying when she stood up but she certainly had tears in her eyes. "Go and stand in the corner with your bottom on display," Molly said as Rebecca stood up.

Molly Dobson had a problem now. She had spanked Rebecca hard so she would have to do the same for little Amy. "Come here Amy," Molly Dobson said. "Over my knee." Amy already had tears in her eyes. She knew what was coming after watching Rebecca get a hard spanking and she was scared. Lifting her skirt she bent over Molly Dobson's lap and shivered. Reaching for the floor her legs came up as Molly lowered her knickers, exposing her small bottom. "Your bottom is red Amy, have you already been spanked today?"

"Yes, Miss," she said. "I got up late and Matron spanked me."

"Well I'm afraid you'll be getting a second spanking, I don't expect you have ever had two spankings in a day have you, Amy?"

"No Miss Dobson," she said.

Molly Dobson had her hand on Amy's small bare bottom trying to think of a way out of this, but there was nothing. "Oh well," she thought to herself as she picked up the hairbrush and spanked Amy hard and fast. Unlike Rebecca, Amy's pain threshold was very low so she started to cry after the second spank and she continued to cry until Molly Dobson stopped spanking her. Strangely Molly Dobson also had tears in her eyes, she didn't like spanking Amy so hard but she had no choice. "Up you get Amy and go back to your desk. You can sit down as well Rebecca, and please remember your homework next time."

"Yes Miss," Amy said as she blew her nose. Rebecca said nothing.

At the end of the class, Molly Dobson asked Amy to stay behind for a minute. When the others had gone she told Amy to come over to her and she hugged her. "I'm sorry I had to spank you so hard Amy, especially after you had already been spanked, but you know you should have remembered your homework."

"I know Miss Dobson, I'm sorry I was naughty," Amy said. As she left the class to go to the break, she knew now that the day could not get any worse than that spanking she had just had. Again she was wrong.

At lunch, Amy's housemaster, Charles Nicholson, stopped her in the corridor and asked her to come and see him in his office after school at five. "Yes Sir," she said and wondered what all that was about.

The afternoon, however, promised to be much better for Amy. She had a free lesson where she could sit on her own and read and then she had Physical Education with the gym mistress Jasmine Pritchard. Amy changed into her green sports knickers and vest that all the girls had to wear for PE. She was lucky, she didn't have any boobs to speak of so she could run up and down without feeling uncomfortable. She was also quite strong so she could climb the ropes that were hanging from the ceiling. Jasmine Pritchard was late for the lesson so while the other girls were standing around chatting Amy climbed a rope right to the ceiling. Katie and Nicole saw what she was doing so they pulled the rope backwards and forwards trying to make her fall. When Miss Pritchard came into the gym all she saw was Amy up the rope and when Amy saw her she fell to the floor. Jasmine ran over to her and examined her. "Are you okay Amy?" Jasmine said.

"Yes Miss, I think so."

"What were you doing climbing up that rope you might have killed yourself. You know the gym equipment is not to be used without supervision. You could have broken your leg with a fall like that, or worse. Go and sit in my office and I'll come and talk to you when I calm down. The rest of you, running on the spot."

Amy had to sit in Miss Pritchard's office for the rest of the PE lesson and when all the other girls were dismissed the PE instructor came to find her. "I'm still very angry with you Amy, you know what would have happened if you had broken your leg, you would have spent the next few weeks in plaster but I would have lost my job. Is that what you wanted?"

"Oh no, Miss Pritchard. I love your lessons and I would never do anything like that."

"Well I would normally call in Mr Nicholson to cane you but I'm so angry with you I will be caning you myself."

"The cane?" Amy was horrified.

"You're lucky to get away with a few cane marks on your bottom. If I sent you to the headmistress you might get expelled. It's a very serious thing to play with the gym equipment without supervision."

"Yes Miss," Amy said. "I understand"

Jasmine stood up and looked for the cane she kept in the cupboard for such an event. "I will let you keep your knickers on for this Amy, I don't want to hurt you, but I will give you a caning you'll remember."

Amy bent over the desk in the office but she was thinking that she would have liked Miss Pritchard to take down her knickers and see that she has already been spanked twice today. Jasmine took a couple of practice swings and then landed the first stroke on Amy's knicker-covered bottom. Amy let out a scream that lasted until the second stroke landed. Four more strokes landed on her bottom and the last two caught the tops of her legs. Amy was sobbing when Jasmine put the cane away in the cupboard and told Amy to go and get dressed.

Amy just had enough time to shower and get dressed again before her appointment with her housemaster. "Oh God," she said, "This day is going to get a lot worse." Strangely she was wrong again.

At five o'clock Amy knocked at the housemaster's office door. Charles Nicholson's office during the day was the lounge in his apartment during the night. He and Sarah had a lovely apartment on the ground floor of the Christie House, named after Agatha Christie. He was given the position of housemaster in a girls' school a few months ago because the headmistress wanted to be progressive. As it turned out he was a very good housemaster for the girls and a father figure for the whole school including the teachers. His nickname by staff and pupils alike was "The Old Man". He wasn't that old at just over fifty, but he was older than the other members of the staff.

"Come in Amy," Charles said.

Amy walked into the office nervously and found the housemaster sitting on the large settee. "Are you going to spank me Sir?" she said and then burst into tears.

"No of course not Amy, come here." he held out his arms and Amy ran to him and sat on his lap. "Why on earth do you think I'm going to spank you?" He asked.

Amy was still crying, "Because I've been spanked twice and caned once today."

"What," Charles was surprised as he offered her his clean handkerchief. "That cannot be, you're such a good girl usually, what happened?"

Amy blew her nose on Charles's Handkerchief and then told him the whole story of her day. Charles had his arm around one of his favourite students and he listened carefully, gently patting her bottom, not interrupting until she blew her nose again and sat quietly.

"So what have we learned from today?" he asked.

Amy looked up to the man she respected more than any other. "I'm not sure what you mean Sir,"

"What have you learned? We must never go to bed without learning something from the experiences we had during the day, otherwise, the day has been wasted. So what have you learned?"

Amy was silent for a while. I suppose I have learned not to use the gym equipment unsupervised and not to forget my homework."

"Yes, but how could you have prevented these things from happening in the first place?"

"Oh," Amy's eyes lit up. "You mean if I had had a good night's sleep, I would have woken up on time, so I would have not been spanked in the morning. If I wasn't tired I probably would have remembered my homework." Amy was still thinking. "But what about falling off the rope?"

"You're a good climber, aren't you?" Charles asked.

"Don't you think you may have made a mistake on the ropes and fallen because you were tired?"

"I see Sir." and Amy did see. "If I had gone to sleep rather than reading until two in the morning, none of this would have happened."

"Well, I can't say that. But you would have had a better chance in making sure that it didn't"

"I get it," Amy said smiling. "Miss Brandon was telling us about Causality in her class. The effect was the spanking but the cause was not the homework, but the lack of sleep. I get it."

"Good girl," Charles said, patting her bottom again. "And if the result of all those spankings is that you have learned all about causality and you have also learned to go to sleep earlier, then I think you have had a very good day, what do you think?"

Amy was silent for a while. "Mr Nicholson?" Amy asked. "Can I kiss you again?"

"Of course Amy," Charles said as Amy kissed him on his cheek.

"Thank you for being there for me, Mr Nicholson."

"You're welcome Amy," Charles said as he helped her up off his lap. "Off you go to dinner now, and you know you can come back and see me any time."

"Thank you, Mr Nicholson," she said as she left the room.

Chapter 15 - Spanking on the Camping Trip

D aisy Andrews, the geography teacher, was sitting in the staff room pouring over a map of Norfolk when Charles came up behind her. "Thinking of running away Daisy?" he said and they both laughed.

"Maybe, want to come with me?" she replied. Daisy and Charles had started to flirt with each other from the first week that Charles arrived at the school.

Sarah, Charles's wife, knew about the fun they had flirting and she encouraged it. "Maybe we could have a threesome one day," Sarah said.

"Maybe," Charles had said, and he quite liked the idea, although Daisy had not shown any interest in anything more than harmless banter and a little spanking like her father gave her.

"So what are you up to Daisy?" Charles said.

"I'm planning a school outing for some of the girls to the Norfolk broads, I'm sure you know that they were originally created by the locals digging peat for fuel, and the sea flooded them creating the famous waterways. I was thinking that we could have a couple of days camping out and exploring the broads."

"Sounds like fun, want me to come with you?"

"Would you?" Daisy said, but she was rather surprised. "I can't imagine you camping out?"

Charles laughed. I was in South Africa for twenty years, remember? We used to do that all the time, but I still like my home

85

comforts. I have my Range Rover back now and I have a tent that fits on top. I can fit two girls in my car and if you take your car with two others we will have enough for a weekend away on the broads. Such fun."

"Will Sarah want to come?" Daisy asked.

"I expect so, I will ask her," Charles said. But Daisy seemed disappointed.

"I can't," Sarah said that evening while they were lying in bed. "I have the flu spreading amongst the younger girls. Anyway, I'm sure Daisy wants you to herself."

Charles laughed. "Yes I'm sure she does, so if you don't mind I will help her on the weekend camping trip."

"You know I don't mind Charles," Sarah said. "You, with four nubile young girls and one old lady that can't keep her eyes off you, what could go wrong?" They both laughed and then rolled over towards each other as they did most nights.

"Well, that's it then," Charles said to Daisy the following morning in the staff room. "Sarah can't make it because of the flu that's infecting the younger girls. So it's just you and me and we can take four senior girls as well. Have you spoken to Amelia?"

Amelia Brandon is the headmistress of St Samantha's school for girls. At thirty-eight she is young for such a senior position but she is a great organiser and an excellent teacher. She was made for the job.

"I'm not sure Daisy," Amelia said when Daisy broached the subject over lunch. "Can you manage on your own?"

"I won't be on my own, Charles has offered to come with me," Daisy said.

"Oh really?" Amelia said suspiciously. Charles was the only man in the school and there was a little rivalry between the teachers for his attention. Both Amelia and Daisy had been spanked by Charles in the past but neither of them knew that the other had been spanked. "Well that's okay then," she said.

The date was set for the following weekend and they asked for volunteers from the upper sixth who wanted to go on the geography camping trip. The whole class volunteered apart from Amy who was looking forward to a weekend with nobody to disturb her reading. "We will take the four girls with the highest marks for the test on Wednesday," Daisy said, and Rebecca groaned knowing that it would never be her. After the test marks were calculated the four girls going on the trip were Mary Becker, Nicole Asher, Katie Owen and Lucy Smith.

There was a lot of excitement on Friday morning when Charles was packing his Range Rover with the equipment. He had already attached the special roof rack that folded out into a two-man tent, and the big army tent was in the back of the car. There were also sleeping bags and cooking equipment, food that the cook had put together for them, thick floor mats for the girls to sleep on and a camp bed for Daisy. By lunchtime, they were all packed and so they left being waved off by Sarah and Amelia.

"I wonder what they will get up to Amelia," Sarah said.

"I hope it will be okay, we haven't had weekend trips away for the girls for a few years," Amelia said.

"I'm sure it will be fine, Charles is very resourceful," Sarah said but they both laughed knowing what Sarah meant.

An hour later, The six travellers had arrived at the designated campsite on a farm owned by one of Daisy's friends, and the girls were helping Charles set up the big tent. There was enough space in the tent for ten people and it was tall enough to walk around in so it would be their base for the weekend and, if it rained, they would all be able to eat in there as well. When everything was set up Daisy took the girls down to the broads to see where the peat was dug hundreds of years ago.

Back at the campsite, Charles was preparing the evening meal so when the girls arrived there was a big pot in an open fire with meat stewing for dinner. After dinner, Charles said to Daisy, "I saw a pub over the hill when we drove here, you and I should go for a drink and let the girls get to be on their own, I'm sure we can trust them."

"What do you think girls?" Daisy said to the four well-behaved girls, "Can we trust you to be good while Mr Nicholson and I go for a walk to the pub?"

"Oh yes, Miss Andrews," Nicole said. "We will go to bed at the normal time, I'm tired anyway, it's been a long day." The others agreed and so Daisy and Charles walked to the pub.

They had a lovely evening. Daisy flirted with Charles outrageously and Charles told her to stop or he would have to give her a spanking. "Promises, promises," Daisy said.

At ten o'clock, Charles said. "We had better walk back before this gets out of hand," and Daisy agreed, hoping to get Charles in the woods before they arrived at the campsite. On the walk back Daisy pulled Charles off the road and kissed him passionately. "I told you what would happen if you carried on like this," Charles said as he turned her around and wrapped his left arm around her body, bending her over slightly. Lifting up her dress and pushing down her knickers Charles spanked Daisy six times on her bare bottom. Then he thrust his hand between her legs and found her to be wet with excitement. "Naughty girl, you're enjoying this."

"Oh yes Charles," Daisy said. "I love to be spanked by a man who takes control."

Charles spanked Daisy again only much harder, and she moved her position so that she was bent over much more and her legs were apart. Putting his hand between her legs again, Charles was able to find her clitoris and he rubbed her hard until she orgasmed. "Pulling herself together Daisy stood up and said. "Thank you, Charles, I needed that. Maybe we can do that again sometime, properly."

"We will have to talk to Sarah about that, she has already said she would like a threesome."

"Oh really," Daisy said, but she was disappointed. "I'm not sure about that."

While Charles and Daisy were away, Katie produced a bottle of wine from her kitbag. "What have you got there?" Nicole asked.

"Just a little something to while away the hours before bedtime," Katie said.

"Oh Goodie," Nicole clapped her hands and they all sat around in a circle inside the big army tent passing the bottle around until it was empty. The girls were having such fun and then Katie spun the bottle around on the floor in the centre of the circle. "Are we playing spin the bottle?"

"Of course," said Katie. "We have to undress for bed anyway, let's play strip spin the bottle."

"But what about the Old Man and Daisy?" Mary Becker said.

"They won't be back until closing time and even then Daisy will pull the old man into the bushes for a little slap and tickle on their way back to the campsite." All the girls giggled at the joke but none of them expected that it would be true."

By the time Daisy and Charles approached the tent, the girls were just a little tipsy and they were slowly taking off their clothes. Mary was down to her knickers and the others were at various stages of undress. Lucy's big boobs were swaying around as she took her turn to spin the bottle and Nicole and Katie were still wearing their bras.

The girls had the big camping light on so Charles and Daisy could see their silhouettes against the canvas of the tent wall. Charles held Daisy back to see what was happening, and they heard lots of laughter and discussion about which article of clothing the girls should take off next. When it was agreed the girl in question would stand up and seductively remove her skirt or bra. Then there would be a call to spin the bottle again. "I think we have heard enough

Daisy," Charles said and he pushed open the canvas of the tent door dramatically to catch the girls.

"What the hell is going on here girls?" He asked as they all scampered to cover themselves with whatever they could lay their hands on. "Oh no you don't," Charles said. "Drop those clothes and let's see what you were doing."

"Come on Girls, you heard the Old Man," Daisy said and then she realised what she had said and all the girls giggled.

It was Nicole who said, "What did you say, Miss Andrews?" All the girls were looking at Daisy now and even Charles was interested."

Daisy was embarrassed as she realised that she had called Charles by his school nickname. "Oh, I'm sorry Charles, it just slipped out," she said.

"I will give you just slipped out," Charles said as he turned her around and lifted up her skirt.

"No Charles, not in front of the girls," Daisy said. But then she said, "NO!" As he pulled her knickers down and spanked her six times on her bare bottom. All the girls were quick to notice that her bottom was already red from the previous spanking.

Daisy was crying with embarrassment as Charles stood her up and said, "Stand over there with your bottom on show. Who's next?"

"But Sir?" Nicole said. "We're old enough to drink wine."

"It's against the school rules," he said. "But you're not old enough to play stripping games in a tent when anybody who walks past can see the silhouette of your bare bodies."

"Oh," Nicole said. "Could you see...Oh dear."

"You can be first Nicole, you're already showing off your breasts, finish taking off your clothes and come over here. You will get six just like Miss Andrews."

"Yes Sir," Nicole said as she slipped down her knickers and walked towards Charles for her spanking. Charles put his arm around Nicole and bent her slightly, then he spanked her bottom hard six times.

"Next!" he said, and the other girls were taking off the remainder of their clothes for their spanking. Mary was next and Charles had spanked her big bottom a few times. He recalled that her bottom was the first he spanked when she was caught smoking behind the bicycle sheds. Charles spanked her bottom six times and loved to watch it wobble as he spanked it, so when she tried to get up he gave her three more.

"But Sir," Mary said. "You only gave Nicole six."

"And you would only have had six if you hadn't had a cigarette earlier on."

"How did you know Sir?" Mary said.

"I know everything," Charles said, and then he looked up at the other girls still holding Mary in place. "And if the other girl who had a cigarette with you doesn't own up you will be getting another three for her as well." Katie and Lucy both put up their hands.

"But I only had a drag of Mary's ciggy," Lucy said. "I didn't like it."

"Smoking is smoking Lucy, you can be next," Charles said as he let Mary get up, "Over there next to Nicole and Miss Andrews, Mary," he said.

Lucy was a shy girl and she was standing naked with her arm across her big boobs and her other hand cupping her pussy as she walked toward her housemaster. "Hands on your head Lucy, no need to hide anything. You weren't shy when you were playing that game, I watched you dancing as you took off your bra."

"Oh God!," Lucy said as she put her hands on her head. When she was beside Charles, he wrapped his left arm around her chubby body and bent her over slightly. His hand couldn't go all the way around and when he started to spank her big bottom his hand slipped down into her curly hair. As he spanked her nine times she was rubbing her pussy against his hand, and she nearly orgasmed. He let Lucy get up and sent her to stand beside the others.

Katie was already walking towards Charles naked and not shy about it either. She draped herself over his lap and said. "Please spank me, Old Man." The other girls gasped and Charles just laughed.

"It will be my pleasure Katie," he said as he started to spank Katie's lovely bottom. After nine spanks she started to get up but Charles held her in place. "What did you call me?" he said.

"I'm sorry Sir, it just slipped out," Katie said.

"And how many spanks did Miss Andrews get for making the same mistake?"

"Oh no, please, my bottom is already sore."

"How many?"

"Six Sir."

"Yes, six," Charles said and proceeded to give Katie another six smacks on her red bottom. When she got up she was crying and Charles sent her to the corner facing the side of the tent just like the others. "Stay where you are girls," he said and they heard the click/whirr of the polaroid camera taking a picture. There was silence in the tent and then Charles said. "Right girls, get ready for bed, you too Daisy, I don't want to hear another squeak out of you until I call you in the morning."

There was silence in the tent and four naked girls and one fully clothed older lady got ready for bed. Once they were all wrapped in their sleeping bags, the girls on the mats and Daisy on her camp bed, they listened for the zip of Charles's tent before Nicole said. "Are you all right Miss Andrews?"

"Oh yes, Nicole. That's not the first time I've been spanked, and I shouldn't have used his nickname. I hope you don't tell the rest of the school."

"Oh no Miss," Katie said. "You're one of us now, we have a new name, we are the "Triple S girls.""

"What on earth is that?" Daisy said.

"Saint Sam's Spanked Girls," They all said together.

"Shush," Daisy said, but Charles was listening to it all, and he smiled.

The following day all was forgiven and forgotten and they all went off tramping over the barren land looking at the broads and how they were constructed. Daisy explained how the rivers Ant and Bure had joined up with the old peat digs and how they had been extended and improved. At lunch, they all sat next to the river and Charles produced sandwiches for lunch plus a bottle of beer for each of them.

"I thought that the school rules said that we couldn't drink alcohol, Sir," Katie said.

"I think you will find that the rules say that you can't drink alcohol on the school property. But we are not on the grounds here, are we? But if you don't want that beer?"

"Oh no Sir, that will be fine, thank you."

They watched the longboats going up and down on the water and all of them longed to be on one of those boats, but nobody mentioned it. That evening Charles produced another special meal and all the girls were very tired so they went to bed early, leaving Daisy and Charles together next to the fire.

"Thank you for coming, Charles," Daisy said. "This trip would not have been the same without you."

"I have really enjoyed myself Daisy, and it beats watching the juniors playing hockey on Saturday." They both laughed.

Sitting quietly watching the fire die down Daisy said. "You know, Charles, I might like a threesome with Sarah and you."

"Okay Daisy," Charles said smiling, "But it's bedtime now."

"Yes Sir," Daisy said.

While all this was happening Katie was listening and she just smiled and then rolled over and went to sleep.

After lunch on Sunday, the tent was packed up and they all went back to the school. Everybody agreed that this had been the best field trip they had ever had. "We even slept in a field," Nicole said and they all laughed.

Chapter 16 - Charles Spanks a Parent

Two weeks later it was Exeat Weekend. The borders were allowed out for the weekend from the time the school finished on Friday to Sunday evening. Many of the girls had parents who lived abroad so it was less than half the school who could take advantage of the Exeat Weekend. Mary Becker's Mum was in Singapore for a few weeks so Mary had to stay in school, but Sophie Lucas, a fifth-form girl, felt sorry for her and invited Mary to come home with her for the weekend. All that would have been fine only Mary had been playing up in class that afternoon and Charles had to spank her quite hard. He had told her that she would not be going out for the Exeat Weekend but she begged him to spank her instead, and he agreed. Again that would also have been fine if she had not been wriggling in Sophie's parent's car all the way home.

When Mrs Lucas asked Mary what the problem was Mary said. "Oh there's no problem, only I was spanked by the Old Man this afternoon."

"Mrs Lucas was horrified. "Which Old Man?" she said and Mary knew that she had made a mistake.

"Mr Nicholson, the housemaster of Christie House. I asked him to spank me instead of stopping me from going out for the Exeat Weekend."

"That's outrageous," Mrs Lucas was obviously angry. "Letting a male teacher spank you, it shouldn't be allowed. Did he spank you on your knickers?"

"Oh no Mrs Lucas," Mary said. She was on firmer ground now. "He always spanks the girls on their bare bottoms."

"What?" Mrs Lucas said. "He makes you take down your knickers?"

"Oh yes," Mary said proudly, "He says that spankings should always be on your bare bottom."

"Well, we will see about that Mary." Mrs Lucas said. "What about you Sophie, does he spank you?"

"Oh no Mum," Sophie said.

"Mr Nicholson only spanks the older girls, Mrs Lucas," Mary said.

"I bet he does." Mrs Lucas said. "We will talk no more about it now, but I promise you that the school governors will hear about this."

The following Monday at about lunchtime, Amelia Brandon, the headmistress, bumped into Charles in the corridor. "Ah there you are Charles, we have a small problem."

"What's up Amelia?"

"This," she said as she passed him a letter that was mailed to the school governors on Friday evening. Charles read the letter out loud.

"Dear Madam. I have just been informed that one of the male teachers at Saint Samantha's school is abusing the children. I have not called the police because I'm sure that the school will not want the publicity, but I want the teacher (Mr Nicholson) fired, and your assurance that no such abuse will happen in the future. If I do not hear from you by Friday next, I will be calling the Police and newspapers. Yours Sincerely. Mrs Lucas.

"Oh," Charles said. "I don't recognise the name so I don't think I've spanked her child."

"No, Sophia is in the fifth form, but Mary Becker went home with her for the Exeat Weekend."

"I spanked her on Friday afternoon," Charles said and Amelia nodded. "I think the best thing to do would be to have a chat with Mary."

"Yes, Charles, I agree, but the head of the board of Governors also wants to have a chat with both of us in my office."

"No Problem, I will go and find Mary," Charles said as he left.

"No Sir," Mary said when Charles caught up with her in the corridor outside the classroom. "I didn't complain to Mrs Lucas at all, I told her that I had asked you to spank me but she didn't believe me, I knew that there would be trouble."

"You're not in any trouble at all, Mary," Charles said. "Don't worry about it, we will sort it all out."

Mary left Charles and called all the girls in the upper sixth form to gather round, then she told them what Charles had told her.

Back in the headmistress's office, Charles was confronted by Mrs Elizabeth Crawley, head of the governors of Saint Samantha's School for Girls. "Hello Charles, good to see you again." Mrs Crawley said. They had met at a governor's meeting three months ago. "Now what's all this nonsense I hear about you spanking the girls?" she asked.

"Well, we agreed..." Amelia said but Mrs Crawley held up her hand.

"I would like to hear it from Charles please," she said.

"Of course Elizabeth," Charles said. "Amelia and I found some old papers about the school in the basement from the last century that talked about the tradition of birthday spankings. That raised the issue of spankings as punishment for all the older girls. Amelia wrote to the parents and we spoke to the girls, they all agreed that it would be a good idea so here we are."

"I see," Elizabeth Crawley said, but it was plain that she didn't see at all.

"Amelia appointed me disciplinarian for the girls over the age of eighteen," Charles continued, "And, as it happens, for the teachers if discipline is necessary."

"The teachers as well?" Elizabeth said. "And how do they feel about that?"

"Well, you had better ask them," Amelia said. She was angry with Elizabeth Crawley for interrupting her before and only listening to Charles.

"Yes, I will," She said as there was a knock at the door.

"Busy," Amelia shouted, but the door opened anyway and Mary Becker interrupted them.

"I'm sorry to bother you," Mary said. "But I think you will want to read this. It's signed by all the girls in the Upper sixth."

"Give it here," Amelia said. "Now back to class." As she read the handwritten note with a lot of signatures at the bottom, she smiled and handed it to the head of the governors.

"I see," she said.

"What is it?" Charles asked.

"I'll read it," Elizabeth said. "The girls from the Upper Sixth at St Samantha's Girls' School would like to assure the governing body of the school that they are in favour of receiving spankings from Mr Nicholson when they are naughty. Nobody likes to be spanked, but that's much better than writing lines, detention or missing the Exeat Weekend." Elizabeth looked up. "Well, it seems that you have a number of fans amongst the girls, Charles, but what about the staff?"

"Most of them will be in the staffroom at the moment, it's their lunch break," Amelia said.

When the three of them entered the staff room there was a lot of discussion and then the room went quiet. Amelia raised her voice. "Ladies, Mrs Elizabeth Crawley would like to ask you a question."

Daisy was the first to talk. "Before she does that Amelia, I may be able to help with your dilemma Mrs Crawley," she said. "We heard about the signed letter that the girls have presented to you today and we have a similar one here. We have all signed it apart from Laura, but she is away today. I'm sure she will sign it when she comes back."

"I see," Mrs Crawley said again.

"Well then," Elizabeth said. "It seems that we have nothing more to discuss. Thank you everybody, and thank you, Amelia, for a wonderful turnout for my surprise visit. I'm very impressed." Then taking Charles's arm she said. "Walk with me to my car please Charles."

As they walked to the car, Elizabeth said. "I will send a note to Mrs Lucas telling her that the board of governors is entirely satisfied and that she should make an appointment to see you during the week. In the meantime I would like to discuss this further with you Charles, could you come and see me next week?"

Charles thought for a while and then said, "Don't you think it would be better if you came to see me Elizabeth? The disciplinarian doesn't usually travel to naughty girls, they usually come to him."

"Oh, I see," Elizabeth said. "You're a very clever man. Shall we say next Wednesday at seven, your office?"

"Okay," Charles said smiling as the driver opened the door of the Bently and Mrs Crawley climbed in.

The following Thursday Charles arrived at Amelia's office and Mrs Lucas was already in the room. "I think it's disgusting that you allow this horrible man to spank the girls, and Mary said that she was spanked on her bare bottom." Mrs Lucas said as Charles walked in. "You must be Mr Nicholas that abuses the girls."

Charles smiled at Mrs Lucas with his hand out, "Hello Mrs Lucas, it's a pleasure to meet you."

"Don't you Mrs Lucas me, you horrible man." Mrs Lucas said.

"Oh, I'm sorry, what's your first name?"

"Synthia," she said. "But that's nothing to do with you."

"Of course it is Synthia, and I'm Charles. Maybe if we sit down we can talk about this like adults."

"I'm talking like an adult."

"No, you're ranting like a child." Charles raised his voice. "Now Sit Down," he said, and Mrs Lucas sat on the chair behind her.

"Well," she said, but didn't say anything else.

"Mrs Lucas," Amelia said when they were all seated. "Before we go any further I should tell you that after you upset Mary with your accusations last Friday, all the girls have signed this petition saying that they prefer to be spanked when they are naughty. It's better than the other punishments we used to give them." Amelia handed the note to Mrs Lucas.

"They must have been coerced." Mrs Lucas said.

"I'm happy to bring them in one at a time with you on your own and you can ask them yourself if you want to interrupt the school day."

"No, that will be fine," she said. "But what about the staff, what do they think about all this spanking lark?" Amelia handed Mrs Lucas the note from the staff without saying a word.

"Right," Mrs Lucas said. "I will be going then."

"Not so fast Synthia," Charles said in his best housemaster voice. "You have caused a great deal of trouble with your stupid letter to the governors and when Mary came back on Sunday from her visit to your house she was crying because she thought she was in trouble."

"Oh, I didn't know," Mrs Lucas was apologetic. "I would like to say sorry to her."

"I'm sure you will have an opportunity to do that sometime," Charles said. "But I would like to ask you a simple question. What would your father have done when you were a child, if you had made so much fuss and upset somebody for no reason."

"Oh," she said. "I see what you're saying and I'm truly sorry."

Charles pushed the point. "Would your father have been happy with a simple apology?"

Synthia felt she was being backed into a corner but she saw no way out. She was looking at her hands on her lap when she said, "No Sir."

"What would he have done?"

"He would have spanked me," Synthia whispered.

"I'm sorry, I didn't hear that," Charles said.

Synthia looked up and said, "He would have spanked me."

"Yes, he would," Charles said. "And that would have been the right thing for a loving father to do?"

"Yes Sir," she said. "But you can't spank me."

"No I can't," Charles said. "Not without your permission, that would be assault. We don't do that in this school. But when you go home tonight you will be feeling very guilty that you created such a fuss in your daughter's school, your daughter will not learn the lesson that everybody must accept responsibility for their mistakes, and Mary Becker will still be upset about raising the issue of spanking when she visited you last weekend."

"I see," Mrs Lucas said.

"But if you ask me to spank you now, you will feel much better because you have been punished for your mistake, your daughter will learn a good lesson and you will be forgiven," Charles said. "So what's it to be?"

Synthia was whispering again. "Please will you spank me, Sir,"

"Sorry, what did you say?" Charles asked. "The Old Man is just a little deaf."

Amelia looked up, surprised that Charles knew his school nickname.

"I said, please will you spank me, Sir?"

"Of course, I will Synthia. Come over here and bend over my lap." Surprising herself, Synthia Lucas stood up and walked the two yards to where Charles was sitting on a dining chair. He patted his lap and she bent over with her hands and toes on the floor on either side of his knees. Lifting her loose summer dress Synthia exclaimed, but Charles said. "Oh come on Synthia, you know that spankings are always on your bare bottom, I'm sure your father told you that."

Then it all came flooding back for Synthia. Her father's punishments on her bare bottom, how much she used to cry and how much she missed her father now. Synthia was already crying as she raised her hips when Charles took the elastic of her big cotton knickers and eased them over her fat bottom. Charles estimated that Synthia was in her late thirties but she had gone to seed as far as her body was concerned. She was probably a slim athletic girl like her daughter when she was younger, but now she had rolls of fat around her waist and her bottom. Charles didn't complain. He took a great deal of pleasure in spanking any bottom no matter how large. This particular bottom, however, was a great pleasure because of all the trouble she had caused.

Charles started to spank the bottom over his lap straight away. Hard and fast, and didn't stop until Synthia was sobbing. "I'm sorry Sir, I promise I'll never do it again."

"Save your apologies until I have finished Synthia," Charles said. Then turning to Amelia he said. "Could you pass me that hairbrush you use sometimes please?"

"Of course Charles," she stood up and got the hairbrush from the mantlepiece, handing it to Charles she mouthed "Thank you" and then left her office.

"These last few with the hairbrush are for the trauma you caused Mary Becker," Charles said and gave Synthia Lucas twenty spanks with the hairbrush on her already sore bottom. She was sobbing when Charles put down the hairbrush and lifted her up. "Go and stand over there and think about your actions Synthia."

Five minutes later Charles called her over and sat her on his knee. Her skirt was down but she had lost her knickers somewhere. Holding her tight on his knee, Charles said. "All forgiven now. All you have to do is to write a letter to the board of governors apologising for the mistake and go and find Mary Becker and apologise to her as well. Synthia looked at Charles and then nodded.

Chapter 17 - Charles spanks a school governor

At six-thirty on Wednesday Amelia was looking for Charles and she found him in his office. "We have another visitation from Elizabeth Crawford," She is sitting in her car at the front of the building.

"I know," Charles said. "She's coming to see me."

"See you?" Amelia was suspicious, "What for?"

"Don't worry, your job is secure," Charles said. "She has a personal matter she wants to discuss."

Amelia thought for a while and then said, "She's coming for a spanking isn't she?"

Charles smiled. "A gentleman never tells," he said.

Amelia turned and walked away laughing.

At seven o'clock Charles was sitting behind his desk when there was a knock at the door. "Come," he said, and Elizabeth Crawford walked in the door. Somehow she looked smaller now. The last time Charles saw her, she was wearing a smart business suit and high heels. This time she was in jeans and flat shoes. Charles guessed that she was in her mid-forties. She had her blond hair pulled right back away from her face and her slim body was encased in a nice cardigan that emphasised the shape of her boobs with a white t-shirt underneath. Charles didn't think she was wearing a bra.

"So you have come for your spanking then," Charles said.

"I didn't say that was what I was coming for."

"No you didn't, but it is, isn't it?"

"I'm not sure." Elizabeth Crawley was uncertain.

"If you haven't come to have your bare bottom spanked, what have you come for?"

"Bare bottom?"

"Spankings are always on your bare bottom."

You are an expert are you?" Elizabeth said and Charles nodded. "We shall see."

Charles needed to take back control of the situation. "Are you here for a spanking for punishment or for erotic excitement?"

"There's a difference?"

"Certainly."

"Well, I guess I felt rather foolish when I visited the school last week. I intended to fire you, give Amelia a written warning and take a lot more interest in the school. I'm an alumnus of the school, or more accurately, an alumna, and I care very much for the school. Bad press is not a good idea. But having seen your results and the support you get from the staff and the girls, I changed my mind. I have also had a letter from Mrs Lucas who seems very supportive of the idea now. Did you spank her as well?"

"A gentleman never tells," Charles said.

"My God, you did, didn't you?" Elizabeth asked and Charles just smiled. "Anyway, I wanted to apologise to you and Amelia and I guess I deserve a punishment spanking, for forming an opinion before knowing the facts."

"Right," Charles said as he got up from behind his desk and moved the spanking chair into the centre of the room. Elizabeth had been standing the whole time she was there, Charles had never suggested that she should sit, so Charles was sitting on the spanking chair and he called Elizabeth over to him. Standing in front of Charles, Elizabeth was very nervous as he undid the button on her jeans and pulled down the zip.

"Are you going to spank me on my knickers?" Elizabeth said.

"Come on Lizzi, you know that spankings are always on your bare bottom," he said. Elizabeth was horrified that Charles had called her Lizzi. It was what her father called her and she wouldn't let anybody else call her that, but from Charles, it seemed appropriate.

"Yes Sir," she said and helped Charles push down her tight jeans and knickers. Elizabeth was now standing naked from her waist to her ankles as Charles guided her across his knee.

"You have been very naughty Lizzi, and I think this spanking is long overdue," Charles said with his hand gently massaging her bare bottom. I will be spanking you with my hand and then you will get the leather slipper. I expect that you will be crying when I've finished but you will be forgiven afterwards."

"Thank you, Sir," Elizabeth said but she had no idea what she was thanking Charles for. She liked the feel of Charles's hand on her bottom, as a single woman it had been a long time since anybody had handled her naked body. As soon as she thought that, she felt the sting of the first smack and it startled her. It hurt. Her logical brain knew that a spanking hurt, but she had forgotten that it might and she was struggling after the first few spanks. Charles stopped spanking her and told her to stop wriggling.

"I will be starting the spanking again now," he said. "And if you continue to wriggle I will stop and then start the spanking again. We will continue to do that until you have settled. This is a spanking and it will hurt. Get used to it."

Charles started the spanking again and now she knew what to expect so she was still. It still hurt and the sting of the spanking got worse and worse. Soon she was crying and apologising but she never wriggled again. "Good Girl," Charles said as he stopped spanking her and massaged her bottom again. "In a minute I will be spanking you with the leather slipper, it will sting but it will soon be over, and then I will hug you until you stop crying."

"Yes, Sir," Elizabeth said. "And I'm sorry to be such a nuisance."

"You're not a nuisance, you're just a little girl lost," Charles said and Elizabeth knew he was right. Soon the slipper was landing on Elizabeth's bottom hard and fast. She was sobbing almost immediately after the slipper spanking started and she didn't stop until it finished. Lifting her up, Charles settled Elizabeth on his lap and he hugged her until she stopped crying, patting her bottom all the time in a comforting way. "All forgiven now," he said.

After about ten minutes, Elizabeth started to stir, so Charles helped her up. "Phew, Charles," she said. "That was intense. I can see why the staff and the older girls like it. Well I guess "like" is the wrong word, I expect they hate it but the feeling afterwards is amazing."

"So I'm told," Charles said as he stood up. He enjoyed the spectacle of Elizabeth pulling her jeans and knickers back into position and then he said. "Feeling better now?"

"Yes, strangely, I do.

Elizabeth Crawley left soon after this and the following day Amelia caught Charles again and said. "I have just had a very long letter from Elizabeth Crawley telling me that she thinks I'm doing an amazing job and apologising for doubting me last week. Did you have anything to do with that?"

"Nope," Charles said. "But she did say that she was going to write to you."

Chapter 18 - Matron spanks two girls for pretending to be sick

With Just two weeks left in the Autumn term there was excitement in the school with most girls looking forward to the coming pleasures of the Christmas festivities. The anticipated presents ranged from a new car for Nicole Asher and the complete Encyclopaedia Britannica Hardcover for Amy Wilson, to the latest Led Zeppelin album for Katie Owen. It seemed that the cost of the presents had nothing to do with how much the parents could afford, but rather how spoiled their children were.

Some of the children would not be going home for Christmas. Mary Becker's mother was still in Singapore and Ella Hall's father was stationed in Hong Kong and it seemed silly for Ella to travel all that way for the short Christmas holiday. Ella was disappointed because the only time she would be with her parents was during the six-week summer holiday. Mary Becker, on the other hand, had spent the Christmas Holidays at the school for the last three years and she was looking forward to it. "You get to see the other side of the teachers at Christmas," she said to Ella, trying to cheer her up. "They are nicer and we have a big Christmas tree and lights and everything. Cook makes a lovely Christmas pudding as well. It's fantastic." Mary didn't really believe it was better to be at school at Christmas, but she was able to cheer Ella up a little.

In the last two weeks of the term, it was hard for the teachers to keep the girls focused on their academic studies. The exams were finished but the results had not come out yet. There would be the

Winter Games to think about. That's what the girls called the Autumn term sports day because it was usually so cold that they all hated to be running around the field in their baggy shorts and t-shirts.

The Matron, Sarah Nicholson, also had the last of the flu epidemic to take care of amongst the younger girls. Surprisingly it didn't spread to the older girls, although one or two girls did complain of flu symptoms, but Sarah was quick to work out which of the girls were just trying to get out of the Winter Games. At seven that morning, Lucy Smith and Ella Hall were both waiting outside the Sanatorium when Sophie Lucas walked out, followed by Sarah who said, "Next".

"Coming now," Lucy said, but Sarah knew the signs, she was waiting for this. Walking back into her surgery Sarah waited and as Lucy walked in she swallowed and then held the back of her hand to her forehead. "Oh, Matron," she said. "I'm sick."

"I'm sorry to hear that Lucy," Sarah said. "Let me take your temperature." and she stuck the thermometer into Lucy's mouth. A minute or so later Sarah looked at the temperature on the thermometer.

"Am I sick, Matron?" Lucy said.

"No, Lucy, you're dead. Your temperature is so high you would be dead from heatstroke by now. I had better take your temperature rectally."

"In my bottom Matron?" Lucy said.

"Yes Lucy, It's the only way to get an accurate reading, and you had better take off all your clothes, you must be burning up."

"I'm feeling much better now Matron, I think I just need to rest awhile," Lucy said.

"With a temperature like that, I can't let you out of here until I have given you a full physical, and maybe an enema as well."

"No really Matron, I'm feeling much better now."

"Come on Lucy, off with those clothes, unless you want me to ask Mr Nicholson to step in here and help me take your clothes off for you?"

"Please Matron," Lucy said, but Sarah had her arms folded and Lucy knew there was no point in arguing anymore. Lucy was a big girl. At five foot eight inches, she was taller than the others in her class and she had big boobs and a huge bottom to go with it. She was very embarrassed by her body and didn't even like to shower in the same room with the other girls, so taking her clothes off for Matron was a punishment.

When she was naked she was standing in the surgery with her left arm across her large boobs and her right hand cupping her pussy. "Climb on the table Lucy, with your bottom in the air so that I can take your temperature."

"Do I have to, Matron, I'm feeling a lot better now," Lucy said.

"Of course you do, girl. You can't possibly have a temperature that high and feel better almost immediately. Up you get." Lucy knelt on the table with her bottom in the air. "Just reach behind you and pull your cheeks apart so that I can insert the thermometer," Sara said as she rubbed vaseline on the glass tube.

Lucy was terribly embarrassed to be in this humiliating position and regretted trying to avoid the sports day. "Nothing could be worse than this," she thought, but she was wrong.

Sarah pulled out the thermometer and declared that Lucy's temperature was normal. "Well that's very strange Lucy, I had better give you an enema just in case."

"No matron, please, I was just joking, I'm not sick," Lucy said in desperation, knowing that having an enema would be worse than having your temperature taken in this position.

"Well, you must have been sick, what other reason could there have been for having such a high temperature?"

"But Matron, I had a mouthful of hot water before I came in," Lucy admitted.

"So you were cheating?"

"No Matron, I was thirsty." Lucy still had her bottom in the air in the most embarrassing position and Sarah had a long wooden spoon in her hand that she keeps under the table for just such an opportunity, so she spanked Lucy with it. "Ouch."

"Lucy, that's a lie and I will be calling Mr Nicholas to come and cane you for lying."

"No, please Matron, I was just trying to get out of the Winter Games. I hate running around the track. My big boobs always bounce up and down and I'm always last in the races anyway."

"If you hate running, why not just walk?" Sarah said. "I had big boobs at school as well, and I hated running, so the school had a walking race as well. Sit up on the examination table Lucy."

Lucy sat up and she was less embarrassed about having big boobs, knowing that Matron had the same problem when she was at school. "Hands on your head Lucy," Sarah said, "I want to test something. Lucy did as she was told and then Sarah cupped Lucy's big breasts with her hands, massaging them. "The doctors will do this for you when you have a physical, they're checking for lumps that may be dangerous. When you have big breasts this is more common. Usually, it's nothing to worry about but you should have it checked out.

"Yes, Matron," Lucy said as she was enjoying the attention. Then Lucy giggled as Matron pinched a nipple.

"You have nice nipples Lucy, and if they're sensitive the boys will love them, some of the girls as well."

"But Matron, is that okay?"

"Of course darling. If it feels good and you both want to do it. It's very okay. How does that feel?" Sarah said as she continued to manipulate each nipple in turn.

"It feels lovely, Matron," Lucy said. "But I'm not sure."

Sarah continued her magic. "What's wrong Lucy?"

"It's only... Well, I can feel it down here." Lucy pointed between her legs.

"That's perfectly natural as well, Lucy. You can try it yourself later." Sarah said as she stopped what she was doing.

"Yes Matron," Lucy said as she jumped off the examination table.

"Where are you going Lucy, you still have a spanking to come for lying."

Lucy looked disappointed. "Yes, Matron," she said. "Shall I bend over the table then?"

"Good girl," Sarah said as she looked at Lucy's large bottom bent over the table. Picking up the wooden spoon again Sarah started to spank Lucy's bottom to the beat of the rock music that was playing in the surgery. When she was appointed Matron at the beginning of the Autumn term, she asked the school janitor to make the surgery soundproofed as much as possible, so that people waiting outside didn't hear the screams of the patients when they had injections. Actually, she wanted to make sure nobody heard her spanking them.

Sarah's wooden spoon was one of the things she brought back from South Africa when she was a school matron there. It was longer than the wooden spoons you get in England and had a bigger spoon shape at the end. It was hand-carved and perfect for spanking naughty bottoms. Lucy was crying after the third spank and Sarah continued for another few minutes until Lucy's bottom was glowing red, then she took a polaroid instant picture of the red bottom to show her husband. "Up you get," Sarah said, and she hugged Lucy until she stopped crying, patting her bottom gently the whole time."Come on now, get dressed and I will see who is next in line outside."

Sarah let Lucy out of the surgery and noticed Ella Hall swallowing something. Sarah smiled as she whisked Ella into the room before Lucy could say anything. Ella also had big boobs and

Matron understood the desire to avoid the Winter Games, but she was also looking forward to spanking Ella, whom she had never spanked before.

Ten minutes later Ella was naked and bent over the examination table. "I'm sorry I lied Matron, do you have to spank me?" Ella said.

"You know I do Ella, you will get a spanking for lying and six extra spanks for making such a fuss over having your temperature taken."

"Yes, Matron, I'm sorry about that." Sarah started to spank Ella with the spoon straight away to the beat of "Yellow Submarine," by the Beatles.

After a couple of minutes, Ella's bottom was very red and she was sobbing. "Right, now for the six strokes for making a fuss about having your temperature taken. Reach behind you and pull your cheeks apart, I will be spanking you right there so that you will never think of making such a fuss again."

"Oh no Matron, not there, that will hurt," Ella said.

"Yes it will, and you will remember that for next time won't you."

"Yes Matron," Ella said as she reached behind her and pulled her big cheeks apart so that her anus came into view.

"Wider Ella," Sarah said and Ella groaned as she stretched her cheeks wider. Sarah then turned the wooden spoon around so that she was holding the round spoon shape. She had spanked girls on their anus before but not since she arrived at this school, and she had been looking for an opportunity to try this out on someone. Bringing the handle part of the wooden spoon vertically down between Ella's cheeks Sarah caught her anus perfectly and Ella screamed. The next five strokes followed in exactly the same way and Ella was sobbing so hard Sarah thought she might pass out on the examination table.

"Well done Ella," Sarah said. "You took your punishment very well."

"But it hurts Matron, I'll never be able to go to the toilet ever again."

"Don't be a silly girl Ella," Matron said as she pulled out a drawer from the cupboard behind her. "I have some antiseptic cream here for you and it has an anaesthetic as well, so your bottom will feel better in no time." Sarah always smiled when she did this. Spanking between the girl's cheeks is very painful, so she does it and then puts on some cream to take away the pain. "Pull your cheeks apart again Ella and I will make it better for you.

"Yes Matron," Ella said but her bottom was very sore, and it hurt to pull her cheeks apart again. Eventually, they were wide enough and Sarah rubbed cream between her cheeks and over her anus, slipping inside just a little with the lubrication of the cream.

After the anaesthetic cream did its magic, Ella stood up. "You're right Matron, the sting has gone."

"Yes, but I hope the memory of that spanking lingers so you don't make such a fuss again."

"Thank you, Matron, I'm sorry that I lied, you're the best," she said strangely as she hugged Sarah. That was the second time a naked eighteen-year-old had hugged her that day. "The day is looking up," she thought.

Chapter 19 - A Birthday spanking in the Staff Room

Sarah walked into the staff room at eight-thirty and was surprised to see everybody there. "What's going on?" she asked her husband Charles Nicholson, who was not only the only male member of the teaching staff, and the Christie House housemaster, but he had also been appointed the school disciplinarian for the older girls and the staff when necessary.

"Lilly's birthday," Charles replied.

Sarah clapped her hands like a little girl. "Oh Goodie, this day is just getting better and better."

Charles laughed as Amelia Brandon, the headmistress, called everybody to order. "Thank you for all coming early to help celebrate Lilly's birthday. I'm sure you remember what happened to Laura a few weeks ago so we all know what's going to happen today. Charles, if you could take your seat, and I expect the others will want to find somewhere to get a good view. And finally, Lilly, would you like to come forward?"

"Not much headmistress," Lilly said, and there was a round of applause as she took her place over Charles's lap. "It's all right for you lot," she said from her awkward position. "But I'm forty-six today." Lilly was wearing a long flowered dress and when Charles raised the dress above her waist she also had on what looked like very expensive silk French knickers and stockings with a suspender belt to hold the stockings up. There was another round of applause in appreciation of the underwear.

"These are lovely knickers, Lilly," Charles said, "it seems such a shame to take them down."

"That's what I was thinking Sir," Lilly said and the others noticed that she called him Sir. It's always quite hard not to when you're over someone's lap.

"Alas Lilly, as much as I would like to spank you over these lovely knickers one day. Today is not that day. The others would be so disappointed." And without any further conversation, Charles eased the knickers down over Lilly's bottom, leaving the stockings and suspenders in place. The spanking started almost straight away with a two-second gap between each spank so that the others could count. "One, Two," they all called together, and Lilly realised that the whole school would guess that she was getting her birthday spanking, and she was right. At twenty spanks Charles stopped for a second or two and rubbed Lilly's bottom. Charles was thinking what a lovely bottom this is to spank. Lilly wasn't fat but you could call her curvy. She had a narrow waist but wider hips so there was plenty of her bottom to spank. Lilly was beginning to enjoy the rubbing of her bottom but then the spanking started again, along with the chanting, "Twenty-one, Twenty-two," they all called out. At forty Charles was rubbing again and Lilly lifted her bottom involuntarily to encourage him, but then the next five spanks were delivered, with a longer break before the last one, which was just a little harder than the others.

Charles knew that this was not a punishment spanking so it wasn't hard and Lilly wasn't crying when she stood up, but she was rubbing the sting away on her bottom as her dress fell back in place. Her knickers had come right off and they were on the floor when Cook burst into the staff room carrying the cake with just ten token candles on it. "That many candles would have been a fire hazard," she explained.

Later, when Lilly went to her classroom, she discovered that the younger girls had placed a cushion on her chair. She laughed but was also a little embarrassed that the young girls knew that she had been spanked. A hand went up as soon as she lowered herself carefully onto her seat. "Miss?" It was Pinky Turner who put her hand up.

"Yes, Pinky?" Lilly said.

"When will we be old enough to get a birthday spanking?"

"There's no hurry for that Pinky," Lilly said. "But I'm sure your friends can help you out if you ask them nicely." There was a rumbling of agreement in the classroom. "But in this school, It's only for your eighteenth birthday that Mr Nicholson gives you a birthday spanking."

"I can't wait until I'm eighteen Miss," Pinky said as she sat down and Lilly smiled.

Chapter 20 - Amelia and Jasmine are caught and spanked

After the spanking in the staff room, Sarah cornered her husband and talked to him about the two girls she had spanked in the surgery that morning. "It's not really fair, you know. Neither girl is going to win their race but they have to present themselves for the race like everybody else in the school and then run with their big boobs bouncing up and down. When they practised during PE last week, I saw Lucy holding her boobs as she was running because they hurt so much."

"What are you suggesting Sarah?" Charles said.

"What about having a walking race for the girls with big boobs. It would still be a race but the girls wouldn't have to worry about their boobs bouncing up and down."

"I think that's a good idea, why not ask Amelia?" Charles said.

"I was hoping that you would ask her, Charles," Sarah said. "You seem to be able to get whatever you want from her."

Charles laughed. "You spanked her as well you know," he said remembering when they both spanked Amelia and Jasmine for being too obvious about their relationship.

"Yes, I know, but you're a man," Sarah said and they both knew she was right.

Charles didn't have a lesson starting until ten that morning so he walked straight to the gym to look for Jasmine, the PE teacher. Jasmine Pritchard was just 26 but she had had a brief Olympic tennis career before becoming a teacher and the school tennis team won all the trophies, with such an experienced teacher at the helm during the summer term. For the other two terms, she ran all the other sports so the Autumn sports day was her responsibility.

The gym was empty when Charles walked in but he heard Jasmine giggling in the changing room. Charles listened for a while and realised that she was with Amelia, which was a good thing, as it would save having two conversations, but then he heard what was going on and decided to listen for a while.

"No, not here Amelia, someone might walk in," Jasmine said.

"It's alright, everybody is busy. I have just watched Lilly being spanked and I'm as horny as hell, get on the floor and lick me or I will have to spank you as well."

"Alright, but we will have to be quick, Amelia," Jasmine said. "I have the fourth-form girls in thirty minutes."

"The more you talk the longer it will take," Amelia said. "Lie on the floor and I will sit on your face, you know how much I like that."

Charles continued listening. He was getting excited at the thought of what was going on in the changing room so he had to adjust his clothing when a couple of girls came running into the gym. Charles turned around and guided the girls back into the corridor. "What are you doing in the gym, you're not allowed in there unless It's an organised PE lesson. I'm sure you heard what happened to Amy Wilson. She was caned last month for unsupervised use of the gym equipment."

"Yes sir," one of the girls said. "But we were desperate for the toilet and there's one in the changing room."

"Well, you had better go to the other toilet next to the dining room." He said as the girls ran to the toilet. "No running in the corridor," he shouted after them and they slowed to a fast walk.

Walking back into the gym he could hear Amelia coming close to her orgasm so he walked straight into the changing room and found Jasmin lying on the floor with Amelia sitting on her face rubbing herself to an orgasm. Jasmin had her hands under Amelia's jumper holding her big boobs. Amelia looked up and said "Charles!"

There was a flurry of activity as Jasmine pushed Amelia off her and they both stood up trying to sort out their clothes. Amelia started to talk and Charles held up his hand. "I don't want to hear it, but you should know that I stopped two junior girls running in here just now to use the toilet."

"Oh my God," Amelia said. "Thank you, Charles."

"I don't think you will be thanking me this evening at seven o'clock in my lounge. In the meantime, I want to ask both of you if some of the girls could do a walking race instead of a running race on Sports day next week?"

"What for?" Jasmine said. "Running is good for them."

"I will demonstrate," Charles said. "Jump up and down Amelia."

"What?" Amelia said.

"You heard me," Charles said using the voice he kept for naughty girls. Amelia did as she was told and then she had to hold her breasts. Charles had correctly guessed that Amelia had loosened her bra so that Jasmin could fondle her boobs. "Hands by your sides,"

She did as she was told but after a while Amelia said. "It hurts my breasts."

"Precisely, the girls with big boobs have difficulty in running fast, if we had a walking race they would still get the exercise without feeling uncomfortable."

"He's right you know," Amelia said to Jasmine. "I wonder why it takes a man to think of these things."

"No, it was Sarah who brought it to my attention." Charles turned and left but then he waited a while to hear what was said.

"Shit," Jasmine said. "We're going to get it now."

"It's just a spanking," Amelia said.

"Maybe not, I heard the girls talking about a new trick Sarah had, of using that wooden spoon between their cheeks. We're lucky that she didn't catch us."

"Oh I don't know," Amelia said. "She could have joined in." They both giggled and Charles decided to chat with his wife.

That evening at seven Amelia and Jasmine were both standing outside Charles's office, which doubled as the lounge of the housemaster's apartment in the evening. It was tastefully decorated with a large desk in the bay window and two leather guest chairs, but the room also had a chesterfield settee and two armchairs around an open fireplace. A Grandfather clock that simply refused to run, and other matching cupboards and small tables. There were also two dining chairs that seemed to have no other use than to support the person spanking one or other of the naughty girls.

Amelia was the headmistress of the school and in theory, Charles's boss, but in practice, she felt less important than Charles ever since he spanked her and Jasmine soon after he was appointed as housemaster of Christie House at the beginning of the term. "Come in," Charles shouted just before Amelia knocked. "Here come two naughty girls who cannot keep their hands off each other."

Amelia tried to explain, but Charles held up his hand just like he had done earlier today. "I'm not interested," he said. "There's absolutely no excuse. It doesn't matter that the girls who nearly caught you were not meant to be there, they were there and you were nearly caught. Had they told anybody it would have been all around the school before lights-out, and I expect the mothers would have been reading all about it in the letters home that the girls write on Friday night."

"But," Amelia said, but Charles interrupted her.

"Yes, it was your Butt that was on display over Jasmine's face, and it will be your butt that pays for it now."

"But, I'm the headmistress," Amelia said.

"Not for very much longer if you carry on like that. I saved your job this morning and the last time we had a conversation about this a few months ago you promised to be more careful. I certainly do not call fucking each other in the changing room next to the gym being more careful."

Amelia relented, "I know, I'm sorry Charles."

"Not yet, but you will be by the time Sarah and I have finished with you," Charles said.

Jasmine hadn't said anything up until this moment but when she heard that Matron would be involved she feared the worst. "Is Matron going to join us?" she said.

"Yes," Charles replied. "She has just gone to the Sanatorium to get something, but she will be back any minute now. We will each spank your bare bottoms and then we have a surprise for you. While we're waiting, stand over there beside the wall and undress." Charles pointed to the blank wall where he often sent naughty girls after they had been spanked. The two sorry-looking adults walked over to the wall like naughty children and started to undress.

"This is your fault," Jasmine whispered to Amelia.

"No talking," Charles said as Sarah walked into the lounge carrying her long wooden spoon. Jasmine looked up and her worst fear was confirmed. Nudging Amelia she pointed to the wooden spoon that Sarah was carrying.

While this was happening Charles had moved the two dining chairs into the centre of the lounge facing each other. He then took the hairbrush and the leather slipper and placed them, one on each chair. Directing Sarah to one of the chairs he sat on the other and then called the naughty girls over. "Sarah, you take Amelia and I will spank Jasmin, then we will swap over. This will be a long spanking, ladies, so don't expect to be able to sit down when you leave here."

The naked thirty-eight-year-old headmistress and the young twenty-six-year-old sports mistress placed themselves over the laps of Sarah and Charles, who then placed their right hands on the bottoms offered to them. This was the best bit for Sarah, she loved the feel of a naked body over her lap and even though Amelia Brandon was rather chubby, Sarah could take the weight so she wrapped her left arm around her body to hold her in place. Then the spanking started. Sarah and Charles had developed the art of spanking pairs of girls like this in South Africa where they had been working for the last twenty years. They would often get the opportunity of spanking a naughty pair of girls and they loved the experience. The spanking was slow and deliberate, making sure that each spank landed at the same time. Sarah had pop music to keep the beat in the Sanatorium but here there was no music, except the sound of two spanked bottoms which was music to their ears.

Amelia was crying very soon after the spanking started but Jasmine was tougher. She was an athlete and used to pain. After about five minutes of hand spanking, Charles indicated that they should pick up their chosen implements, so Charles had the leather slipper that belonged to Daisy's father, and Sarah had her wooden flat-backed hairbrush. Again the spanking started and Charles was determined to get Jasmine crying. The slipper was landing on Jasmine's bottom and the hairbrush on Amelia's. That lasted another five minutes and finally, they were both sobbing. "Go and stand facing the wall again while Sarah and I take a break, it's hard work spanking naughty girls. And no rubbing."

"Shall I make some coffee Charles?" Sarah asked as she stood up and stretched.

"Good idea Sarah. Thank you." Charles said and when Sarah looked at the naughty girls facing the wall, Charles shook his head "No."

Charles and Sarah had their coffee and chatted while they watched the two naked ladies facing the wall. "Right ladies, time to swap over. Amelia over my lap and Jasmine over Sarah's. No need to start with the hand spanking Sarah, their bottoms are already warmed up so we will go straight to the implements."

Once the ladies were over the appropriate knees, Sarah and Charles picked up the leather slipper and the hairbrush and started to spank the red bottoms over their laps. Amelia started to cry straight away but it took Jasmine six or more spanks with the hairbrush before she was crying. They were spanked for another ten minutes after they started to cry and they both knew that they had been punished. Once the spanking was finished the crying girls were held on the laps of the spankers until all the tears had finished.

"Right you two," Charles said. "Get up and sit on the settee, I want to tell you what will be happening in the future." Charles stood up and paced the room. "It seems I can't trust you to be discreet. You promised to dispel any rumours and you managed to do just that. Amelia, you're an excellent headmistress and all the staff love you. Jasmine, you're fantastic with the girls and your record proves you're an excellent sports mistress. I'm very fond of you both and I hate to see you ruin your careers like this. What the hell are we going to do?"

It was Jasmine that said it first. "Charles, I'm sorry and I promise we will never get caught again."

Amelia followed suit, "Yes Charles, I'm sorry too and I really appreciate the fact that it was you that found us, not the girls."

"Good," Charles said. "But your punishment has not finished." Charles picked up the wooden spoon that Sarah had brought from the Sanatorium. "You will each get ten strokes with this nasty-looking wooden spoon between your cheeks. I'm told that this hurts and it will be a reminder that you should never put your jobs at risk like that again." They were both horrified but they knew they had no choice. "You first Jasmine. Kneel on the floor with your bottom in the air and your knees separated, and then reach behind you and pull your cheeks apart.

"Please Sir," Jasmine said. "Not too hard."

"It doesn't need to be hard to sting between your cheeks," Charles said, handing the wooden spoon to Sarah. "You do the honours, Sarah," Charles said as if she was going to be pouring a cup of tea.

"Thank you, Charles," she said as she took the long wooden spoon by the round spoon end and stood with her legs on either side of Jasmine's body. "Wider Jasmine please," Sarah said as she looked down between Jasmine's spread cheeks. Jasmine did as she was told and the narrow handle part of the spoon whipped down and landed on Jasmine's anus.

"Jees," Jasmine said but she held her cheeks apart. Again the wooden spoon whipped down and caught Jasmine between her cheeks. Sarah leaned over for the next stroke and it caught Jasmine on her pussy so she screamed but still she kept her cheeks wide apart. The next few strokes landed on her anus or her pussy and each was excruciatingly painful. When the spanking was finished Jasmin was sent to the wall again, but this time her steps were tentative as her cheeks rubbed together, reviving the sting.

"You're next Amelia," Charles said, "And I think I will take the wooden spoon for this one Sarah."

"Of course," Sarah said as she handed the spoon to Charles.

Amelia had seen the exposed position that Jasmine had been in, so she didn't need to be told what to do. Kneeling on the rug she put her head on the floor and eased her knees wider, then she reached behind herself and pulled her cheeks apart. She could feel the cool breeze on her anus and pussy so she knew that they were exposed. Strangely her pussy felt damp. Was she getting excited by showing Charles and Sarah her secret places? She didn't know but her body was certainly reacting as if she was. Just like Sarah, Charles stood on either side of Amelia and aimed the handle of the long wooden spoon at her anus. Looking over the top of Amelia he could see her anus twitching in anticipation of the spank so he didn't keep her waiting. The wooden shaft of the spoon landed squarely on Amelia's anus and she screamed. She had expected it to be painful but it was worse than she thought. Again the wooden spoon landed and again she screamed. She was not sure if she could manage another eight strokes like that and then the next stroke landed on her pussy. The pain was intolerable and she let go of her cheeks and fell sideways on the floor sobbing. "I can't take any more Charles, I just can't."

Charles took pity on her and let Sarah throw a blanket over her. Looking at Jasmine he said, "You had better get dressed and get going Jasmine, Sarah will take care of Amelia."

"Yes Charles," Jasmine said. When she was dressed she was about to leave when Charles said. "Just a minute, I want to have a word with you." He walked out with her and they stopped at the front door of Christie House. "Are you and Amelia serious?" Charles asked. "I know It's none of my business but you didn't seem too keen when Amelia asked you to bring her off this morning."

"You were listening?" Jasmine said and Charles nodded. "Well, it was fun to start with. Amelia was my boss and so I did as I was told. I enjoyed it. But after a while it became a problem and when you spanked us last time I told her that it must never happen again. I like my job here and I don't want to get into trouble. In a way, I was delighted that you caught us, and I promise it will never happen again."

"Okay Jasmine," Charles said. "That's what I thought." Charles pulled a small tube of cream from his pocket. "This is anaesthetic cream. Put this on your bottom and you will feel more comfortable. I would offer to do it for you, but I have to talk to Amelia now."

"Thank you, Charles," Jasmine said as she kissed him on his cheek. "Next time maybe," then she laughed as she left the building.

Back in the lounge of their apartment, Amelia was sitting on the settee with a blanket wrapped around her and Sarah was giving her a cup of coffee. "Oh that's a good idea, can I have a cup?"

"Of course," she said and wandered off to the kitchen, but Charles followed. When they came back Charles sat next to Amelia. "It's no good, you know. You have to leave Jasmine alone."

"But I love her," Amelia said.

"No you don't, you lust after her, which is a very different thing."

"Well, whatever it is, I seem to be horny all the time around these girls and the staff and when you spanked Lilly this morning I had to have some relief." Amelia was horrified that she was sharing these things with Charles and Sarah but she didn't seem to have any choice.

"Okay, I thought you might say that so I have had a word with Sarah. She likes you and I'm sure you like her, next time you need relief, go and see her in the sanatorium. She can lock the door and even if you're caught with your clothes off, it would be okay because she's the matron." Amelia looked up at Sarah who nodded her agreement.

"But that doesn't mean you get away with your punishment. You're still owed eight more strokes of the wooden spoon between your cheeks, and Sarah has agreed to do that for you tomorrow."

Amelia looked up and then nodded. "Yes you're right and I do deserve it for being stupid. Thank you Charles and Sarah for being so caring."

A little later Amelia left the apartment and Sarah said to Charles. "Take me to bed Charles, I need some relief after all that excitement. You had better bring that wooden spoon with you, I think I'm going to be very naughty tonight."

Charles laughed as he locked the door and switched off the lights following Sarah to the bedroom with the wooden spoon in his hand.

Chapter 21 - Spanking a Parent again

The autumn sports day was a big event at St Samantha's School for Girls. There was lots of running and jumping of course, but nobody took it too seriously because they also had the greasy pole pillow fight for the stronger of the girls and the new walking race for the girls with big boobs. Nobody said that was what it was for, but everybody knew. Many of the parents were there to support their children because it was the last day of term so they could take the girls home for the two weeks holiday over Christmas. It was a festive occasion. After lunch, there would be an inter-house hockey match which was always strongly contested, although the hockey skills were not all that good.

There was a good turnout of parents this year and Amelia was delighted to see some of the governors there as well. The head of the governors, Elizabeth Crawley, was standing next to Amelia watching the walking race when she said. "Good idea, I used to enjoy running but I'm sure you would have found running in a t-shirt quite uncomfortable."

"Yes," Amelia said. "Of course, we don't tell anybody what it's for, but everybody knows. I have to keep telling the girls who are well built in that area, that the boys will love them."

"And girls of course," Elizabeth said.

"Yes, and girls," Amelia said but she was wondering if Elizabeth was flirting with her.

"What size are yours?" Elizabeth asked.

Amelia was surprised. "Double D cup size," she said.

"Mine are so small they're measured in egg cup sizes," Elizabeth said and they both laughed at the joke. "But my nipples stick out like organ stops and they are sensitive. In this weather, if they start to rub on my clothing I can have an orgasm. Are yours sensitive?"

Amelia knew that Elizabeth was flirting now. "They are at the moment," Amelia said.

"Oh really, I would love to see them, maybe we could go to your office to discuss something terribly important."

"Yes," Amelia said and they walked off together. Charles had been watching the interaction and he could recognise the signs. "I hope they are careful," he said.

"Sorry?" He heard the person next to him talking.

"Oh, did I say that out loud?" Charles said and then he looked at the parent standing next to him. "It's Mrs Lucas isn't it?"

"Oh, Synthia please," she said.

"I nearly didn't recognise you. You have lost weight haven't you?"

"Nice of you to notice," Synthia said. "After that time when you... you know."

"When I spanked you?" Charles said.

Synthia looked around. "Yes, when you spanked me. Well, I had a look at myself and I thought if you could stand to spank my bottom and get excited by it. Then the least I could do is to lose some weight and get fit. I have been going to the gym.

"Well it really suits you Synthia, you look like a million dollars. But how did you know that spanking your bottom excited me"

"I may have been fat, but I could still feel your excitement poking into my tummy." Synthia laughed and Charles joined her. "Actually, I'm glad I've found you, I was wondering if you would give me another spanking to keep my enthusiasm going, then maybe you could show me your excitement and I could help you with it."

"It would be my pleasure Synthia," Charles said. "It looks like they're taking a break now, if you come with me we can take a break in my office." Charles and Synthia walked slowly to the Christie House as if they were just going to have a quick word as parents and housemasters often do. Once they were inside Charles's office he took control. "I was certainly disappointed with your behaviour Synthia," Charles said but Synthia was surprised. She had no idea what was going on.

"What would your father have said if he saw you flirting with one of the male teachers?"

"Yes, Sir," Synthia caught on. "He would not have been happy at all."

"No, he would not, I'm going to have to teach you a lesson to make sure you think twice next time." Charles moved one of the spanking chairs into the centre of the lounge and sat down, making sure that the leather slipper was ready when he needed it. "Come here Synthia," he said.

"Yes Sir."

"I have always believed that the punishment should fit the crime, so pull that dress over your head and show me what you're wearing underneath." Synthia did as she was told and stood shivering in her knickers and huge matching bra. She was also wearing a corset and tights that did nothing to flatter her body. "Let's have that corset off, you have a lovely body and I want to see it all." Synthia was embarrassed as she struggled to remove the corset and the tights, now she was barefoot in knickers and a bra. "That's much better, Synthia," Charles said as he brought her closer and then felt her body tenderly. "You have lovely smooth skin Synthia. I know you're losing weight but don't lose too much. I like to be able to feel your body and I'm looking forward to running my hands over your bottom. Turn around."

Synthia did as she was told. She was very self-conscious but she was also very excited to be talked to in this way. She had had a low opinion of herself when Charles spanked her before and it had improved slightly while she was losing weight, but the way Charles was talking to her now, she felt really good about herself. "Bend over and stick out that lovely bottom Synthia," Charles said and she did as he told her. Synthia's bottom was just inches from Charles's face as he was sitting on the spanking chair, then he took the elastic of her knickers and slowly pulled them over her bottom.

"Christmas has come early this year," Charles said. "And I'm opening my first present." Kissing Synthia's bottom he said, "You have a lovely bottom Synthia, I just need to adjust the colour a little."

"Yes Sir," Synthia said as she was guided over Charles's lap. Her knickers were around her ankles now and Charles loosened her bra with practised efficiency. The weight of Synthia's boobs pushed at her bra and as soon as it was loosened her boobs fell free and she let the straps fall down her arms and onto the floor. Naked now, Synthia felt a sense of freedom. She didn't need the corset and bra to be attractive to men. This man, Charles Nicholson, has given her nothing but compliments.

Reaching his left hand down under Synthia's breast he cupped a boob as best as he could and massaged it gently. "I thought you were going to spank me, Charles," Synthia said.

"I'm sorry, I cannot resist such beauty." He said to Synthia's delight as he started to spank the large bottom over his lap. Over and over again his hand came down on her lap reddening her cheeks in preparation for the leather slipper. After twenty spanks Charles rested his hand on Synthia's bottom and massaged gently to add to the excitement of the sting. Reaching beneath her he held an erect nipple at the same time and Synthia moaned. "Not yet my darling," he said and started to spank her bottom again. The sting was building up so she started to shift uncomfortably, then Charles stopped the spanking again and continued with his massaging, letting his fingers drift between her cheeks as her legs seemed to part of their own accord. Picking up the leather slipper that Daisy gave him, Charles started again on Synthia's bottom. She was crying now with the sting of the leather slipper, so he knew that she didn't need many spanks. After ten or so hard smacks with the slipper, he put it on the floor beside him and massaged her cheeks with both hands. Pulling her bottom cheeks apart she could feel the breeze on her anus and very wet pussy.

As Synthia spread her legs wide apart the aroma of her excitement was impossible to miss. Slipping his fingers between the lips of her large pussy he found he was able to slip two fingers inside, then three. "God yes," she said. "More."

With a series of rapid movements in and out, Synthia thought she needed more so she eased her right hand under her body and found her clitoris. With the combination of Charles in her vagina and her own fingers rubbing her clit, she orgasmed loudly and then clamped her fat legs together, securing Charles's fingers where they were. Eventually, Synthia relaxed and Charles was able to retrieve his hand. Slipping off his lap, Synthia found herself on her knees undoing Charles's pants and pulling down his zip. Charles eased his bottom off the seat so that Synthia could pull down his pants and then his erection sprang into view at full alert. "Yes," Synthia said as she opened her mouth and devoured his erection, pulling out and then in again she was hungry to please him, as he had her. He felt himself building up to an orgasm and he told her so, but she said, "Don't get any on me, come in my mouth," so he did, and she swallowed every last drop.

Ten minutes later Charles and Synthia were walking back to the playing field where the next event was taking place, looking to all the world as if they had had a teacher/parent meeting, which, of course, they had.

Chapter 22 - Two girls are spanked

As Charles arrived back at the races he bumped into Sarah. "All okay?" she asked.

"Yes Darling, I was just having a parent/teacher meeting with Mrs Lucas," Charles said smiling.

"But you don't teach young Sophie, do you?"

"No, good point." Charles said smiling, "But there's nothing wrong with improving teacher/parent relationships."

"No, of course not, darling," Sarah said. "And how is that going?"

"Oh, very well I think. I don't think she will be complaining about the spankings at the school any time soon, unless It's a complaint that she's not getting enough of them." They both laughed and that was interrupted by an argument they overheard.

"But you cheated," Lucy Smith said to Ella Hall, as she pulled at her t-shirt.

"I did not, I won fair and square," Ella said.

"You were running. I saw you, I was behind you and I was watching, you were running."

"I was not, it was just a fast walk," Ella said and they started to scuffle as Charles and Sarah pulled them apart.

"What's going on here?" Charles said.

"Ella cheated in the walking race," Lucy said.

"I didn't cheat, I just walked faster than that little bitch." Ella said and then Lucy shook herself free and slapped Ella on the face. Ella started to cry as she rubbed her face.

"Get into my office you two, and be quick about it," Charles said.

"You see, that was your fault," Ella said.

"And if I hear one more word from either of you it will be the cane. Just one more word, and don't tempt me, I haven't caned anybody today yet." Charles said but Ella stifled a laugh, as far as she knew, he hadn't caned anybody since he started at the school.

Back in his office again, Charles realised that he hadn't put the spanking chair back since he spanked Synthia just a few minutes ago. The girls noticed that as well. They were sitting on the settee feeling very sorry for themselves. "Now listen to me girls. It's the last day of term and we will all be going off for our Christmas holidays soon, but I will not have you arguing like that in front of the parents. It will give us a bad name. I know the headmistress was watching you arguing and she was with the head of the governors, so she will ask me what I did. You will both get a spanking and I hope it's the last one I have to give anybody this term."

"Yes Sir," they both said together.

"You first Lucy," Charles said as he sat on the spanking chair. "Stand in front of me."

The girls were just wearing baggy shorts and a white top. Both girls had large boobs and their shape was obvious under the t-shirt. Taking the shorts, Charles pulled them down with her knickers at the same time and then he turned her and pulled her over his knee. Charles loved his job but his favourite part was spanking eighteen-year-old bottoms. Lucy's skin was very white and the first spank clearly showed his handprint. He thought that you could almost take a fingerprint of that mark. It was so clear. Charles continued to spank Lucy and soon she was apologising and crying. He didn't want to leave bruises for her to take home so it was just a short sharp spanking. "Up you get Lucy, and go and stand facing the wall. Your next Ella."

Charles went through the same process with Ella and was surprised to see that she had shaved when her knickers were pulled down. "What's this?" He said.

"All the girls in America are doing it, cool eh?" Ella said with a smile.

"No, it's not cool, and what does that word mean anyway? I will speak to Matron to have an inspection to make sure it doesn't spread to the other girls, in the meantime I want you to report back to me in two weeks' time and show me you're growing it back."

"Yes Sir," Ella said but she was disappointed.

Charles bent Ella over his lap and he was angry with her so he spanked her a little harder. She was crying when he finished and then he sent both girls back out to the playing field.

The rest of the Sports day went without a hitch and after the house hockey competition, which Christie House won, the girls left with their parents to go home for the holidays. Some of the girls had to sleep another night at the school and then took the train in the morning back to their homes, others had to fly, but by Sunday morning the term was finally over and Charles and Sarah could relax.

Mary Becker and Ella Hall were the only two upper-sixth girls who didn't go home for Christmas, and they were joined by Amelia Brandon, Charles and Sarah Nicholas, Daisy Andrews, Lilly Armstrong and Laura Taylor who all had decided to stay this year. None of them had a family to go home to and in any event, the school was their home.

In book five we will see how the Christmas festivities progress in the school. Amelia has a new relationship and Sarah has that threesome that she wanted with Charles and Daisy. Mary and Ella are also spanked with surprising results.

Chapter 22 - A spanking at Breakfast

Charles Nicholas surprised them all by walking into the dining room on the first day of the Christmas Holliday wearing a checked shirt and jeans. For the whole term, nobody had seen Charles in anything other than a dark suit, white shirt and tie. Even on the field trip with Daisy Andrews and a few of the girls, he had worn dark suit pants and an open-neck white shirt so this was quite a shock.

"Good Morning everybody," he said as he walked into the dining room. There was a stunned silence for a second and then they said good morning. Sarah said to Amelia later that her husband likes to make an entrance, but actually what he was doing was letting everybody know that they can be more relaxed over the Christmas break. Everybody else was already eating their breakfast. There were two girls from the Upper Sixth, Mary Becker and Ella Hall and three from the lower sixth. Amelia Brandon, the headmistress, was there and three other teachers, Daisy Andrews, Lilly Armstrong and Laura Taylor. Charles's wife Sarah was there of course, and there was a place laid up for Cook but she was in the kitchen frying more eggs. So the twelve of them would be having meals together.

"So what are we going to do today Amelia?" Charles asked as he was tucking into his breakfast.

"Well," she started, "I have a few things planned, and I'm hoping that you will all join in but it's not obligatory for the teachers and the sixth form girls. They are all over eighteen and old enough to do what they like."

"Oh, Goodie," Mary said.

"Thank you, Mary," Amelia said, but she was not amused. "I'm delighted to tell you that the Governors have agreed to allocate some funds for us to have a good time over the holidays, and they have booked a longboat for us on the Norfolk Broads at the weekend as well, which will be fun. We are also going to have a Secret Santa game where each of you will be given two pounds and you have to buy two presents with that money, then we will all have two presents to open on Christmas day, on top of the gifts your family have sent for you."

The younger girls were getting excited and whispered to each other. "Settle down now girls," Amelia said. "I thought it would be a good idea to go to the Market on Saturday to buy these gifts, there are always nice things at the market."

"What about TV?" Ella asked.

"Oh yes, I forgot about that. I'll ask Charles to carry my TV into the library and we can all watch it there if you like. I know you girls will like Doctor Who although I'm not sure I should allow the younger girls to watch The Goodies, they're always a little extreme... so I'm told."

"With pleasure Amelia," Charles said. "I'll do that straight after breakfast."

"One last thing," Amelia said. "We can't expect Cook to do all the cooking and washing up as well, So I've prepared a rota and we will all take turns to clear the table and wash up. Mary and Ella will do the breakfast today, and Laura and I will be doing the dinner tonight. There will be no organised lunch, but Cook will leave out some bread and cold meat if you want to make a sandwich for yourself. Any questions?

"Mr Nicholas?" Mary Becker said.

"Yes, Mary."

"I have a question," Mary hesitated, "Will there be any spanking over the Christmas Holidays?"

Charles pushed his chair back. "Come over here Mary."

"Oh," Ella exclaimed, "Watch out Mary."

Mary walked over to Charles as instructed and he guided her over his lap. "Now, what was that question again," Charles said as he had his hand on her jean-covered bottom.

"Oh Sir," Mary said. "I was only asking."

Charles gave Mary a light smack. "What do you think Mary?"

"Well," Mary said from her position over Charles's lap, "I was just thinking that maybe there should be a moratorium on spanking because of the holiday," Charles spanked her again, just a little harder this time. "At least we should not be spanked on our bare bottoms, just for the holiday." Charles gave her another smack a little harder again. "Okay, okay, I get it, Mr Nicholson, If we're naughty we will be spanked."

One more spank and then Charles helped Mary up. "Well done Mary, you just learned another lesson even if it's the holiday."

"Thank you, Sir," Mary said, rubbing her bottom as she sat back in her chair.

"What about the teachers Mr Nicholson?" It was Ella talking now.

"What about them," Charles said.

"Well we all know that you spank the teachers on their birthday and probably at other times, will you be spanking the teachers during the holidays."

"Oh, I see," Charles said and everybody was expecting him to call Ella over and spank her softly as well, but he didn't

"Laura," Charles said. "Perhaps you would like to help with Ella's question. Come over here."

"What?" Laura said. "Oh please no, not in front of the girls."

"I'm sure you don't want a real spanking Laura like you got in the staff room when you had your thirtieth birthday," Charles said as he patted his lap. "Just for the holidays I think we should all be just one happy family, don't you agree Amelia?"

"Oh yes, Charles," Amelia said. "You had better do as he says, Laura."

"Alright," Laura said as she stood up and walked over to Charles who was sitting waiting to put her over his knee with a smile on his face. "But not too hard Charles, please."

"Well," Charles pulled Laura over his lap, "You made more fuss than Mary," he said as he pulled up her short skirt to spank her on her knickers.

"Not on my knickers Charles, what about the girls?" Laura said.

"I'm sure they have all seen a pair of knickers before, and I must say they're really nice knickers," Charles had his hand on Laura's white lace knickers. Then he spanked her. "What do you think, Ella? Do you think that the teachers will be spanked as well if they're naughty?"

Ella smiled, "I'm not sure Mr Nicholson." she said and Laura said. "Ella!" as Charles spanked Laura again, just a little bit harder than last time.

"What about now Ella?" Charles said.

"I'm almost certain," Ella said as Charles spanked Laura again. "Yes, now I'm certain that the teachers will be spanked as well."

Laura got up and was rubbing her bottom under her short skirt as the rest of the room broke into a round of applause. "Well, I think that has answered all of the questions. Does anybody want to ask anything else?" Charles said, but nobody wanted to ask any questions at all. "Right," he said, putting his hands on his knee, "I'll go and move the TV into the library."

Although Amelia was the headmistress and effectively Charles's boss, she didn't mind him taking charge in this way. She had already been spanked by Charles a couple of times and she liked it. For the

Christmas holidays, she was happy that Charles would be the man of the house.

Chapter 23 - Spanked in the Sanatorium

"Right girls," Sarah said as Charles left the dining room. "I need a volunteer to help me sort out the Sanatorium. It will only take a couple of days but I need to get organised for next year. Any volunteers?"

The room was silent for a second and then Ella put up her hand. "I'll help Matron," she said.

"Good Girl," Sarah said. "I'll be starting at nine."

By now the rest of the people in the dining room had gone off and that just left Ella and Mary. "I thought we were going to play Monopoly today," Mary said to her friend.

"Yes, sorry Mary," Ella said. "But I thought it would be fun helping Matron, anyway, I've something I want to talk to her about."

"What?" Mary asked.

"Mind your own beeswax," Ella said and that was the end of the conversation.

At nine o'clock Ella was knocking at the door of the Sanatorium. "Come in Ella, the door is open," Sarah said and Ella walked in but she was surprised to see all the stuff from the glass-fronted cupboard lined up on the examination table. "Thank you for volunteering to help Ella, I was hoping it would be you. I'm sure we will have some fun sorting this lot out."

Ella was not sure it would be fun, but as it happened, it was. They emptied all the cupboards and washed them out, making sure they were properly sterilised before putting the bottles, glass jars and instruments back in the right order. Ella and Sarah chatted like close friends while they were working and Ela found out all about what it was like to work in South Africa, while Sarah found out about Ella's family.

At lunchtime, Sarah told Ella to finish up the last cupboard while she went to the kitchen to make them both a sandwich. Ella finished and then sat on the examination table. She had really enjoyed working with Sarah that morning but she had a nagging question she wanted to ask, so when Sarah came back carrying a plate of sandwiches and two bottles of Coke, Ella said, "Matron?"

"Yes Ella," Sarah said as she put the sandwiches on the table.

"I have a question, but it's rather embarrassing."

"No matter, I'm a nurse and your Matron, you can ask me anything," Sarah said, but she was thinking that she liked the embarrassing questions the best.

"Well," Ella hesitated, "Do you remember when you spanked me a couple of weeks ago, it was a sore spanking and then you put some cream on for me?"

"Well, it was a sore spanking because you were naughty, and you made such a fuss about having your temperature taken in your bottom."

"I know Matron," Ella said. "And I'm sorry about that, only it was how I felt afterwards that I want to ask you about."

"How did you feel afterwards?" Sarah asked, but she thought she knew the answer.

"I don't know, it felt rather strange between my legs, here," Ella held her right hand over her pussy."

"You see Matron, when you spanked me I got excited, and then when Mr Nicholson was asking at breakfast if there were any more questions after Mary was spanked, I asked a question because I wanted to be spanked as well. It makes me feel strange."

"What sort of strange Ella?"

"Nice strange, like I want to... you know, rub it."

"You mean when you masturbate?"

"Ooh Matron, that is a bad word," Ella said.

"Of course it isn't a bad word. Would you prefer jilling?"

"Matron!"

"Now you listen to me young lady, we all do it so we have to have a name for it."

"What do you mean, we all do it? I know the girls do it in the dorm sometimes, but surely not you?"

"Of course I do," Sarah said. "You can't expect the young to have all the fun."

Ella was stunned into silence, "Lucy said that you probably did, but I didn't believe her. She said that you probably played with yourself after you spanked us that time." Sarah nodded and smiled.

"Really?" Ella was not so shocked about Sarah's admission, but the fact that she admitted it. Ella had never admitted it to anybody apart from her best friend Pamela who lived in Hong Kong and would never tell anybody.

Sarah was pointing at Ella, "That's a secret between you and me, if you tell anybody I'll know and you will get the hardest caning from Mr Nicholson."

"I'll never tell anybody, only I didn't get spanked at breakfast so I wondered if you would spank me now?"

"You want to feel that strange feeling again then?" Ella nodded. "Take off your clothes and get up on the examination table as you did before when I took your temperature."

"Okay Matron, but why."

"You'll see Ella, just trust me."

"Yes, Matron, I'll always trust you," she said as she started to take off her jeans and jumper. Sarah locked the door to make sure they would not be disturbed and then stripped down to her bra and knickers. When Ella turned and saw her she was surprised but she wanted to sound like an adult so she said, "That's a lovely bra, Matron, with matching knickers as well. You look lovely."

"Thank you, Ella, but I usually wear a corset, I'm putting on a little weight," Sarah patted her tummy.

"Me to Matron," Ella patted her tummy as well. She was now naked and sitting on the examination table.

"Spanking first Ella, and it will be a proper spanking, not just a play spanking like you do with Mary sometimes."

"How did you know?" Ella said, but Sarah just smiled. Actually, they had only tried it once, bending over each other's lap with their knickers on and getting a light spanking but that didn't do it for either of them. Sarah was just guessing.

"Kneel up on the table with your bottom in the air and your head on the table, I'll spank you with my hand and then six with my wooden spoon. It will hurt and I expect you will cry. Don't worry about making a noise, nobody will hear."

"Yes, Matron," Ella said nervously. Ella got into position as instructed and she felt Sarah's hand on her bottom and between her cheeks. She shivered with delight and then the spanking started, softly at first and then built up just a little with a few spanks, and then Sarah massaged her bottom again. The pain from the spanking was intense but it seemed to change to pleasure when her bottom was massaged. Then Sarah spanked her again. This mixture of pain and pleasure lasted for a few minutes and then Sarah picked up the wooden spoon. "Oh no Matron, you're not going to spank me between my cheeks are you?"

"No Ella, not this time, but there may be a time when you ask me to do that again,"

"I don't think so, Matron, it stung terribly," Ella said, but she was wrong.

"Just six with the wooden spoon on your bottom Ella,"

"Yes, Matron," Ella said and then she screamed when the first spank landed on her bottom. Sarah was making sure that the wooden spoon really hurt this time and after just two smacks Ella was sobbing and begging Matron to stop.

"Just four more Ella, and then you will thank me."

"No, Matron. No more, please," But the spanking continued until they got to six.

"Good girl, Ella," Sarah said, "All over now, stay in position so that I can spread some cream on your bottom."

"Will it be that anaesthetic cream you used last time?"

"No Ella," Matron said. "That will spoil the fun. Just relax and let me help you enjoy the moment." Sarah spread the cream on Ella's bottom which was still sticking in the air. She smoothed the cream all over Ella's bottom and then her fingers slipped between her cheeks and over her anus.

"Ooh Matron," Ella said. "That's rude."

"No Ella, nothing is rude if you enjoy it, how does it feel?"

"It's nice Matron, sexy."

"Yes, it is, just relax your bottom for me." Ella did as she was told and felt Sarah's finger slip inside, lubricated with all the cream. Then she pulled it out. "How did that feel, Ella?"

"It was funny, but nice I think," Ella said.

"See what you were missing when you made all that fuss last time about having your temperature taken."

"Yes Matron," Ella relaxed. "Can you put it in again, please?" Sarah's finger slipped inside Ella's bottom again and she moaned with pleasure. "I had no idea, Matron," she said.

"Did you know there are more nerve endings around here than in any other part of the body, that's why it can feel so good if you relax."

"Yes Matron, I'm very relaxed."

"How is the sting of the spanking Ella?" Sarah asked.

"Oh, I forgot about that. My bottom still stings if I think about it, but it's not a bad sting."

"No, spanking helps, it releases endorphins into the body. Endorphins are the feel-good hormones that numb the brain to the pain just a little, but more importantly, they make you feel a lot better after the spanking has stopped. Just like you feel now. I had to give you a hard spanking to release the endorphins."

"Maybe that is what Mary and I were doing wrong?"

"Yes maybe, Ella," Sarah was still pushing her finger in a little and pulling it out, and Ella was enjoying the intrusion. Soon Ella was pushing back to let Sarah's finger go deeper. "Put your hand between your legs Ella and feel for your clitoris. Remember we talked about that in the Sexual Education lessons."

"Yes," Ella said. "I know where that is."

"I'm sure you do, darling. Now just turn your head the other way, and rub yourself there. Does that feel good?" As soon as Ella was looking in the other direction Sarah pushed her left hand into her big knickers and rubbed her clit at the same pace as Ella

"Ooh Matron, it has never felt this good, I'll come very quickly."

"Just hold back until I tell you, I'm sure you can do that."

"I'll try Matron," Ella said as Sarah was trying to catch up. Both of them were rubbing their clits furiously and just as Sarah felt herself coming she said, "Come for me now Ella." and she did, wetting the examination table with her excitement. They orgasmed together.

Sarah was the first to pull her hand out of her knickers, and Ella had not noticed what the Matron had been doing. Ella rolled onto her side and then realised that the examination table was wet. "Oh no Matron, I must have peed on the table."

"That's not urine Ella, that's your natural lubrication, sometimes when you're having the best orgasms, you will splash out a little just like you have done there. It's not a problem, in fact, it's a compliment to the person you have been playing with."

"Well, you deserve that compliment Matron, can we do that again sometime?"

"Of course, Ella. But for now, I think we had better get dressed and see what the others are up to."

"Yes, Matron."

Chapter 24 - Daisy spanked again

The first week of the holiday was progressing nicely. They all managed to fit into three cars and drove to Norwich with their two pounds to buy a small gift for the Secret Santa. Charles managed to get away and get something for Sarah and the others as well. Amelia did the same thing so there would be a lot of gifts around the tree on Christmas day. There was also the Christmas tree to purchase and Charles bought the biggest he could find and strapped it to the top of his Range Rover, luckily he remembered the roof rack.

They were all exhausted at the end of the day and Nicholas suggested that Daisy should come to the apartment and have a drink to celebrate a good day.

When they were sitting around the open fire in the lounge, drinking their Mulled Wine, Charles's speciality, it was Daisy who said. "What did you get up to in the Sanatorium with Ella?"

"Nothing," Sarah said in a tone that meant she was hiding something.

"Oh come on, Sarah," Daisy said. "I've never seen Ella so happy when she walked out of the San, and she was singing and dancing all afternoon. Whatever you gave her, I want some."

"Are you sure?" Sarah said. "Be careful what you wish for."

"What do you mean?" Daisy said as she shuffled uncomfortably on the settee.

"I mean, Ella wanted to know why she felt good after a spanking and I had to tell her about the endorphins that spanking releases, and how they make you feel good even though the spanking is painful."

155

"Oh, I see," Daisy said. "And did you just tell her, or did you demonstrate?"

Charles decided that the conversation needed a little authority to get it going in the right direction. "Why not show Daisy what happened in the San with Ella, Sarah."

"That's a good idea if you like Daisy?"

"That will be lovely," Daisy said.

"Okay, Daisy, but from now on you have to do exactly what I tell you to do, okay?"

"What if I don't want to?" Daisy was nervous now.

"Bad luck, if you want to feel like Ella felt you have to have everything that Ella had, okay?"

"Okay," Daisy said.

"Right, stand up and take off all your clothes," Sarah said.

"What?" Daisy was shocked.

"You have to do exactly what I say, if you question me again, this will stop and you will never know why Ella was so happy."

Daisy stood up and thought for a second. "Okay," she said and started to undress to the delight of Charles and Sarah who were sitting watching in the comfortable armchairs. Daisy was a slim lady and very attractive for her forty-eight years. Always dressing well, she took her time to be careful with her dress and sexy underwear. She was wearing matching lace knickers and a small bra, but she was wearing tights rather than stockings which spoiled the view just a little. Very soon the tights were gone leaving her in just a bra and knickers.

She looked at Sarah, "Everything," Sarah said. So she reached behind her and undid the bra and let it drop down her arms. Next came the knickers, but she decided to turn around and slip the knickers down her legs bending right over giving the audience a lovely view. Sarah and Charles clapped and Daisy turned back to them and smiled then curtsied. "Right, my turn," Sarah said as she pulled her dress over her head and took off the corset. "I hate wearing these things, but I had to today, I was wearing jeans when we went out." But neither Daisy nor Charles knew how uncomfortable a corset can be.

Sarah stood there in the knickers and a bra and said, "We need an examination table. Charles, can we use your desk?"

"Yes, of course, I'll clear it for you." While Charles was clearing the desk Sarah went to the airing cupboard and found a few towels to cover the desk and then told Daisy to climb up and get on her knees with her head down.

"God, did you make Ella do this?" Daisy said, and Sarah nodded and rubbed her hand over Daisy's small bottom.

"Spanking first Daisy. As I explained to Ella, it has to be a hard spanking and then six with the wooden spoon to release the endorphins. A soft spanking won't do it."

"What did Ella say to that?"

"She said that she trusted me," Sarah said and Daisy nodded as the spanking started. Softly to start with, then the spanking got a little harder and then the rubbing came to change the feeling from pain to pleasure, and then the spanking started again. As soon as Daisy was feeling uncomfortable with the pain the spanking stopped and the massaging started. Over and over again this happened until Daisy could not tell if it was pain or pleasure she was receiving.

Sarah stopped spanking and ran her fingers between Daisy's cheeks and she moaned with pleasure as Sarah concentrated the action around her anus. Then she picked up the wooden spoon and spanked Daisy's bottom hard. Just like Ella, Daisy screamed at the first stroke of the wooden spoon. She had never felt pain like it. Then the spoon landed again, and Daisy was sobbing. "No more," she said but Sarah ignored her. Four more hard strokes landed on Daisy's unprotected bottom and when Sarah put down the wooden spoon Daisy was sobbing hard.

Turning to look at Sarah, Daisy said, "Surely you didn't spank Ella that hard." but Sarah simply nodded. "And that made her happy?"

"We haven't finished yet, stay in that position."

Daisy had no idea what was coming next but she stayed in the position as she was instructed to do and then Sarah applied the cream all over her bottom. As the cream was massaged into Daisy's bottom she started to relax and feel the pleasure, and then Sarah's fingers slipped down between her cheeks and over her anus, Daisy had never felt like this with anything over her anus, it had always been a no-go area sexually until now. For Daisy, it felt good, actually, it felt very good and she pushed back encouraging Sarah to slip inside her. Sarah was happy to oblige and her index finger slipped inside Daisy's bottom, lubricated with the cream. Daisy moaned and simply said, "yes."

By now Sarah had her hand in her own knickers and Charles needed to loosen his clothing because his erection was pushing at his pants uncomfortably. He stripped down to his boxer shorts and played with himself as the girls were doing the same thing.

"Reach between your legs and massage your clit," Sarah said to Daisy and she did as she was told, discovering that she had never been so horny. Her clit was already enlarged and poking out from under its hood. She knew she wouldn't take long to orgasm and she was moaning when Sarah said. "Don't come yet,"

Daisy looked towards Sarah for the first time and saw that she had her hand in her own knickers rubbing her clit. Charles was also masturbating in his pants so Daisy said. "Wait Charles, don't waste that. Come in my ass." They all stopped what they were doing and Charles suggested that they would be more comfortable in the bedroom. As soon as they were there, Charles and Daisy had a kissing competition and Sarah took off her bra and knickers. Daisy pulled down Charles's boxer shorts and his erection sprang free.

"That's what I want, Charles," Daisy said as she crawled on the bed and stuck her bottom in the air. "Just where Sarah had her fingers."

Sarah didn't want to miss out so she climbed over Daisy and lay at the top of the bed with her legs on either side of Daisy's face. Sliding closer, Sarah's pussy made contact with Daisy and she rubbed up and down. As Charles entered Daisy from behind her face was pushed into Sarah's pussy and she started to lick hard, swallowing and then licking again like a hungry cat.

Daisy couldn't wait any longer so she stuck her right hand between her legs and pulled on her engorged clit, then rubbed hard and she knew she would come soon. Both Sarah and Charles were close as well, and while they didn't come together, it was close. Charles was the first to explode shooting his excitement deep inside Daisy, this pushed her right into Sarah's pussy who orgasmed, followed closely by Daisy, rubbing her own clit.

They all stayed in that position for a few minutes, unwilling to spoil the effect of their lovemaking. Eventually, Charles's erection shrank and he pulled out, Daisy rolled onto her side and Sarah sat on the side of the bed. "Phew," Sarah said. "Anybody for a shower?"

Chapter 25 - Spanked by Father Christmas

"Are you awake," Ella asked Mary at eleven o'clock on Christmas eve.

"No," Mary replied and then turned over in her bed.

"We could go downstairs to the library and see what presents are under the Christmas tree."

"Go back to sleep," Mary said. But Ella was already out of bed.

"Come on Mary, it will be fun."

"Going back to sleep would be fun," Mary said but Ella had already pulled the covers off her bed leaving her shivering. "Ella, please, I'm cold. And the old man said that there would be no going downstairs hoping to see what Father Christmas had brought until breakfast on Christmas day."

"Come on. You're not scared of the Old Man are you?" Ella passed Mary her dressing gown.

"Okay, I'm coming, but just for a minute and then I want to go back to bed."

The old school building had its own sounds at night. Lots of creeks and bangs in the wind starting all sorts of rumours that the house was haunted. Ella had a flashlight to help them find their way without banging into anything but they were both a little scared as they made their way to the library where the Christmas tree had been set up. All the girls had helped decorate it when Charles set it up after their trip to Norwich, and it looked magnificent with lights, glass balls and tinsel. Now it looked a little creepy in the dark and the girls decided not to put the lights on in case anybody was still up. Once inside the library, they scampered to the tree and sat on the floor looking at all the presents.

There was a creaking sound coming from the corner of the darkroom. "What was that?" Mary said.

"Nothing, just the wind."

The sound came again. "No really, I can hear something." Mary was scared. "In the corner, let's go back to bed."

"And what do we have here?" A deep voice came from the corner of the room and both girls screamed, as the small table lamp was switched on and Father Christmas was sitting in one of the leather wingback chairs in the corner of the library. "Two naughty girls looking at the presents before Christmas."

The girls were hugging each other in fear, but then Ella whispered, "it's just the Old Man."

"Old Man?" Father Christmas stood up and both girls thought that this didn't look like Mr Nicholson at all. "Old Man?" he repeated with the deepest of deep voices and now towering over them, the girls knew it was not Mr Nicoloas at all. "I'm Father Christmas, some people call me St Nicholas or Kris Kringle, but you can call me Santa Clause if you like. And naughty girls who come downstairs to steal the presents around the tree before Christmas day get spanked."

"No, we were not going to steal them, just look at them," Mary said. "Please, Santa, we will go back to bed now."

"Yes, you will, as soon as I have a look at the Naughty or Nice book." Nick picked up a huge old leather book and started to page through. Are, there you are," he said. "Mary Becker. Smoking behind the Bicycle sheds every day, eating in bed at night, and being nasty to the junior girls at the end of term. I had better give you a spanking or there will be no presents for you on Christmas day. Come here."

Mary stood up almost as if she was dreaming and she wondered how Santa knew about all that. There was a stool conveniently placed next to the tree so he put his foot on the stool and pulled Mary over his knee. Pulling up her dressing gown and nightie, he pushed down her knickers and started to spank her straight away. "I'm so sorry Santa," Mary said. "I won't be naughty again."

"Well if you are, you know what will happen," he said but he continued spanking Mary on her bare bottom until she was crying. Lifting her off his knee he said. "You stand over there with your spanked bottom on display, while I have a look in the book for Ella, where are we." Santa was paging through the book again. "Ella Hall. Are yes, here we are. Oh, dear. Cheating in the Maths test, taking a shortcut in the cross country race, eating after lights-out. There seems to be a very long list for you, Ella. I'm not sure if there will be any presents for you tomorrow."

"But I didn't really cheat, I just looked at Amy's answer to see if I had it right. Please Santa, can't you just spank me as you did to Mary?"

"I'm not sure," Santa said in a very deep voice.

"Please."

"Well, okay," he said eventually. "As long as you promise to be good next year."

"Oh I will Santa, I promise," Ella said and she stood up and undid the rope holding up her flannel pyjamas and pushed them down with her knickers before she bent over Santa's lap. The spanking started straight away and Ella was soon crying. It was a hard spanking and she regretted cheating and taking that shortcut, but she did wonder how he knew. Ella's spanking lasted a little longer than Mary's but soon they were both standing next to each other with their bottoms on display.

"I have to take a picture for the naughty book," Santa said and both girls heard the click/whizz of the instant camera. "Mrs Clause will want to make sure I spanked you properly. Now come here and give me a hug, then off to bed with you." Mary hugged Santa first, followed by Ella, and each of them got a few pats on their sore bottoms, and then they scampered off to bed. "Merry Christmas," Santa called after them, and they both replied "Merry Christmas Santa Clause."

"Ho, Ho, Ho," Charles said as he pulled off the uncomfortable false beard and put away the old leather ledger that he had found in the basement.

Back in their bedroom Mary and Ela pulled their covers back up to get warm again. "That wasn't really Father Christmas," Ella said.

"Of course not," Mary said. "There is no such thing as Father Christmas."

"But who was he then? He didn't sound like the Old Man, and that outfit was very convincing. And how did he know those things about us?" They both lay back in silence for a while and then Ella said, "God I'm horny."

"Ella!" Mary said.

"Well aren't you? Spanking always makes me horny."

"Well, yes," Mary said. "But I thought that was just me." Ella got out of bed and slipped in next to Mary. "What are you doing?"

"When Matron spanked me last time she showed me some things, do you want to try it?"

"Try what?" Mary said but Ella had already slipped her hand under Mary's nightie and was feeling for her knickers. "What are you doing Ella? Mary said, but she didn't stop Ella as her hand slipped inside Mary's knickers and felt for the clitoris.

A little later Charles walked back into his bedroom. "How did it go?" Sarah asked.

"Perfect. It was Ella and Mary, as we expected. Clever of you to ask the others if they suspected either one of them of cheating or something. Ella was shocked that I knew."

"Did they know it was you?"

"I don't think so, but they will work it out I guess. I won't admit it, just let them guess."

"What does it say in the naughty book about me?" Sarah asked, smiling.

Charles was still in the Santa suit although he was not wearing the beard. He paged through the book. Ah, here we are. Sarah Nicholson. Oh dear, Oh dear me. Such a long list of naughtiness."

Sarah giggled. "I expect you will have to spank me then," she said as she got out of bed and pulled her nightie over her head leaving herself naked for Santa Clause.

Chapter 26 - Spanked in wet knickers

New Year's Eve was on a Thursday this year and they had a party in the library with the TV on to check the time was exactly midnight, and then they sang Auld Lang Syne and Charles surprised everybody with his baritone singing voice. "That sounds like Santa Clause," Mary said to Ella and they both giggled.

"Right everybody," Charles said when all the fuss had died down. "Time for bed, we have an early start and then we're off to the Broads.

"Hurray," everybody said and there was a lot of clapping and excitement. This may have been because of the rum punch that Cook had made, which tasted a little stronger than the recipe Charles had given her.

"That was a lovely evening Charles," Sarah said when they were in bed that night, "It has been a lovely Christmas holiday, best I can remember."

"Yes, it has been good," Charles said, hugging his wife. "And I'm looking forward to taking out that boat on the Broads. They looked so attractive when we had that field trip and I'm sure everybody wanted to go on the water rather than just stand beside it."

The following morning there was a hive of activity with the teachers loading the cars and one or two of the girls feeling the effects of the rum punch from the previous night. By ten o'clock they had loaded the cars and they all piled in. Cook wasn't coming on the trip. "I get seasick," she had said, "Anyway, I would like a bit of a break from cooking for you lot."

It was then that Amelia realised that Cook had not had a holiday at all. "Why don't you take a bit of a break, Cook," she said. "We will take turns to do the cooking for the rest of the holidays."

Cook smiled. "Well I could go and spend a week with my sister in Bournemouth, she keeps asking me to come down."

"Well, that's settled then, we will see you back here the day before the term starts." Cook seemed very pleased as she waved the three cars off and turned to pack her bags.

They arrived at the harbour in Great Yarmouth an hour later and Charles went with Amelia to meet the owner of the longboat. "It will sleep twelve, as long as there are a couple of small kids amongst the group, and it's very easy to run, I'll show you, Charles." Amelia got the impression that she was not needed so she organised the offloading and storage of the luggage and allocation of the beds. They were all very impressed with the interior of the seventy-foot boat. There was a nice kitchen, or gally as the owner called it, and a toilet with a shower, or head, as the owner called it. All the beds folded back into seating apart from the double bedroom at the front, or bow as the owner called it, and Amelia suggested that Charles and Sarah should have that. There was so much to learn it was making the girls dizzy.

"This longboat is a seventy-footer so you will not be able to turn around in many places," The owner was saying to Charles. "But I've marked a couple of different routes on the map that will take you until Monday to get back here."

The engine was started and Charles took the helm as he guided it out of the harbour up the river Yare to connect with the broads. There was no hurry so after an hour of moving forward at a slow pace Charles pulled over in a secluded spot and the girls tied the longboat up.

"Okay ladies," Charles said. "Gather round, we just have to chat a little bit about safety. We will take turns steering the boat, but there must always be two people at the helm just in case one makes a mistake. Now, who is going to be responsible for the cooking?"

"I'll do that, Charles," Amelia said. "I used to do a lot of cooking but I'll need some help in the kitchen and everybody must help with the washing up."

"Excellent, thank you, Amelia," Charles said. "Remember we're all here to have some fun, but I don't recommend any swimming, it's cold in there. The first person to fall in will get a spanking on their wet knickers to warm them up." There was laughter and general approval of this comment because everybody knew that they would never fall in.

Charles pulled the boat away and at the same time, he was showing Daisy what to do. "Oh, I know what to do with a longboat," Daisy said. "We had holidays on the broads when I was younger." So Daisy took over and Charles encouraged Mary to come into the cabin and watch what Daisy did so that she could take her turn later.

There was lots of excitement with the girls running around and having fun. "Remember what I said, girls," Charles said as Ella turned and slipped off the narrow gunwale into the water. "Man overboard," he shouted and Daisy stopped the engine. Charles ran to the little dingy tied to the end of the longboat, expecting to have to go and fetch Ella who was now twenty yards back, but she was a good swimmer and got to the boat easily climbing the rope ladder that hung off the side. Ella was shivering but everybody else was laughing, including Charles. "What did I tell you?" Charles said.

"I know," Ella said as she started to undo the button on her jeans. Pushing them down she bent over and Charles spanked her wet knickers six times. "That stings," Ella said as she went into the cabin to change.

"Okay Daisy, off we go again," Charles said and the rest of Friday was uneventful. That evening they moored the longboat where the owner suggested, just a few hundred yards from a very nice country pub. After dinner, Charles walked to the pub with Laura, Lilly and Daisy, but Amelia and Sarah decided that they were tired and wanted an evening in. Charles was suspicious but he didn't say anything. It had been a busy day so after the girls went to bed at ten, Sarah and Amelia went quietly into the double bedroom and closed the door. They were kissing almost immediately and then Amelia said. "What will Charles do if he finds us here?"

"He will probably spank us," Sarah said.

"Oh goodie," Amelia said and they both laughed.

"Anyway, he had three lovely ladies to entertain, I'm sure he will not be back until after closing time."

Thirty minutes later they were both rolling around naked on the bed when Charles opened the door. "And what do we have here?" he said in a soft voice so as not to wake the others.

"What have you done with the others?" Sarah said as if nothing was wrong.

"I knew you two were up to something so I came back early, you're lucky that one of the girls didn't wake up and catch you."

"So what are you going to do?" Sarah was still defiant.

"Well you will both get a spanking, but not now. You will have to pretend to fall into the water and then you will be spanked in front of the others. Both of you wear dresses tomorrow but no knickers, you will be getting a spanking on your bare bottoms."

"Not in front of the girls, surely Charles?"

"Yes, in front of the girls, it serves you right for taking a risk in here. Now get dressed Amelia and leave my wife to me."

"Yes Charles," Amelia said.

The whole of this conversation was whispered and amazingly none of the girls woke up.

"Well, that seemed to work," Sarah said when they were on their own. "Amelia didn't suspect a thing."

"It looked like you were having fun anyway," Charles said.

"Oh yes, I'll certainly be looking forward to a repeat performance when we get back."

Once Charles was undressed he slipped into bed beside his wife and finished what Amelia had started earlier.

They were all up early on Saturday looking forward to a fun day. They had only been travelling an hour or so when Sarah slipped up and fell in the water. "Man Overboard," They all shouted and Mary, who was at the helm, instantly stopped the engine and pulled over to the side. They were getting used to this now so Sarah swam up to the side of the boat and Charles helped her in. The others started the chant, "Spanking, Spanking, Spanking." and then Sarah pretended to whisper something to Charles.

"Well that's your own fault, come on, over my knee." Charles sat down on a stool and pulled Sarah over his lap. Pulling up her skirt they were all surprised to see that she wasn't wearing any knickers. "No, knickers?" Charles said. "Naughty girl," and he spanked his wife on her big bottom. It was a longer spanking than he gave Ella the previous day, and everybody appreciated it, except perhaps, Amelia, who knew she would get the same this afternoon.

When Charles had finished there was a round of applause from the girls and two fishermen who had been watching from the side of the river. "Oh," Sarah said as she stood up and brushed down her skirt quickly, she hadn't anticipated that there would be other men watching as well.

"Later, after lunch, it was Amelia's turn to fall in. She had been showing one of the younger girls how to crochet when a ball of wool rolled forwards and threatened to fall off the boat, Amelia reached out to get it and fell in herself. Interestingly she hadn't meant to do it now, she had planned to fall in later so this was an accident. Luckily she fell right next to the rope ladder so she held onto that while the "Man overboard," cry went out and the boat was stopped yet again.

"We will never get there if you're going to keep falling in," Charles said as he sat on the stool that everybody knew as the spanking stool. Again the chorus of "Spanking, Spanking." was heard on the boat and when Amelia pulled herself up the rope ladder with a little help from Charles he pulled her over his knee and pulled up her skirt. Amelia also has a fat bottom and Charles really went to town spanking her. "Not so hard Charles, not in front of the girls," Amelia said, but he didn't stop until she had a really red bottom. Again the girls on the boat clapped and they were joined by at least ten fishermen on the bank. "Oh my God," Amelia said as she stood up, "I didn't know they were there."

"Well you should have picked a better spot to fall in then, Amelia," Charles said.

"But I fell in by accident," Amelia said as one of the girls gave her the ball of wool she had been reaching for.

That evening Charles walked to the pub before dinner and brought back three bottles of wine and some beer. Amelia looked at him with a question in her eyes. "Oh come on Amelia, they're all old enough to have a glass of wine with their dinner." Amelia agreed, so they had another lovely evening playing Cluedo and eventually they discovered that Colonel Mustard did it in the Library with the lead pipe.

On Sunday it rained and the sensible members of the group stayed in the cabin reading. But Charles said that they had to keep moving or they wouldn't get back to the boatyard by Monday. The younger girls played on the boat and got soaking wet but they were running around in their knickers and a t-shirt so it didn't matter. "They will catch their death," Daisy said but Amelia said that they could have a hot shower when they had finished. When Charles pulled over for their lunch, the three girls jumped into the water.

"Men Overboard," Charles shouted but the girls were just swimming around without a care in the world. "Come out of there," Charles said. "Or you will get bitten by the eels."

"Eels?" one of the girls shouted

"Or the bloodsucking leeches will get you," Charles said, but by now all the girls were fighting to climb up the rope ladder. Standing on the boat they all stripped off to see if there were any leeches on them. Charles sat on the stool and looked at the three girls standing there naked, "Who's first?" he said.

They looked at each other and then queued up to be spanked. Charles had not spanked any of them before and he really enjoyed the experience, which is more than can be said for the girls. Again there was a round of applause when he had finished.

The rain had stopped just after lunch and the sun came out to dry the ground so when they parked for the evening it was a warm night and Charles announced that he would be cooking that evening. Setting up an open fire he wrapped up potatoes in layers of aluminium foil and put them in the coals to cook. "They will take about an hour," he said to his helpers Lilly and Laura. Sarah had noticed that the pair of teachers had been hanging around Charles trying to get his attention the whole weekend, but she didn't mind. "They will get a spanking before the weekend is up," she said to Amelia who agreed

"Serves them right," she said, laughing.

Charles put a grill over the fire and cooked the steak. "Oh Goodie," Mary said, clapping her hands. "A Barbeque."

"In South Africa, this is called a Braai," Charles said. "Something special for our last night."

They all enjoyed their dinner and went to bed early, the fresh air was getting to them, Amelia thought.

On Sunday they had a lovely breakfast of bacon and eggs and then they were all talking at once. Charles raised his voice and asked everybody to stop talking and they did. "Definitely Father Christmas," Mary whispered to Ella.

"Mary, come here please," Charles said in his best baritone voice. And as soon as she was in reaching distance Charles pulled her across his knee and pulled up her skirt, then he spanked her on her knickers softly. "What did I say?"

"Um, you said to keep quiet, Santa," Mary said and everybody laughed, except Mary who got six hard spanks on her bottom.

"Ho, Ho, Ho," Charles said as he lifted her up, but even Mary could see the funny side. Then he cleared his throat and said, "This is our last day on the water, so no falling in, we don't want to be carrying home wet clothes. We will head for Great Yarmouth but then stop somewhere quiet for lunch before we drop off the boat in the afternoon.

Chapter 27 - Two spankings after lunch

Lunch was a quiet affair. Everybody had such fun that they didn't want it to finish. After lunch, they were sitting around the table but it was Sarah who said. "You know Charles, Lilly and Laura haven't had a spanking yet on this trip, everybody else has."

"Oh no, wait a minute," Laura said. "We have been good girls, we helped with everything and didn't fall in once."

"Sarah makes a good point." It was Amelia who was talking now. "It would be a shame to leave them out of the fun."

"I don't mind missing the fun of a spanking," Lilly said. "Anyway, we have to get back so let's clear up lunch and get going." She stood up from the table and started to stack the plates. Charles saw his chance so he pulled her over his knee and raised her skirt. "Oh no, please Charles, not in my bare bottom."

Charles was not going to pull down her knickers but he realised that that was exactly what she wanted him to do. The rest of the girls encouraged him, so he pulled down her knickers and she raised her hips to make it easy for him. Lilly had a lovely curvy figure and at forty-six, she had looked after herself. This was not the first time he had spanked Lilly but this time he intended to give her a hard spanking. Over and over again his hand came down on her wide bottom and she was crying when he helped her up. Rubbing her bottom she looked at Charles through the tears in her eyes. "That was a hard spanking,"

"No more than you deserve for chasing after me all holiday," Charles said and Lilly hung her head.

"Sorry Charles," she said.

"Your next Laura," Charles said but Laura looked worried, she was now expecting to get a hard spanking the same as Lilly, and she was right. "And take off those jeans, they will only get in the way."

"Yes Charles," Laura said as she undid the button of her jeans, pushed down the zip and let them slip to the floor. Next came her knickers and she stretched across Charles's lap. Charles didn't waste any time and gave Laura a hard spanking as well. Everybody was silent for these spankings, worried that they might be next. Everybody had been spanked on the boat except Daisy, and she was certain that Charles would find a reason to spank her, but she was wrong.

Lifting Laura up from his knee he said. "And that goes for you too."

"Yes Charles," she said as she pulled up her knickers and jeans.

Not long after the spanking, Charles pulled the boat out again and they motored back to the boatyard where the owner was waiting for them. "All okay," the owner asked.

"It was fantastic," Laura said, rubbing her bottom. "Only, my bum is a bit sore."

"Yes," said the owner, "Those seats are a little hard." and everybody laughed.

A Housemaster in a girl's school - Spring Term

Charles Nicholas spanks girls and teachers at St Samantha's School
By Paula Mann

Introduction

The story is set in 1971

Charles Nicholas is the housemaster of Saint Samantha's school for girls in Norfolk, England, and his wife Sarah is the Matron. Charles and his wife love to spank naughty girls on their bare bottoms and there's plenty of opportunity at the school.

Chapter 1 - Nicole gets the first spanking of the term

The new year had only just started when the girls at Saint Samantha's Boarding School for Girls arrived back to start the Spring term. It was called the Spring term even though it was the middle of winter and you wouldn't really see any let up in the weather for a couple of months. However, the governing body decided that having a term called Winter was asking for trouble.

So on Saturday the second of January, the boarders started to arrive in their chauffeur-driven cars, ancient Rolls Royces and the coach that picked up some of the girls from Norwich Station. Nicole Asher arrived driving her new red Mini Cooper and when she pressed the horn it played a tune loud enough to frighten the birds in the field next to the school. The headmistress, Amelia Brandon, was standing at the impressive entrance of the old building and she walked over to Nicole and suggested that if she did that again her next trip would be to go and see Mr Nicholas. Charles Nicholas was the disciplinarian at the school so Nicole knew what that meant.

"Can I park my car at the front of the school Mrs Brandon?" Nicole asked.

"You can't park your car anywhere, as soon as you have offloaded your trunk that car has to go straight back home."

"But Mrs Brandon, it was my Christmas present."

"I don't care, girls are not allowed to have a car at school, the only thing you're allowed is a bicycle."

"But Mrs Brandon?" Nicole said as Amelia walked away. "Silly old bat," Nicole said under her breath to her boyfriend, Brian, who was sitting in the passenger seat.

"I heard that Nicole," Amelia said. "Go and see Mr Nicholas before dinner this evening."

"Yes Mrs Brandon," Nicole said and then she turned to Brian. "You had better help me with the trunk and tuck box, and then drive the car home."

"What will Mr Nicholas do?"

"Oh, I'll probably just get a spanking," Nicole said

"I could spank you," Brian said.

Nicole laughed, "Not in your wildest dreams."

As Brian was helping Nicole with her tuck box, Amy Wilson was climbing off the bus carrying three huge red books. "Hi Amy," Nicole said. "I see you got your Encyclopaedia Britannica for Christmas."

"Hi Nicole," Amy said. "I just brought three volumes with me, A to Braille. I should have read them by the end of the term."

Nicole just shook her head and followed Brian into the school.

There was lots of laughter and excitement as friends met for the first time since Christmas and told each other about their presents.

While they were unpacking their trunks in the dormitory, Leah Robson asked Mary Becker what Christmas at school was like.

"We had a great time," Mary said and then went on to tell Leah about the trips to Newcastle, the cruise on the Broads and the fact that Mr Nicholas wore jeans and a checked shirt for much of the holiday."

"No," Leah was shocked. And did you have a spanking moratorium for the holiday?"

"Not really," Mary said. While they were on the long boat on the Broads everybody had been spanked including the Headmistress and Matron, but the girls were all sworn to secrecy, so Mary was hesitant.

"What did you get for Christmas," she asked to change the subject, and they chatted for another hour.

Once Nicole had waved goodbye to Brian and listened to the car horn one last time as he churned up the gravel drive and swerved to avoid the gatepost, she decided that she had better go and see Mr Nicholas, and she found him in his office at Christie House.

Charles Nicholas was the housemaster of Christie house. He had been employed at the beginning of the school year and, although he was the only male member of the teaching staff at St Samantha's, he had fitted in rather well. During the last term, he was made disciplinarian for the school so he does most of the spanking and other punishments as well as a birthday spanking for all the staff and the girls when they get to eighteen.

"Come," Charles called out as he heard a knock at his study door. "Hello Nicole," he said. "Have a good holiday?"

"Yes, thank you, Sir," Nicole said. "How was your holiday here?"

"Very nice, thank you," Charles said. "The Headmistress said you might be visiting me before dinner."

"Oh, she told you, did she?" Nicole was nervous. "What did she say?"

"Why don't you tell me what you think she might have said."

"Well, she might have said that she misheard me. My boyfriend asked me about something and I said 'Millie Told Pat'," Nicole said.

Charles laughed. "How long did it take you to come up with that?"

Nicole couldn't help joining in the laughter, "Most of the afternoon Sir,"

"Well, I give you ten out of ten for creativity," Charles said as he stood up and came around his desk to pull the dining chair into the centre of the room and sit on it. "But you still have the honour of being the first person to be spanked this term. Over my knee."

"Yes Sir," Nicole said. She actually didn't mind being spanked, it gave her a lovely tingle between her legs when Mr Nicholas pulled down her knickers, and she was used to the sting of the spanking. Nicole had a crush on Charles, which was not surprising because most of the girls in the school had a crush on Mr Nicholas. Charles was a tall man going prematurely grey which, together with his military walk, made him look very distinguished. Charles was also permitted to take their knickers down when he spanked the girls, and that may have made him more attractive. Whatever the reason, Charles Nicholas was the subject of many of the early evening dreams the girls had in bed, with their hands in their knickers.

What made Nicole more interesting was that she also had a crush on the twenty-four-year-old sports mistress, Jasmine Pritchard.

Charles loved spanking Nicole, she was a short girl with a small bottom and she was the second girl he had spanked in the school when he joined the teaching staff last year. He pulled her over his knee and lifted up her short school dress. The school rule about dresses was that they had to be no more than six inches above the centre of the knee. It was Matron's pleasant task to enforce that rule and spank the girls who were breaking it. The problem with the rule was that six inches above the knee for the shorter girls may mean that they were showing their knickers.

Nicole didn't mind showing off her knickers and she would do it to her boyfriend Brian all the time, but she never let him inside her knickers, not like she did with Mr Nicholas. She may also have been attracted to Charles because he had a similar surname to her first name. Her friend caught her daydreaming at her desk one day, having written Nicole Nicholas twenty times on a page to see what it looked like. Nicole thought that she would be teased about it, but Katie just laughed and gave the paper back to her. Katie knew she had a similar page in her secret journal so she wasn't going to tell anybody.

So Nicole bent over Charles's lap and wiggled a little as he pulled up her short skirt. "These are not regulation knickers Nicole," Charles said as he rested his hand on her sexy lace knickers.

"No Sir," Nicole said. "Sorry Sir. I didn't think I would be spanked on the first day of term."

Well," Charles said. "I'll let you get away with the knickers as the term doesn't really start until Monday, but you can't go around calling the Headmistress a Silly Old Bat. She is not old and not at all Silly."

"Does that mean that you think she is a B..." Nicole's sentence was stopped just in time with a sharp smack on her knickered bottom.

"I see you're still in a holiday mood Nicole," Charles said. "Maybe it would be a good idea to keep your mouth shut until you get back into the school routine."

"Yes Sir," Nicole said as Charles took down her lacy knickers and started the spanking.

Charles loved spanking naughty girls, he always had and he imagined that he always would. He had spent twenty years teaching in South Africa where he spanked most of the girls when they were in the sixth form, and while he was an excellent teacher, one of the parents had complained and the headmaster of that school suggested that he may like to work in another school, "The other side of the world, maybe?" he was told. So he returned to England and promptly got a job in a girls' school, which amused him. Being a housemaster of this private school he was paid well but when he was appointed to the position of disciplinarian and was told by Amelia Brandon, the headmistress, that there would be no extra money for the additional responsibility, he thought he would have paid them if they had asked.

Over and over again his hand landed on Nicole's small bottom and when she started to cry he realised that he might have got carried away. He stopped spanking her and turned her around on his lap so that he was hugging her. Patting her bottom gently he waited until she stopped crying and then said, "That's the last time I want to see you in here for a spanking this term Nicole,"

"Yes Sir," she said as she stood up and pulled up her knickers letting her school skirt fall into place. "It will be, I promise." A promise she broke within a week.

Chapter 2 - Six girls spanked in the dormitory

S arah Nicholas loved her job as the school Matron. She also loved the opportunities it gave her to explore her other passion, spanking naughty girls. Charles and Sarah were perfectly suited and having spent twenty years together exploring their joint passion in South Africa, Sarah counted herself as being very lucky that she could continue now that she was at Saint Samantha's School for Girls. It was past nine o'clock at night and Sarah was wandering around on the second floor of Christie House making sure that the lights-out rule was being adhered to. The girls were all excited to be back with their friends and there was plenty of noise in the dormitories but at nine o'clock the lights go out and the conversation should stop.

By nine thirty most of the dormitories were quiet but the girls in the upper sixth were still sharing stories about new boyfriends, shared experiences and the occasional first kiss. There was lots of giggling as Sarah opened the door and the room went silent instantly. "Come on girls, it's long past your sleeping time. Settle down now."

"Yes Matron," Lucy Smith said. Lucy was meant to be the leader of the dormitory, and it was her job to keep the others in check.

"Any more noise from this room and I'll be back with the leather strap," Sarah said.

"Yes Matron," Lucy said.

Sarah closed the door and listened and the giggling started. "Come on girls," Lucy said to the others, "Keep the noise down, I don't want to go to sleep with a sore bottom on the first night."

Sarah went back downstairs to the ground floor where the housemaster's flat was situated. "All quiet?" Charles asked as she walked into the lounge. Charles was sitting in an armchair next to the fire with a glass of whisky in his hand.

"No, not really." Sarah said, "Where did the tawse go?"

"Are you going to be doing a little spanking this evening?" Charles said smiling, "Need some help?"

"No, I don't think so, Charles. They will probably be quiet when I get back upstairs but if not there will be a few red bottoms in room seven."

"Oh, the upper six girls," Charles said. "Nine o'clock is too early for them to go to sleep really."

"I know, but it's nearly ten now."

Sarah found the tawse and as she left Charles said. "Have fun," and Sarah laughed.

Back upstairs outside the dormitory, Sarah didn't need to listen too hard to hear all the chatter but Lucy was trying valiantly to get them to quieten down. "Please girls, Matron will be back in a minute I'm sure."

"Matron is as deaf as a post, silly old bat," Nicole said as Sarah walked into the dormitory shining her torch at Nicole. "Was that you again Nicole?" Sarah said. "Isn't that what you called the Headmistress this afternoon?"

"I'm sorry Matron, that was what I was calling Lucy," Nicole said.

"Nice try, Nicole," Matron said as she turned on the light. "Up you get everybody, and bend over the end of your beds, you will all be going to sleep with a red bottom tonight."

There was lots of grumbling and rubbing of eyes against the harsh light, but eventually, all six girls in room seven were bent over the back of their beds. The beds in the dormitories were all the same. A metal headboard and footboard with a wire mesh holding up the mattress. The footboard seemed to be a perfect height for a girl to bend over and Sarah briefly wondered if they had been made with that in mind. "Come on girls," Sarah said. "You have only been away a couple of weeks, surely you remember that spankings are on the bare bottom." More grumbling as they all pull the cord on their regulation striped pyjamas and then they drop to the floor. Next came the knickers and eventually they were all bent over the end of their beds with their bottom bared for a spanking. Sarah looked around the room with delight. Six bottoms of all sizes waiting to be spanked. Nicole and Amy with small bottoms, Lucy and Katie with big bottoms, and Mary and Leah in between. A wonderful sight for a spanker.

Sarah put the leather tawse down, she wanted to feel her bare hand on each bottom so she walked around the room giving each girl six hard spanks. They were all used to getting their bottom spanked so this was not a surprise to any of them, but it seemed to set the tone for the coming term. "Now pull up your knickers and go to bed. You have got off with just a hand spanking now, but if I hear another word, it will be the tawse for all of you."

"Yes Matron," Lucy said.

"And I want to see you tomorrow in the San, Lucy. After the church service."

"Yes Matron."

Sarah switched off the light and closed the door, not another word was heard from room seven all night, but had you listened carefully, you would have heard Nicole and Amy pleasuring themselves ever so quietly a little later on.

"So did you spank them?" Charles asked Sarah when she came back downstairs.

"I did, and now I need a little spanking myself, let's go to bed," Sarah said with a smile.

Chapter 3 - Lucy is Spanked in the Sanatorium

Breakfast was unusually quiet on Sunday morning. The girls had got over their initial excitement of seeing each other again and were now settling down to the fact that they are stuck at school for the next few months. Straight after breakfast, there was the church service to attend. The school had its own church at the end of the grounds and the vicar from the village church would run their service for them. The church choir was very good and performed in competitions from time to time, so the service was mostly hymns with a short sermon.

After the service on Sunday, the girls were free to do their own thing until lights-out at nine.

At ten thirty Lucy knocked on the door of the sanatorium. "Come in, Lucy," Matron said.

Lucy was surprised to see that things were a little different. "You've changed things around Matron."

"Yes, Ella and I worked on it during the holidays, what do you think?" Sarah said.

"It looks much more like a doctor's surgery now, very professional."

"Thank you Lucy, that was the look we were going for," Sarah said. "Now, I wanted to have a talk with you about the noise in the dorm last night. You're meant to keep the girls quiet, you know."

"I know Matron, but they just wouldn't listen."

"And what should you do if they don't listen?" Sarah asked.

"I know I'm allowed to spank any girl who talks too much in the Dorm, but I'm not sure I could."

"I don't see why not, Lucy," Sarah said. "You're bigger than all of them. You'll have to make an example of one of them tonight. The first one who makes a noise after lights-out, you get up, pull them out of bed and spank them."

"But how Matron?"

"Let me show you," Sarah said as she took Lucy's ear with her left hand and twisted it a little.

"Ouch, that hurts," Lucy said.

"Once you have a girl by her ear, you can pretty much do whatever you like, for instance." Sarah kept hold of Lucy's ear with her left hand, then sat on the stool and pulled Lucy over her lap. "You see, I can put you anywhere I want to when I have your ear. And by using my left hand for that I can flip up your skirt with my right hand, pull down your knickers and spank you." As she was saying that she did what she was saying and spanked Lucy on her bare bottom. "See what I mean?"

Lucy tried to get up but Sarah held her in place. With her hand on Lucy's bottom, Sarah said. "Now you know how to do it, I'll be listening outside your dormitory this evening and if I don't hear spanking coming from your room, I'll expect you to report to me on Monday morning and I'll be spanking you instead. Understand?" To support her message, Sarah spanked Lucy one more time and then helped her up.

"I understand Matron," Lucy said, pulling up her knickers. "Thank you."

That evening Sarah was doing her usual rounds checking all the dormitories had their lights out and she heard the sound of spanking from room seven. "Good girl," she said to herself and then went back to the flat on the ground floor.

Chapter 4 - Two Birthday Spankings

The headmistress, Amelia Brandon, was trying and failing to get everybody's attention in the Staff Room on Monday morning. Charles thought he had better intervene so he banged the table and said in a commanding voice, "Quiet Everybody," and the room was instantly silent.

"Thank you, Charles," Amelia said, but she was just a little annoyed that she didn't have the same control over the staff as Charles did. "Good morning staff members, I have a few announcements to make. Unfortunately, Molly Dobson has taken a leave of absence to look after her sick mother but she will be back next term I'm assured. Luckily the governors have made a temporary appointment and Clara Harrison will be joining us this year as the housemistress for Shelly House and she will also be teaching History. I hope you will all join me in welcoming Clara to our happy family." There was a round of polite applause for Clara Harrison.

Clara looked like a battle axe of a woman and Charles wondered how she would manage in this school. Amelia had made the point that she was appointed by the board of governors, and he wondered if she had been consulted, it seemed not. Clara Harrison was a tall woman with large breasts that seemed to be permanently hidden as she had her arms crossed. Her short black hair and penetrating eyes seemed to add to the illusion and Charles thought that she might be pretty if she would only just smile.

Charles was only half listening to Amelia's other announcements. She had already discussed the change in the staff rota with him and he was happy with all the changes, but his ears pricked up when he heard the word birthday.

"I'm pleased to announce that Alexandra Dixon achieved the ripe old age of forty-eight during the holidays and so she will be getting her birthday spanking today. There was a loud cheer of approval and the usual chorus went up, "Spanking, spanking." Looking around Charles noticed that everybody was joining in except Clara Harrison, who had a look of pure shock on her face.

The chair that Charles always used for birthday spankings was moved into the centre of the room and Amelia invited Charles to sit down. "Alex, I think you know the routine by now."

"Yes, Headmistress, although I'm not at all sure with the 'ripe old age' bit," she said as she pulled her loose dress up displaying her silk knickers. She got another round of applause for the quality of her underwear and bent over Charles's lap.

"Forty-eight eh?" Charles said. "You had better get comfortable, you may be here a while."

Clara was obviously horrified but she gasped when Charles took the elastic of Alex's expensive silk knickers and lowered them gently, baring her bottom. "Nice knickers," Charles said.

"Thank you," Alex was looking back at Charles and smiling. "I thought I might have to upgrade from my Marks and Sparks cotton ones for today, I'm glad you like them."

Charles rested his hand on Alex's bare bottom when Amelia said. "Enough flirting you two, we all have classes to teach in ten minutes."

"Of course headmistress," Charles said formally and started to spank Alex's bottom. As usual, all the staff counted the spanks but when Charles stopped halfway through and started to rub Alex's bottom, there was an argument about the number he was on when he started again. Some people thought it was twenty-four and others thought it was twenty-five. Charles knew the number should have been twenty-five but he said we would start again at twenty-four. "It would be terrible if I missed one," he said.

"Oh yes, terrible," Alex said.

Charles was not harsh with the spanking but Alex was sore when he rested his hand on her bottom and everybody said Forty-Eight. Everybody that is, apart from Cora, who was still horrified and determined to talk to the governors about it later today.

Alex got up and rubbed her bottom. "That was sore Charles," Alex whispered as she got up. "Maybe I could come around this afternoon and you could finish it off for me."

"That would be my pleasure, Alex," Charles said. "Shall we say two o'clock?"

Charles had some spare time in the afternoon and he was happy to help Alex in whatever way she had in mind, this morning he had two lessons to teach but it was the Upper sixth he was looking forward to. Walking into the classroom all the girls stood up and greeted him in unison. As he placed his books on the teacher's desk he was thinking that this was a far cry from the slovenly behaviour that he experienced when he joined the staff at St Sam's at the beginning of the last term. "Thank you girls, you may sit now," Charles said surveying the room. "No new faces then, just a handful of girls hungry to continue with their logarithms." There was a groan from the room. "Today we will be continuing with the Exponent of Log Rule. Open your books at page one hundred and twenty-eight."

"Sir," Charles didn't need to look up, he knew it would be Nicole who would want to attract his attention.

"What is it Nicole, do you want to explain the Exponent of Log Rule to us," Charles said.

"Oh no Sir," Nicole said. "You do that so much better than I would. I just wanted to remind you that there was an eighteenth birthday during the holiday, and as Alex, I mean Miss Dixon, received the traditional celebration on her birthday this morning in the staff room, I expect you would like to extend the same courtesy to Rebecca who had her birthday on Christmas day."

"Nikki!" Rebecca exclaimed then she turned to her teacher. "You don't have to, Sir, I'm sure you have much more important things to do."

Charles knew about Rebecca's birthday. He had a special calendar on his desk that showed when the girls would get to eighteen, but he also knew that Nicole, or someone else in the class, would remind him. "There's nothing more important than looking after the girls in this school. Rebecca and I would hate to break with tradition so you had better come up here and receive your special birthday spanking. I'm sure you will want to thank Nicole later for reminding me."

"Oh I certainly will Sir," Rebecca said and she walked towards the front of the classroom. Charles stood up from behind his desk and sat on the chair in the front of the class that was there as a reminder that any of the girls could be spanked at any time. Rebecca came to Charles's right-hand side and bent over his lap. Rebecca was an athlete and she was extremely fit. She was a weekly boarder so she usually went home on Friday and came back on Monday but she would often be at the school at the weekend to participate in any athletics or team sports that were being held. Bending over Charles's lap was easy for her and she raised her legs as instructed when Charles lifted her skirt and pulled down her knickers.

Charles also knew that Rebecca was tough and he had never known her to cry while being spanked. On the contrary, she seemed to enjoy the endorphin rush that the spanking created. He spanked her hard ten times and the girls counted in unison. Leaving his hand on her bottom he said, "You're not feeling this at all are you?"

"Oh Sir," Rebecca said. "Have you started?" The rest of the girls burst out laughing and Rebecca joined them, bent over Charles's lap

Then he said, "No, I haven't started yet. Nicole, please go to the cupboard behind my desk and bring me the table tennis bat that's in there." Nicole did as she was told and was smiling when she handed over the table tennis bat.

"Oh Sir," Rebecca said. "I was only joking."

"And a fine joke it was, but I think the joke will be on you now."

"Yes Sir," Rebecca said as she felt the table tennis bat land on her bottom. This was a different type of pain altogether and she certainly felt it this time.

The girls called out "Eleven," but Charles said. "Oh no girls, Rebecca didn't feel the first few, so I've started again, that was one." Charles spanked her again. "Two," The girls called out but they could see that Rebecca was getting a proper spanking not just a few light taps on her birthday. Ella Hall was especially worried because it was her eighteenth birthday coming up next month. At ten spanks Charles was resting his hand on Rebecca's bottom as he said. "Did you feel those Rebecca?"

"Oh yes Sir," Rebecca said. "I'm certainly feeling this spanking," Charles reminded himself that this wasn't meant to be punishment, it was a spanking to celebrate her birthday so he eased up a little for the last eight spanks. Finally, Rebecca stood up and was rubbing her bottom when she said, "Thank you for my birthday spanking," but Charles noticed that she had tears in her eyes.

"You're welcome," Charles said.

At the end of the class, the bell rang for the lunch break and Charles asked Rebecca to stay behind. When they were alone in the room, he said, "I'm sorry I spanked you so hard for your birthday spanking Rebecca, but do you know why I did?"

"Because I was cheeky?"

"Yes, because you were cheeky, but there's also a consolation gift." Charles reached into his drawer and pulled out a parker pen in a gift box. "This is for your birthday Rebecca, but don't mention it to the others or everybody will want one."

Rebecca was very excited. "Thank you Sir," she said and came to his side of the desk and hugged him with a kiss on the cheek.

Charles took advantage of his sitting position by patting Rebecca on her bottom a few times and said, "Off you go now, and remember, don't tell anybody." Charles had given every one of the girls who got to eighteen a parker pen in a gift box, and he told each one that they were not to tell their friends.

Chapter 5 - Alex Dixon gets another spanking from Charles

At two o'clock Charles was sitting in his lounge at Christie House when Alex knocked at the door. "Come," he called and Alex Dixon walked in. She was wearing the same white blouse as she was wearing this morning but she had a knitted cardigan over the top and a tight pencil skirt. This was more like the clothing she would normally wear at school. "Hello Alex, you changed."

Alex was smiling. "I knew I would get a spanking from you this morning so I wore a loose skirt, I wasn't going to strip off in the staff room."

"And now?" Charles said

"Oh, I don't mind if it's just you and me."

Alex smiled and Charles laughed. "So what can I do for you, Alex."

"Well, for a start you can finish what you started this morning," Alex said as she undid the zip on the side of her skirt and let it drop to the floor. Alexandra Dixon was a well-built lady by any standards. She was about five foot eight inches with broad shoulders, a heavy breast and large hips. She was now standing in her blouse and cardigan with silk knickers and suspenders. When the skirt fell to the floor she kicked off her shoes. "Do you like what you see?" she asked Charles.

"I'm not sure, I'll need to see more before I make up my mind," Charles said.

"Yes, of course," Alex said as she shrugged off the cardigan and began to undo the buttons of her blouse. Letting that fall off her shoulders she was now just in her underwear. "And now?"

Charles stroked his chin, "Um? Still not sure."

"Charles Nicholas, you're a dirty old man. What would Matron say?" Alex said.

"Oh she would say that she was not sure yet, either," Sarah said from the corner of the room. She had been sitting on a chair right in the corner of the lounge and hadn't made a sound when Alex walked in.

"Oh Shit!" Alex said, reaching for her blouse that was on the floor. "I didn't know you were there Matron."

"I'm sure you didn't, Alex," Sarah said. "Trying to seduce my husband while you thought I was away."

"No Matron, it's not like that at all, I was just going to ask for a proper spanking, not the soft spanks I got this morning."

"Oh is that all?" Sarah asked. "Only it looks to me like you were wanting to fuck him."

"Oh no Matron, I promise."

"Well if you were only looking for another spanking I can give it to you can't I?"

Alex knew she was in a corner and the only way to get out of it was to agree. "Of course Matron, if you have time."

"Oh I have a little time Alex," Sarah said as she stood up and walked to the centre of the room carrying the spanking chair that was always in the lounge. Sitting down, Sarah said. "Finish taking off your bra and knickers and get over my knee."

Stripping down to just her suspenders and stockings, Alex felt very vulnerable and bent over Matron's lap. She had heard that Sarah likes to spank the girls but she had no idea that desire extended to the teachers as well. When Alex was over her knee, Sarah pulled her tight against her body and started to spank her fat bottom. Over and over again Sarah landed hard spanks on Alex's bottom. "This will teach you for trying to seduce my husband," Sarah said. "It's a pity you didn't know that you only had to ask me."

When Sarah finished spanking the forty-eight-year-old she patted her bottom twice and looked at her husband. "There you go Charles, I've warmed her up for you, a little more spanking and she will be ready I think."

"Thank you, Sarah," Charles said as Sarah stood up abruptly and deposited Alex on the floor. Charles kissed his wife and she left, leaving Alex astonished. "And as for you," Charles said to Alex. "Roll over and get on your knees, stick your bottom right up in the air, I haven't finished with you yet."

"Yes Sir," Alex said. She found it very sexy to be controlled by a strong man and Charles was just that sort of man. Going behind his desk he took the leather slipper that Daisy had given him last term and walked back to Alex, who was displaying herself quite lewdly, to Charles's delight.

"Ten strokes with the leather slipper and then I'm going to fuck you up your ass."

"Oh, does it have to be there?" Alex asked. "I've never done that before."

"Yes, it does," Charles said. "Anything else is saved for my wife."

"Okay," Alex was about to say but she was cut short when the slipper landed on her bottom. Sarah hadn't spanked her all that hard but when the slipper landed on an already spanked bottom it hurts. "Ouch," Alex said and reached behind her to cover her bottom.

"Take your hand away or we will start again," Charles said.

"Yes Sir," Alex said and held her hands together in front of her just in case she was tempted to cover herself again. Alex was crying when Charles got to ten spanks but he put the slipper down and felt between Alex's legs. She was soaking wet and he massaged her pussy vigorously. Using her natural lubrication he pushed one finger into her bottom, and then two. "Stop, I can't do this Charles."

"Of course you can, push back and you will see it's a lot easier." Alex pushed back and was surprised to find he was right. Charles had two fingers working inside Alex's anus now and she heard a zip being lowered. She knew what that was. He pulled his fingers out and she felt his erection against her pussy. He didn't enter her, just rubbed it up and down on her pussy and then pushed against her sphincter.

"Oh God," Alex said as he entered her just a little. "Too much," she said.

"Just relax Alex, you'll get used to it." Surprisingly she did get used to it and inch by inch Charles pushed himself inside her. To start with she hated it and was hoping he would come soon, but after a while, she got used to it and pushed back against him to make sure he went deeper. She had never felt so full and the feeling was wonderful.

Reaching between her legs, Alex found her clitoris and as Charles was pumping himself in and out of Alex's bottom, she was bringing herself off by rubbing her clit. They came together. As Alex felt Charles come inside her she exploded in a glorious orgasm.

A little later, when Charles was dressed and Alex came out of the bathroom she said, "Well that was a first, Charles, thank you."

"You're welcome, and I'm sure Sarah will enjoy spanking your lovely bottom any time you like."

"Oh really, thank you, I'll remember that." Alex faced Charles and kissed him on his cheek and then left as Mary Becker knocked on the lounge door with a message from the headmistress.

"Excuse me Mr Nicholas, but the headmistress would like to see you," Mary said. "Sounds important, are you in trouble?"

"Don't be cheeky Mary," Charles said. "I allowed a little flexibility during the holiday, but we are back at school now."

"Yes Sir. Sorry Sir." Mary said. Then she giggled, "But it was a fun holiday wasn't it."

By now Charles was standing right next to her and he spanked her hard. "Yes it was, Mary," He said smiling. "Okay, tell her I'll be along shortly," Charles said.

Chapter 6 - Charles meets the head of the governors

C harles knocked at the headmistress's door and then walked straight in without waiting for an answer and found Elizabeth Crawley with Amelia. "Hello Lizzi," Charles said and instantly got a look from her, with a slight shake of the head. Charles glanced in the corner and saw Clara Harrison sitting on a chair.

"Ah there you are Mr Nicholas," Elizabeth Crawley, the head of the school governing body, said. "Thank you for coming along. I've received a complaint that sex orgies are going on in the staff room."

"Oh really?" Charles said. "Sex orgies, I'm sorry I missed them."

"This is serious Mr Nicholas," Mrs Crawley said.

Charles cleared his throat, "Yes, of course it is. What precisely do you mean by sex orgy?"

"Oh come on Mr Nicholas," Clara Harrison said. "I saw you bearing Mrs Dixon's bottom this morning in the staff room."

"Oh, you mean the birthday spanking?" Charles said. "That's a tradition that goes back to the last century in this school, and we are keen on tradition, aren't we Headmistress?"

"Yes, of course," Amelia was ready for this comment. "I have the documents here that talk about the tradition." Amelia went to her cupboard and pulled out a pile of papers that she found in the old basement last term.

Elizabeth Crawley was relieved that there was an excuse for the birthday spankings. "Well if that's all it is, and everybody involved was over age, I see no problem with a little harmless fun, as long as everybody agrees, that is."

"Of course Mrs Crawley, everybody agreed to it last year," Amelia said.

"Well," Elizabeth Crawley said. "Unless there's anything else, I'll be off."

"Aren't you going to fire Mr Nicholas then?" Clara Harrison said.

"Certainly not, he is the best housemaster we have ever had at this school." Mrs Crawley said. "And I suggest if you don't want to take part in the birthday celebrations, you stay out of the staff room."

"Well really," Clara Harrison said as she made her way out of the office. As she walked past Mr Nicholas she said, "Don't imagine you will get me across your knee for a spanking on my birthday."

"I'll try not to imagine that," Charles said as he watched her bottom walking away, and, try as he might, he did imagine it."

Mrs Crawley closed the door behind Clara Harrison. "Phew, that was close," she said. "That woman is the sister of one of the board members and when I announced that we would have a temporary vacancy, I had no choice but to put her forward. We will have to be a little careful what we say around her."

"When's her birthday?" Charles said to Amelia.

"Charles," Elizabeth said. "You're not thinking what I think you're thinking are you?"

"I'm just seeing how long I have to get her across my knee," Charles said smiling.

"March 21st Charles," Amelia said, putting down the paper she was reading.

Elizabeth was smiling, "Just you be careful, Charles, it may get you into trouble and I would have no alternative but to fire you."

"What?" Charles said in mock shock. "The best housemaster you've ever had?"

Elizabeth laughed. "You're the only housemaster we have ever had at the school."

"Good point," Charles said smiling.

After Elizabeth left, Amelia said," That was close Charles, we do not want all the Governors poking their nose into the school affairs."

"Don't worry Amelia, I'll have Clara over my knee before her birthday."

"Okay, but just be careful," Amelia said.

Chapter 7 - Amelia gets a spanking

The first few weeks of the Spring term progressed comfortably. Cold weather prompted warmer clothing and the dormitories were particularly cold. "I walked into the upper sixth dormitory this morning," Sarah told her husband in the staff room, "And there was frost on the inside of the windows. The girls would freeze to death if they weren't sleeping together."

"What do you mean?" Charles was interested.

"There are six beds in that room and only three of them were slept in last night," Sarah said.

Charles was laughing, "Oh I see." he said. "As long as they're enjoying themselves."

"I'm serious Charles, we have to do something about the heating in this school before we have a real problem."

"Okay, I'll speak to Amelia."

Later in the day, Charles was in the headmistress's office explaining the problem. "Can't you spank all the girls before they go to bed and then they will at least have warm bottoms," Amelia said.

"Another comment like that and I'll be spanking your bottom, Amelia," Charles said.

"Oh yes please, I get cold too you know," Amelia said. Charles Nicholas has spanked the headmistress a few times during the last term and the holiday, but there hadn't seemed to be an opportunity this term yet.

"I know, I'm sorry, we seem to both be too busy to do the important things," Charles said.

"Like spanking my bottom?"

"Like spanking your bottom. Come around tonight after lights out. Sarah will be in the sanatorium with that sick child, I'm sure. If not, she can join in."

"Okay, Charles, but I want you to treat me like one of the girls, I miss that."

"Okay, in the meantime have a word with the board of governors and see if we can install some radiators in the dormitories at least."

"Yes Sir," Amelia stood up and saluted.

"And don't be cheeky," Charles laughed.

"Or what?"

"You will find out tonight."

Charles and Sarah had dinner in the main dining room that evening. They would often have food delivered to their dining room in the housemaster's apartment, but sometimes they liked to chat with the other teachers and the girls over dinner. "I had a chat with Amelia and she will ask the board to install some radiators in the dormitories. The heating system will have to be upgraded I expect, but the weather isn't going to get any warmer before the summer."

"I don't expect it will get warmer then, sometimes I miss the old school," Sarah said. Charles had spent the last twenty years teaching in a boarding school in South Africa and Sarah was the Matron there so the English weather was just a little difficult to get used to.

"By the way, Amelia will be coming over at nine tonight, she has been naughty, do you want to join us?" Charles asked.

"Naughty?"

"Like a little girl," Charles said. "I'll be spanking her, and then we will see."

"I would love to join you but I have to stay in the San, probably all night. Little Pinky Turner is really sick. If she gets any worse she will have to go to the hospital so I'll be with her all night."

"Would you like some more apple pie, Mr Nicholas?" Amy Wilson was standing behind Charles serving the dessert.

"Oh hello Amy, are you on dinner duty tonight?" Charles said.

"Yes Sir, I overslept again and missed the bell for assembly," Amy said.

"We've talked about this before, why did you oversleep?"

"I was reading my encyclopaedia. I'm halfway through the first book and last night I was reading about Africa, I didn't realise they were so primitive there, living in huts and all."

Charles laughed, "Well there's another side to Africa as well you know. Modern buildings and infrastructure, come and talk to me about it sometime and I'll share some of my experiences with you."

"I would love that Sir, thank you," Amy said as she walked away.

"Do you think she heard what we were talking about Charles?" Sarah was concerned.

"I don't think so. Too late now if she did."

Later that night Charles was sitting in his lounge when he heard a tap at the door. Standing up he walked to the door and opened it. Amelia was standing there in a dressing gown and somehow she looked younger than her thirty-eight years. "Why it's little Amelia, isn't it? What can I do for you?"

"I'm sorry to bother you Sir, but Matron said I must come and ask you to spank my bottom, I was up after lights-out."

"I see, well that's very naughty, so you had better come in." Charles stood to one side and thought he saw a shadow in the half-light, but dismissed the thought as he was looking forward to spanking Amelia. The spanking chair was already set up in the centre of the room in anticipation of Amelia's visit and Charles sat on it guiding Amelia in front of him. There was a cushion on the floor at Charles's feet and he said, "Kneel down, Amelia, I want to have a serious talk with you. You're such a naughty girl for getting out of bed after lights-out, you need your sleep, that's why there are rules."

"Yes Sir," Amelia was kneeling down in front of Charles. She was looking down at the carpet and she felt very small at this moment.

Charles lifted her chin and looked down at her. "What have you got to say for yourself?"

"I'm sorry Sir, I promise I'll never do it again," Amelia said, and she meant it.

"Well that's as maybe, but you know I still have to give you a sharp spanking don't you?" Amelia nodded. "And it will be on your bare bottom." Amelia nodded again, looking up at Charles.

"Stand up and take off your dressing gown and nightie, I think I'll add a little humiliation as well, I'll be spanking you in the nude."

"Oh no Sir, please, I'm shy."

"Maybe this will help you to remember not to be so naughty," Charles said as Amelia stood up and let her dressing gown fall down her arms followed by her nightie. Amelia was standing there naked as Charles reminded himself of her body. Her large boobs fell free as she bent to gather up her nightie and gown, she had broad hips making her bottom nice and round. Perfect for a spanking, Charles thought to himself. "Put your clothes on the table and then get over my knee, you will be getting a sound spanking from me to teach you not to be so naughty in the future.

"Yes Sir," Amelia said as she bent over his lap and waited for the spanking. Charles had his hand on Amelia's large bottom and he curled his fingers between her cheeks. "Oh Sir," Amelia said, but at that moment he raised his hand and started to spank her. He spanked each cheek twenty times and she was wriggling uncomfortably when he stopped and massaged her bottom. "That was a sore spanking Sir," Amelia said, and I was only out of bed for a few minutes after lights-out."

"But Amelia, the spanking is not over, I was just warming up your bottom before I spank you with this leather slipper." Charles held up the slipper that had been on the floor next to the chair.

"Really Sir?" The slipper?"

"Yes Amelia, the slipper, and I hope this will teach you not to be so naughty in the future." Charles used the leather slipper to great effect. Amelia was making lots of noise and wriggling trying to get away from each spank, then she put her hand on her bottom to protect it and Charles spanked the back of her hand.

"Ouch, Charles, that hurt," Amelia said, breaking out of character.

"Well, you shouldn't try to protect yourself with your hand."

"Sorry Sir," Amelia said.

Charles continued with the slipper on her sore bottom and then stopped putting the slipper back next to his chair. Using both hands Charles massaged Amelia's sore bottom. "Oh Sir," Amelia said. "That's nice." Amelia's legs seemed to have a mind of their own as they drifted apart displaying her hidden places. Amelia was no longer pretending to be a little girl when she said. "You know what I want, Charles," she said and his massaging hands slipped between her cheeks and found her very wet pussy. "Yes, there Charles, down a bit, yes there. Faster."

Charles didn't mind being guided in this way. The spanking was for his pleasure and to get Amelia excited. Massaging her pussy was for her pleasure and he loved to see her orgasm which she would do quite loudly. Luckily the old building that was Christie House had very thick walls and heavy wooden doors so the room was soundproof unless you stood with your ear to the door.

It didn't take Amelia long before she was bucking her bottom up in the air and then she came loudly, clamping her legs together as she slowly calmed down.

"Oh thank you, Charles," Amelia said as she got up and started to dress. "I needed that." Wrapping her gown around her she opened the lounge door, looked to see that there was nobody there and then she was gone.

Later Charles thought that it was probably instinct that made him think that there was somebody in the hall. He wasn't sure but he thought he had better check. "You can come out now Amy," he said to nobody, and nothing happened. Listening carefully, however, he thought he heard something, so he went to look and he found little Amy Wilson crouched behind the big grandfather clock shivering in her nightie. "Oh Amy, you will die of the cold sitting there, come with me." Charles bent down and picked up Amy's slight body and carried her into the lounge. Putting her on the rug in front of the log fire, he said. "You wait there."

"Yes Sir," she said shivering.

Five minutes later Charles came back into his lounge carrying two steaming mugs of cocoa. "Here you are Amy, drink this."

"Thank you Sir, but I had better get back to the dorm," Amy said.

"I don't think so Amy, we have to have a little chat first." Charles sat on the settee and then said, "Come up here and sit on my knee, you're too close to the fire." Amy was just five feet tall and her short hair made her look much younger than her eighteen years. She had a boyish figure with a slim waist and almost no boobs at all so it was easy for Charles to wrap his arms around her and hold her on his lap. "So what were you doing, hiding in the entrance hall?"

"I just came downstairs to get a glass of water Sir,"

From his position, it was easy to reach Amy's bottom so he spanked her hard. "That was a lie Amy," he said. "You're already going to get a spanking for being out of bed and for every time I hear you lie it will be the cane, understand?"

"I'm sorry Sir, but I don't want to tell you what I was doing. I'm embarrassed."

"I see, let me guess," Charles said. "You heard me talking to Matron at the dinner table." Amy looked up and nodded. "And you knew the headmistress was coming to see me this evening," Amy nodded again. "And you listened at the door to see what would happen."

"Oh no Sir, I didn't hear anything." Charles spanked her again. "But Sir, it's very difficult to hear anything so I watched through the keyhole."

"Amy, that's very naughty, isn't it?"

"Yes I know Sir," Amy said. "But is it true that the headmistress enjoyed being spanked by you?"

"What do you think, Amy?"

"Well, Sir," Amy thought for a while. "It looked like she was enjoying it very much after the spanking finished, but I don't understand why she would ask you to spank her first."

"Well, the spanking helps her enjoy the aftereffects much more," Charles said. "You know you're going to get a spanking for spying on us don't you?"

"Yes Sir, I know."

"Then get over my knee and I'll show you what I mean," Charles said.

"Should I take my nightie off like the headmistress?"

"Yes, that would make sense," Amy is one of the brightest girls in the school and she isn't spanked very often but Charles loves the look of her slim body and flat chest as she pulled the nightie over her head and stretched across his lap. Charles put his hand on Amy's bottom and started spanking straight away, this spanking is for being a little spy Amy,"

"Yes Sir," Amy said but she had already started to cry. Her small bottom was very red after just twenty or so spanks and so Charles stopped spanking and started to rub her bottom a little.

"Now that I've stopped spanking you, how does it feel if I start to rub your bottom for you."

"Oh Sir," Amy said. "My bottom is still sore but your rubbing makes the sting go a little deeper, to my... well you know."

"To your pussy Amy?"

"Yes Sir,"

"So you see that a spanking can make you feel nice afterwards even if the spanking stings."

"Yes Sir, I see," Amy said. "Could you... you know?"

"No Amy, this is as far as I go, and anyway this is meant to be punishment. But it's just the start. I want you to report to me tomorrow in the first break and we will discuss your behaviour today and come up with the appropriate punishment, okay?"

"Okay Sir," Amy said. "I guess I deserve it."

"Yes you do," Charles said as he spanked her again. "Off to bed with you, and if you discuss what you saw this evening with any of the girls I'll know about it and I'll be very disappointed, understand."

"Yes Sir, I understand," Amy said as she stood up and pulled her nightie over her head.

As Amy was leaving the room she said, "Thank you, Mr Nicholas. You're the best teacher in the school and I won't let you down, I promise."

"I know Amy," Charles said and then he patted her on her bottom as he sent her on her way.

Closing the lounge door he said to himself. Well, I survived another "Get behind me Satan," moment. Then he laughed out loud as he made his way to bed.

Chapter 8 - Amy is excited about her punishment

"Come In," Charles Nicolas shouted from his desk in the study at Christie House. His first lesson on a Wednesday was not until eleven so Charles likes to spend the morning in his study preparing for the day. "Ah, there you are Amy. I trust you slept well after our little bottom warming last night."

"Yes, thank you Sir," Amy said. She had been caught spying on Charles and the headmistress the previous night and she had been spanked, but this morning she expected more punishment for the incident.

"Come here and stand beside me Amy," Charles said as he sat at his desk. "I've prepared a list of your punishments for your disgraceful behaviour last night. We will go through it together."

Standing next to Mr Nicholas, Amy felt him put his hand under her school skirt and rub her bottom through her knickers. This was not a surprise, she was expecting it. Ever since Charles Nicholas had been made school disciplinarian, all the girls would feel his hand on their bottom from time to time, even if they were not to be spanked. He thought the girl's bottoms were his domain. Amy was also a very small girl at just five feet, and she had a small bottom, so Charles's hand could cover it all, and rub or squeeze as he liked.

"I see that there is not a lot of chatter about the headmistress and me, so you have kept that to yourself I guess," Charles said.

"Oh yes Sir, I promised."

"Good, let's keep it that way. Many of the staff come to me for a little entertainment from time to time and I would hate that to get out, I don't think the junior girls would understand."

"No Sir, you're right," Amy said. "But I've just one question Sir, does Matron know?"

Charles squeezed Amy's bottom painfully. "Of course she knows, Amy. You don't think I would do anything like that behind her back, do you?"

"Oh no Sir," Amy said.

"In fact, she's part of your punishment so you can ask her. Now, you read out what is on the page, and then I'll want you to sign it."

"Yes Sir," Amy said as she concentrated on the list Charles had written out. "Miss Amy Wilson accepts that she was very naughty, sneaking downstairs after lights-out and spying on the housemaster in his private lounge. In this regard, she accepts the following punishment. One. She will do dinner duty every day for a week starting today. Two. She will report to Mr Nicholas at seven every evening for a week and tell him what she has learned about Africa. Three. She will report to Matron on Saturday for an extended lesson about the human reproductive system." Amy looked up. "But Sir, this is not really punishment, apart from the dinner duty, I would love to do the other things."

"You had better read the last item on the list," Charles said.

Looking down, she read the last item and then said, "Oh, I see."

"Read it out loud," Charles said

"She will report to Mr Nicholas after dinner on Friday when she will get twelve strokes of the cane." Looking up, she said. "Yes, that bit is punishment. Can't I have that now, I would hate to have to wait?"

"No Amy, the waiting is the punishment."

"Yes Sir," Amy said.

Charles squeezed her bottom again. "Right Amy, you must sign at the bottom and then off you go or you will miss the next lesson, what have you got?"

"Oh, it's just 'old Harry'."

"Pardon?" Charles was surprised.

"Oh sorry Sir, that just slipped out." Amy was embarrassed. "I meant to say that the next lesson is with Miss Harrison, and she doesn't care if we're late."

"I see, that will get you an extra smack this evening."

"Yes Sir," Amy said as she left. Strangely she was smiling all the way to her next lesson.

Charles decided he would find out what Clara Harrison was doing in the class so he walked slowly behind Amy and discovered she would be doing history with the rest of the upper sixth. Amy didn't know he was there and she just walked into the class and closed the door behind her. There was a lot of noise coming from the classroom and he recognised Nicole's voice organising the mayhem. He thought that there was no teacher in the room but then he heard Clara Harrison trying to calm the girls down.

"Okay girls, that's enough now," Clara said. "That's enough," she shouted but the noise continued. Charles walked into the classroom, there was instant silence and the girls all stood up and hurriedly got back to their own desks. "Good Morning Mr Nicholas,' they all said in unison."

"Sorry to bother you, Miss Harrison. But can I have a word with Nicole, please?"

"Clara was shocked that all he had to do was to walk into a room to get the girls to be quiet. "Yes of course," she said.

"Nicole?"

"Yes Sir?"

"Come and see me at four, please. My study."

"Yes Sir," she said and then Charles left.

Chapter 9 - Nicole is spanked again

Just after lunch, Clara Harrison approached Charles. "Sorry to bother you Charles, but can I have a word?"

"Well I have the upper sixth in five minutes and you know how rowdy they can get if they are left on their own."

"Yes, I guess that is what I want to talk to you about."

"Well I have Nicole coming over at four but you can come at half past, if you like,"

"Thank you Charles, I'll be there," Clara said.

"What was all that about?" Sarah said as she walked up behind her husband, "You look like the cat who got the cream."

Charles was smiling, "Old Harry wants to talk to me. I think that is the first time she has said anything more than good morning since she got here."

"Old Harry?"

"That's what the girls are calling her, apparently."

"Do you want me to stay away?" Sarah said.

"I don't think so, I doubt it will be that sort of discussion." They both laughed and then Charles hurried off to teach the upper sixth.

At four o'clock it was Nicole who was knocking on the door of the study in Christie house. "Come in, Nicole," Charles said and a very subdued schoolgirl entered the study. The housemaster's study in Christie house was their lounge in the evenings, in addition to an elegant desk in the bay window and office chairs to sit on. There was also a chesterfield settee and two matching chairs. One addition to the room was two dining chairs that Charles put against the wall in the far corner, and these were for spanking naughty girls and teachers sometimes. Charles was sitting at his desk and he invited Nicole to stand beside him. Nicole was only an inch or so taller than Amy and she had been in this position before, so she was not surprised when Charles's hand found its way up her skirt and felt her bottom.

"I don't think these are regulation knickers, are they Nicole? In fact, I would guess that these are the lace knickers you were wearing the last time I spanked you on the first day of term. Am I right?"

"Yes Sir,"

"I think I better have those Nicole, I'll return them at the end of term." Charles held out his hand and Nicole reached under her school skirt and pulled down her knickers. Stepping out of them, she put the warm material onto Charles's hand. "Right," Charles said as he put the knickers in the top drawer of his desk and put his hand back under Nicole's skirt feeling her naked bottom. "Now, what was all that fuss I heard you orchestrating in Miss Harrison's class this morning?"

"It was just a bit of fun Sir."

"Well, in that case, I'll be having a bit of fun on your bottom before you leave here this afternoon."

"But it wasn't just me Sir, it was everybody."

Charles squeezed Nicole's bottom. "Here's the thing Nicole. As you know Ruby Grant has to go back to Holland in two weeks and she will be finishing her studies there. I'll be looking for a new head girl for Christie house and you would be the perfect candidate if you weren't so naughty. You're a born leader and the others respect you, but if you organise rowdy behaviour like you did this morning, I'll have to start looking for another candidate."

"Oh Sir," Nicole said excitedly. "I had no idea."

"Well, you do now," Charles said. "I haven't made up my mind yet, and you will be getting a spanking for your behaviour this morning, but I'll be looking for something more from you over the next two weeks."

"Yes Sir,"

Charles pushed his chair back away from his desk. "Come on then, you know the position by now."

"Yes Sir," Nicole said. As she stretched across his lap, Charles had his hand on her bare bottom the whole time, holding her, his fingers curled between her cheeks and felt for her little anus. "Oh Sir," Nicole said but she wasn't worried, this was not the first time that her housemaster had felt her butt hole. As soon as she was in position, Charles started the spanking. He had no intention of giving her a hard spanking or making her cry for that matter, he just wanted to warm her bottom to give her something to think about the next time she decided to be naughty. After thirty or so spanks, Charles lifted her back in position next to him. "Now, I'll be watching you. You have a natural talent for leadership, I want you to use that talent to help Miss Harrison, okay?"

"But she's so..." Nicole was interrupted.

"I don't want to know. She's your teacher and she needs to be respected, starting today."

"Yes Sir," Nicole said and as she left, Clara Harrison was at the door. "Good afternoon Miss Harrison," Nicole said politely. Then she shocked Clara and Charles by curtseying.

"Hello Clara, come in," Charles said.

"What was all that about Charles?"

"All what?" Charles said as if he didn't know what she was talking about.

"That curtsey," Clara said. "I didn't know the girls here were taught to do that."

"Oh yes," Charles said casually, but he hadn't seen anybody curtsey at the school either. "Now what can I do for you?" he said as he directed Clara to one of the guest chairs across the other side of his desk.

"Well, I know we didn't get off to a good start Charles."

"Really?"

"Well, all that stuff about the spanking in the staff room, I was shocked and I felt I had to report it."

I expect that you thought it was in the school's best interest." Charles said.

"Precisely," Clara said. "Only, I think I was wrong."

"In what way?"

"I see the respect you command from the girls and, as it happens, from the staff. And I was wondering how you do it?"

"I see," Charles said. "I spank them when they are naughty."

"Yes, well, apart from that." Clara was embarrassed. "Anyway, I've never seen you spank any of the girls."

"Only because you haven't been watching. Actually, I've only ever spanked girls from the upper sixth, but my reputation as a spanker is well known in this school, and even the young girls think they may get spanked if they're naughty."

"There must be more to it than that, I can't go around spanking all the girls to get respect."

"You don't have to, just spank one of them and the word will soon spread," Charles said.

"I can't do that, I don't know how, for a start. No, there must be another way."

"I'm afraid I don't know of any other way," Charles said standing up. "But if you find one, let me know. In the meantime, I think you will find the upper sixth better behaved in the future."

"Oh I do hope so, they run me ragged. Thank you for listening, Charles."

"Any time Clara," Charles said as she left.

Chapter 10 - Mrs Elizabeth Crawley is Spanked

"How are you getting on with Clara Harrison?" Elizabeth Crawley, the chairperson of the school Governors, asked.

"She's doing okay," Amelia said but the tone of her voice said something different.

"Oh, I see," Elizabeth said. She was making a surprise visit to the school and she was in Amelia's office going over the books. "I've had a look at the plans for the new heating system for the dormitories. I must say it's long overdue, I still remember how cold it got when I was a student here and I think the heating system is just the same. It must be pre-war."

"Which war?" Amelia said in an unusual attempt at humour.

"Point taken," Elizabeth said. "I'll have to reach out to the parents again, and we are still funding the new swimming pool as well. It should be okay though, we have a few parents who have sent their little darlings to the school recently, who could pay for the complete system out of petty cash."

Amelia laughed, "I suppose a pay rise is out of the question then."

"Ah, yes, well..." Elizabeth said obscurely.

"Don't worry, I know it's not due until September, but we will have to prepare for that when we look at the school fees for next year," Amelia said.

"So what are we going to do about Miss Harrison?" Elizabeth found a way to change the subject

"I'm not sure. She knows her stuff, but she's failing to get the respect of the girls, especially the senior girls. I know that she has had a chat with Charles about it, so we will see what comes out of that."

Elizabeth pretended that she had just thought of something. "That reminds me, I want a chat with Charles, will he be available this afternoon do you think?" In fact, Charles was the reason she had driven all the way from London today. She hadn't called Charles because she didn't want to be turned down.

"I expect he will make himself available for the chairperson of the board of governors, anything, in particular, you want to talk about?" Amelia knew what she wanted, and she knew Charles would spank Elizabeth this afternoon so she was just a little jealous.

"No, not really," Elizabeth said obscurely. "Just a little matter of discipline."

"Yes, of course. I'll get Emily to call him for you."

"No, don't worry, I expect I'll find him in his study if he hasn't got any classes," Elizabeth said as she left the headmistress's office.

Charles was sitting in his study chatting to Sarah at lunchtime when there was a knock at the door. "Are you expecting anybody?" Sarah asked. Sarah and Charles had developed the habit of meeting in his study after lunch, and they didn't like to have that time disturbed.

"No," Charles said as he stood up. "I'll get rid of them." Opening his study door he found Elizabeth Crawley standing there. "Hello Mrs Crawley, I wasn't expecting you."

"Sorry to disturb you, are you busy?"

"Well I am a little," Charles said on impulse. "But I'll be free in ten minutes."

"Oh. Okay," Elizabeth was not used to being told to wait. She wasn't sure how to handle it. "Shall I wait here then?" she said pointing to the chair outside his door.

"Yes, okay. I'm sure I won't be long."

Back in the study, Sarah was wondering what was going on. "Who was that?" she asked.

"Elizabeth Crawley."

"Oh, I had better leave you to it, didn't you invite her in?" Sarah said.

"No need to hurry, she's waiting outside until I'm ready to see her," Charles was smiling. "I think she wants another spanking."

"Charles!" Sarah was shocked. "You can't leave the chairperson of the board of governors sitting outside your study."

"I just did," Charles said, but I'll let her in now. Give me a passionate kiss when I open the door, okay?"

Sarah shook her head. "Okay."

Charles opened the door and then kissed his wife passionately, "See you later darling," he said. "I'm free now Lizzi."

"Matron," Elizabeth said dismissively.

"Hello Mrs Crawley," Sarah said but she felt she had to explain. "Sorry to keep you, we had a very important discussion to finish."

"Okay," Elizabeth said as she followed Charles back into his study.

Sitting behind his desk he let Elizabeth Crawley stand. "Now, what can I do for you, Lizzi?"

"Oh God, Charles, you don't make this easy do you?"

"I always say to my students that if maths was easy everybody would be good at it, but it isn't easy," Charles said. "Life isn't easy either."

Elizabeth was angry now, she had been kept waiting and now she was being treated like a child. "I didn't come here for a lecture, Charles."

"What did you come here for then?"

"A spanking."

So you want to be treated like a child then?"

"Well, yes, I guess," Elizabeth said as she slumped into one of the guest chairs on the far side of Charles's Desk.

"Stand up," Charles commanded and Elizabeth was on her feet again. "I'll not have slovenly behaviour in my office, do you understand?"

"Yes Sir," Elizabeth said.

"That's better. I'll help you out today, but I expect you to make an appointment the next time you want a spanking, do you understand?"

"Yes Sir."

"Good, now you had better slip off that tight skirt, you know spankings are always on your bare bottom, and you'll be getting the cane as well today."

"The cane?" Elizabeth said. "Oh, I don't think I could..." Her sentence was cut short when Charles slammed the desk hard.

"I'll be the judge of what you could or could not. Understand?"

"Yes Sir," Elizabeth said as she undid the zip on the side of her black pencil skirt and let it drop to the floor. Mrs Crawley was in her mid-forties with blond hair that was always tied back away from her face. Her slim body was immaculately dressed and Charles was delighted to see she was wearing satin french knickers and matching suspenders.

Charles made no attempt to hide the fact that he was enjoying watching Elizabeth removing her clothes. "Now the blouse, Lizzi. Then I want you to go and stand in the corner and think about your behaviour."

"But Charles, what behaviour is that?"

"Well, rudeness for a start. You were rude to me by just turning up without an appointment. I also want you to consider who else you have been rude to this week, I'm sure there are plenty of occasions that you need to be punished for."

"Yes Sir," Elizabeth said as she walked to the far corner of the room wearing a matching set of satin knickers, suspenders and bra. The corner had been left with no pictures or furniture for precisely this purpose.

Charles allowed Mrs Crawley to stand in the corner for a full ten minutes which felt like an hour to her. "Right, come here Lizzi," Charles said. Turning she noticed that the spanking chair was now in the centre of the room and there was a leather slipper on the floor next to the chair and the cane on the table. Mrs Crawley shivered. "Cold?"

"No sir, I'm just worried about the cane."

"And so you should be, the cane stings, but you will only be getting three strokes unless you add to them during the spanking," Charles said as he sat on the chair and told Mrs Crawley to kneel in front of him on the cushion he had put there. "So tell me how often you have been rude to others this week."

Elizabeth was looking at the floor when Charles lifted her chin so that she was looking up at him. "I was rude to you of course, but I'm not sure how else I may have been rude this week?"

"Your number of cane strokes has gone up to four, Lizzi."

"Oh no Sir," Elizabeth started to cry. "I guess I was rude to Amelia for arriving unannounced this morning."

"Good Girl, that's a start. Who else?"

"Nobody," Elizabeth said uncertainly.

"Five."

"No, wait. I was rude to the chauffeur this morning, I didn't even say good morning, I just told him where to go."

"Who else?"

Elizabeth was worried she may get more cane strokes; she was talking quickly now, in the hope that this would stop Charles from adding another. "The gardener," she said. "I was rude to the gardener when he pruned the roses too harshly, and the maid when she got in the way, and... and... I can't think of anybody."

"Six."

"No, really," Elizabeth was crying loudly now. "There's nobody else."

"What about Matron? You were rude to her this morning as well."

"Oh yes, I'm so sorry Charles," Elizabeth said through the tears. "I had no idea I was such a terrible person."

Lifting her chin again Charles looked into her eyes. "You're a wonderful person Lizzi, you just need a little correction for your rudeness."

"Yes Sir," she said

"I'm going to spank you now and then you will get the slipper and six with the cane. When I've finished I expect you to go and apologise to Matron and the headmistress. On the way home I expect you to apologise to the chauffeur and tomorrow you have to apologise to the maid and the gardener. Okay?"

"Yes Sir."

"Then you will write me a letter explaining what you said to them all."

"Yes Sir."

"Now stand up and push your knickers down, I'll start by spanking the tops of your legs." Mrs Elizabeth Crawley was totally defeated and she lowered her satin knickers and let them drop to the floor. Charles started to spank the front of her legs. It was not a hard spanking but her legs were not used to being spanked so the smacks stung terribly. Charles liked this position and he had spanked his wife like this recently. In this position, he could watch Elizabeth's pussy through her trimmed hair. It was already glistening and if she was asked if she was enjoying being humiliated in this way she would have denied it, but her body was telling a different story.

Charles turned her around and started to spank the back of her legs from the seated position. To keep her in position, his left hand was on the front of her body over her pussy. Elizabeth shivered as she cried. "Take off that bra now Lizzi and get across my knee. Your proper spanking is about to start." Although Mrs Crawley was a thin lady she had larger boobs and they fell forward as she bent across Charles's lap. Holding her in position with his left hand, Charles used his right to spank each cheek in turn. Over and over again his hand came down on Elizabeth's sore bottom but she didn't try to get away, she just lay in position crying.

After a while Charles stopped spanking her and rested his hand on her bottom, massaging in the sting. Elizabeth liked this part of the spanking, he had done the same the last time he spanked her and it was the part she remembered most. It was probably the main reason why she decided to come to the school on impulse this morning.

"Slipper, next Lizzi," Charles said and she groaned. The groan was not so much in anticipation of the slipper, but rather in disappointment that the bottom rubbing had stopped. Charles picked up the slipper and landed the first spank on Elizabeth's bottom reminding her how much the slipper stings. Strangely, she also felt her pussy getting very wet. By the time Elizabeth had had ten spanks with the slipper, she was feeling erotically charged. This was the real reason why she was here and Charles instinctively reached for her nipple and squeezed it. The electricity of the pain on her nipple shot into her brain and then down to her pussy as she orgasmed loudly.

"Naughty Girl," Charles said but Elizabeth wasn't listening; she was still wallowing in the aftermath of the orgasm. Charles waited for a while with his hand on her bottom and then she stirred. "Up you get Lizzi, you have six with the cane to come."

"Oh no, I couldn't take it, Charles."

"You have had your pleasure. Now you must have your punishment for being such a rude girl. Get up and get over the desk."

Elizabeth knew that she could just run away, but she also knew that she would do as she was told. Stretching across the desk, she spread her legs to get more comfortable and her pussy came into view. It was red and swollen from the orgasm and Charles picked up the polaroid camera that was always available and took a picture of Elizabeth from behind. Sarah would enjoy that picture, he thought.

Mrs Crawley was stretched across the desk with her legs apart but she was still wearing her suspenders and silk stockings. Charles thought that this framed the target nicely. "You will count each stroke, Lizzi,"

"Yes Sir," she said and when the cane landed on her bottom she said. "Ouch, one."

"That one was for expecting me to see you without an appointment."

"Ow, Two."

"And that one for disrespecting my wife"

"Ouch, Three."

"That was for being rude to the gardener."

"Owie, Four.

"The maid."

"Ouch, Five."

" The chauffeur."

"Ow, Ow, Shit!"

"That was the hardest one for being rude to Amelia. She's doing a very good job of being the headmistress here and I expect you to apologise to her and give her a pay rise. She's underpaid for the work she does."

Elizabeth turned to look at Charles. "I can't do that, what would I say to the board?" Charles still had the cane in his hand so he gave her another hard stroke. "Oh Shit. Alright, I'll see what I can do."

Ten minutes later Mrs Crawley was standing next to the fireplace in Charles's study drinking a cup of tea and rubbing her bottom with her other hand. "Phew, Charles, that was a real stinger."

"I'm glad you enjoyed it," Charles said.

"I'm not sure I would say that I enjoyed it, not until that sting goes down anyway, but it was certainly an experience I'll remember. Thank you."

"Just remember what you promised. Go and find Amelia and Matron before you leave and have a word with the chauffeur as well."

"Yes, yes, all right," Elizabeth said testily.

"And if you talk to me like that again you'll be back over my knee."

"Yes, sorry, Sir. But I still have to sit in the back of a car for the next two and a half hours on the way home."

Charles laughed.

Mrs Elizabeth Crawley apologised to Amelia and Sarah before she went home and when she got to the car to have a word with the chauffeur she noticed that there was a large rubber ring to sit on in the back. "It's such a long journey," The chauffeur said. "I thought you might appreciate that ring to sit on Madam."

"Thank you, Smith," Mrs Crawley said. "You certainly do look after me, I should tell you more often how much I appreciate you."

"Yes, Madam, you should." The chauffeur thought. What he actually said was "Yes, Madam." Brian Smith, the chauffeur, had spent most of the day at the back of the school chatting to the kitchen staff and he had found out what was probably happening to his boss in the Old Man's study. There were very few things that the kitchen and cleaning staff didn't know about in the school, and they are usually very quiet about it all, but as the chauffeur was almost family they told him about the spankings and other things.

Chapter 11 - The wrong words to the school song

"Okay, settle down." Amelia was trying to get a little quiet at the school assembly but that was proving to be challenging, this time, however, Charles decided not to interfere. He had seen Amelia's disappointed face when he did that in the staff room and he didn't like to upset her.

"Quiet please everybody," she said again and eventually, it was quiet. "I've just a few announcements to make. Firstly I noticed that there is a tendency to change the words of the school song during assembly. I know the other words are funny but they must not be used at assembly. Any girl using those words will be punished, and in that regard, I would like to ask Katie Owen and Mary Becker to report to Mr Nicholas during the lunch break." She then turned to Charles. "If you have time Charles?" she said and he nodded. "I've asked Miss Pritchard to get the school choir to have extra practice sessions so that they, at least, get the song right.

Jasmine Pritchard is the sports mistress and she's an Olympic tennis player, so the tennis team in the summer outperforms all the other local schools. As Molly Dobson is away and she normally looks after the school choir, Jasmine volunteered to fill in for the term and it seems she's doing a fine job.

"Also Matron will be doing her medicals over the next two weeks. She has issued a rota to the teachers and I would be obliged if the girls could make sure that they are on time for their appointment. I'm assured that each medical will only take fifteen minutes, so it should be over quickly. Finally, I'm delighted to tell you that the Chairperson of the School Governors was here last week and she has written to me telling me how impressed she is with the school. She made a special mention about most of the staff and she was impressed with how polite the girls were. Well done everybody, I've asked Cook to prepare some cakes to be available at the morning break today to celebrate."

There was a cheer from the girls and some of the staff, but Clara Harrison looked disappointed and she stopped Amelia on the way out. "Excuse me, Mrs Brandon," she said. "I didn't know that we had a visit from the board, I just wondered why I wasn't informed?"

"Nobody was informed, Clara," Amelia said. "It was a surprise visit, but to be honest your name did come up in conversation. I'm a bit concerned with the noise that's coming out of your classroom sometimes, you really must get control of your girls or they will not learn anything. Have a word with Mr Nicholas and see how he does it."

"Oh I know how he does it, and I'll not be going there."

"Well, I suppose that you will only be here for the term so it won't matter all that much. Excuse me, I must have a word with Charles." Amelia walked away leaving Clara Harrison very concerned. She had hoped that she might get a permanent position in the school but that was looking less likely now.

"Charles," Amelia called to Charles as he was leaving the hall. "I just wanted to thank you."

"Oh yes, what for?"

"I mentioned that I had a letter from Elizabeth Crawley, but what I didn't tell the school was what she said about me. Apparently, she thinks I'm an excellent headmistress and she has asked the board to increase my salary from this month instead of waiting until the end of the year. Did you have anything to do with that?"

"Certainly not, I've said before she's a good judge of character."

Amelia was smiling. "I don't believe you, but thank you anyway," Amelia squeezed Charles's arm. "I'll find some way to make it up to you I promise."

Charles looked at her and saw the sparkle in her eye. "Naughty girl," he said.

"And what happens to naughty girls?" Amelia said but then a crowd of girls came up behind them so Charles couldn't answer the question.

"Oh Charles," Amelia said so that the girls could hear. I take the school song seriously, please cane Katie and Mary when you see them during the lunch break."

"Of course Headmistress," Charles replied, knowing that she wanted the girls to hear.

During the lunch break, Charles was in his study with Sarah as usual when Katie and Mary knocked at the door. "Oh Sorry Sir," Mary said. "If you're busy we can come back tomorrow, or next term, maybe?"

Charles laughed. Mary Becker was the first girl he spanked at the school for smoking in the bike sheds, and she had spent the Christmas holiday at the school so she probably thought she could get away with a comment like that, and she was probably right. Teachers are not meant to have favourites, and Charles would never admit it to anybody, but Mary, Nicole and Amy were his favourites this term.

"No, it's alright Mary, I've made time for you."

"Thank you Sir, but there is a rumour going around that we are to be caned for forgetting the school song and we were thinking that's a bit harsh."

"Well, that depends on how hard I use the cane on your bottoms doesn't it."

"I guess so Sir,"

"Let's find out, shall we?"

"But Sir, Matron's here as well."

"So?"

"Well, I was thinking that you might be easier on our poor bottoms if we were on our own," Mary said.

"Well Mary, you're going to get a slightly harder caning than Katie here because you're being cheeky. You will have to ask Katie what sort of caning you would have got."

"Oh," Mary said and then had the good sense to keep quiet.

"Right you two, knickers down and bend over the desk side by side, I'll be caning you together and Matron will be watching to make sure I'm not too soft on you." Mary and Katie had both been spanked often by Charles and Sarah so they knew the routine. Reaching under their school skirts they eased down their knickers and let them fall to their ankles. They both bent over the desk and flipped up their skirts as Charles retrieved the cane from the tall cupboard and swished it through the air. "Six each," Charles said and proceeded to cane them one at a time with practised efficiency. After twelve strokes, neither of the girls were crying but both knew that they had been caned. Standing up they were each rubbing their bottoms as Charles said. "There you go, not too bad was it?"

"No Sir," Katie said, but Mary was too busy rubbing.

"Pull up your knickers and get back to classes, and if either of you is caught singing the wrong words again, it will be a much harder caning, pass the word around for me."

"Yes Sir," Mary said. "I certainly will."

When the girls had left Charles said, "Did you get a picture?"

"Oh yes," Sarah showed Charles a lovely picture of the girl's bare bottoms each with five lines where the cane struck. "Nice parallel lines, well-done darling."

"And it's about time I put some parallel lines on your bottom as well."

"Yes Sir," Sarah said and giggled.

Jasmine had the last word as far as the school song was concerned. She was in the gym with the school choir practising the song as Charles walked past. He was thinking that the choir had never sung the harmonies of the school song so beautifully until he concentrated on the words. "Oh my God," Charles said when he heard, "In God, we trust" had become "Bob feels my bust." and "In church and steeple" became "and squeezed my nipple."

He walked into the Gym as the girls had just finished. "What the hell were you singing?" he said to nobody in particular.

"Oh Christ!" Jasmine said. "The choir had finished practising and they asked me if they could sing the wrong words just one more time, I said they could for the last time."

"Get rid of the choir and we will have a quiet word," Charles said.

"Yes Sir," Jasmine said. The whole choir knew that Jasmine was in trouble and as they walked away most of them said, "Sorry Miss."

"Let's go into the changing room where we can have a little privacy." Charles guided Jasmine into the changing room and then said. "I'm sorry Jasmine, but you know I'll have to cane you. I've just caned Mary Becker and Katie for singing those words and if you get away with it we will lose the motivation to get the song right."

"I know Charles," Jasmin said and she went to her locker at the back of the changing room and pulled out a cane. "Will this do?"

"I'm not going to ask why you have a cane in your locker, mostly because I don't think I would like the answer. Just push your knickers down and I'll give you six light strokes, so you can say you have been caned if they ask."

"I'm afraid that won't do, Charles," Jasmine said. "The senior girls will want to see my bottom and they will know if you didn't cane me properly. I probably deserve six hard ones anyway." Jasmine reached under her short sports skirt and pulled down her knickers. Bending over easily she placed the palms of her hands on the floor. "I'm ready," she said.

Jasmine's short skirt hid none of her bottom as she bent over but Charles flipped it up anyway. Standing back he swished the cane through the air and it landed on Jasmine's bottom. "Harder, please," Jasmine said. "I don't want the girls to think you have been soft on me." Jasmine was a sportswoman and she was used to pain, or rather ignoring the pain until the endorphins clicked in. Again Charles swished the thin cane on Jasmine's bottom. "Harder," she said.

Charles took a step back and made sure the swing of the cane came from his shoulders and to add to the stroke he flicked his wrist at the end. "God, Yes," Jasmine said. "That's it, now five more like that."

Charles put a lot of effort into the rest of the caning and when he inspected the damage he was grateful that he hadn't broken the skin on Jasmine's bottom. Jasmine stayed bent over as Charles stroked her bottom and she shuffled her legs apart just a little. "Thank you, Charles, that was a resounding caning, I wonder if you wouldn't mind helping me out a little." Saying that Jasmine pushed her legs wider apart and her anus and pussy came into view. As her pussy opened up Charles could see that she was very excited so he ran his fingers through the folds making a sloshing sound. Charles went to her clitoris and found the little pebble in the pond. Rubbing vigorously, Charles brought Jasmine close, and then slowed a little. "No please, I want an orgasm now."

"Naughty girls don't always get what they want," Charles said, but he went back to work on her pussy and she orgasmed loudly.

Ella and Rebecca were both in the choir and they were waiting outside the gym to apologise to Jasmine when they heard the noise of an obvious orgasm. Giggling they ran down the corridor before Charles came out.

Chapter 12 - Spanking in the Sanatorium

The medical check every term was usually performed by a few nurses and a doctor from the local town, but it was expensive and a little demeaning to have all the girls lined up in a row in their underwear to have their temperature checked and their blood pressure taken. Sarah Nicholas also made the point that it wasn't very effective so the whole process was cancelled in favour of a much more personal approach. She calculated that it would take about fifteen minutes for each girl to be checked by her in the Sanatorium, and she could have it done in a few weeks. Matron also suggested that this would help with infection prevention, any undiagnosed eating disorders and, as happened last year, pregnancy. Amelia agreed, partially because it was good for the budget.

So the rota was set up and the girls started filing into the San for their checkups. The system worked well for the younger girls and Sarah was getting through them faster than she expected. One or two minor issues were uncovered and dealt with straight away. One day-girl seemed to have chickenpox but she was sent home and told not to come back until her doctor said it was completely cured. The problem started to occur when it was the turn of the older girls to have their medical checks. There was often a plausible excuse for being late or not arriving at all, but it was making Sarah's life difficult.

Ella Hall was one of the girls who didn't turn up for her medical and Sarah had to send word for her to come immediately. She arrived thirty minutes later and Sarah was furious. "Where have you been Ella?" Sarah said.

"I'm sorry Matron but we were watching a very interesting programme on TV and I didn't want to miss it," Ella said.

"So, you missed your medical check because you were watching TV?"

"Well, yes Matron," Ella said. "But it was an educational programme and the whole class watched it with the teacher."

"And you knew I was waiting here for you while you were watching TV."

"Yes, Matron."

"Well, I'm sure Mr Nicholas will have something to say about that, I hear he's using the cane a lot more at the moment."

"Yes I know Matron," Ella said. "Jasmine, I mean Miss Pritchard, was given the cane for allowing the choir to sing the other words to the school song. She showed Rebecca and me the marks, they were vicious."

"Well, I'm sure he will give you the same punishment for keeping me waiting if I ask him."

"Oh please Matron, I don't want the cane from Mr Nicholas, can't you punish me?"

"It will either be my wooden spoon or his cane. You choose."

"Can I have the wooden spoon from you then Matron," Ella said.

"Okay, but let's have the medical first. Strip off and stand on the scales, I'll check your weight and height."

Ella got down to her bra and knickers and looked up at Sarah. "Everything?" she asked.

"Yes everything Ella," Sarah said but she was delighted that Ella had chosen the wooden spoon, she had a trick with that spoon that Ella had had before. Ella Hall was a tall girl with the biggest boobs in the upper sixth. She was embarrassed by her size although Sarah had told her that the boys will love them when she gets older.

Sarah made a note about her weight and height and then said, "Now get on the examination table on your back."

"Yes Matron." Naked now Ella clambered onto the examination table and lay back feeling her large boobs falling on either side of her body.

Matron was well practised in taking her blood pressure and listening to her lungs and heart. She checked Ella's head and neck, then her tonsils. At each stage, she would make notes on the form she had designed. "Roll over and get on your knees. I want to take your temperature."

"In my bottom Matron?" Ella was uncertain.

"Of course in your bottom Ella, it's much more accurate that way. Just pull your cheeks apart from me."

Ella reached behind her and pulled her bottom cheeks apart displaying her most private of places. Putting a little vaseline on her finger Sarah rubbed Ella's anus around the rim and then pushed her finger inside. Pulling it out again she put vaseline on the thermometer and pushed it deep into Ella's rectum. "That's uncomfortable, Matron," Ella said.

"Just relax and let the feeling spread. Maybe you'll learn to like this in time."

"I don't think so Matron," Ella said but even as she was saying that, she decided that the feeling was not so bad after all.

Sarah pulled out the thermometer and declared that her temperature was normal. "Roll over again and bring your knees up for me Ella," Sarah said. "That's it, a little wider. I'm just going to check your vulva."

"My what Matron?"

"Your vulva," Sarah said. "The vulva is the part of your genitals on the outside of your body. your labia, clitoris, vaginal opening, and the opening to the urethra (the hole you pee out of). While vaginas are just one part of the vulva, many people say "vagina" when they really mean the vulva."

"Oh, I didn't know." Ella said, "I just call it my pussy."

"Well, that's the slang of course, but that's okay. I'm just going to check your pussy."

"Okay, Matron."

Sarah was not surprised that Ella was wet. Most of the girls found the medical erotic in one way or another. Ella's clitoris was also just poking out and Sarah rubbed it. "Ooh Matron, That's nice," Ella said. "Can you do that again?"

Sarah continued playing with Ella's clit but stopped just before Ella had an orgasm. Ella groaned. "Punishment first Ella, then we will see. Back over on the table and up on your knees, you're about to get my favourite wooden spoon for being late."

"Yes Matron," Ella said, disappointed that she didn't have an orgasm even though she got very close. Kneeling on the examination table, Ella felt her boobs falling free until Matron told her to put her head down and her bottom up in the air. "Knees apart Ella," Sarah said, and Ella did as instructed.

Sarah couldn't resist running her hands over Ella's large bottom and especially between her cheeks. She knew Ella would not complain because she was close to an orgasm. Then Sarah picked up the wooden spoon and placed a hard spank on each cheek. The wooden spoon was well known in the school. Sarah brought it with her from South Africa when she came to the school last year and it was longer than most wooden spoons you would find in England, with a larger spoon face. The first two spanks with the wooden spoon were Sarah's favourite. They left two circular rings on the receiver's bottom. After a while, those rings would have mixed into the general redness of the bottom but the first two spanks were always memorable.

After ten spanks on each cheek, Ella was crying and so Sarah stopped spanking and rubbed her bottom. "Just six more between your cheeks Ella," Sarah said.

Ella had experienced being spanked between her cheeks by Matron and she didn't want to repeat that. "Oh please Matron, not on my butt hole?"

"Just six for being naughty Ella, and then we will see if I can finish what I started earlier."

"Yes Matron," Ella said as she reached behind her and pulled her cheeks wide apart. Sarah turned the wooden spoon around so that she was now holding the face end and she had the long handle aimed at Ella's anus. With a quick flick, the handle of the wooden spoon landed on Ella's anus and she screamed. "That hurts Matron," Ella said through the sobbing cries.

Sarah smiled as she gave Ella five more spanks on exactly the same place and she was impressed to see that Ella didn't let her cheeks go. "Good Girl," Sarah said as she rubbed Ella's bottom. "I have a little cream for that anus of yours, would you like me to put some on?"

"Oh yes please Matron, I'm so sore." Sarah rummaged around in her drawer and pulled out a tube of cream. Applying some to Ella's bottom and anus, Ella started to feel much better. The spanking had hurt but it was almost worth it for what Matron was doing at the moment. Ella pushed back and Sarah's fingers slipped forward towards her clitoris. Sarah knew what she was doing and very soon Ella was close to orgasm again. Sarah continued rubbing and Ella exploded loudly. Luckily the Sanatorium was away from the main areas of the school and it was almost soundproof. Sarah played loud pop music for the girls, or that's what they thought, actually, it was to cover the sound of the spanking Sarah enjoyed in the San and sometimes it was to drown the sound of loud orgasms, like today. Ella remained on her knees with her bottom in the air while she calmed down and Sarah pulled out her polaroid camera and took another photograph for her collection. She would be sharing that with Nicholas this evening in bed.

Ella was sent back to her classroom when she was dressed and the word soon spread that anybody who was late for their medical exam would get the dreaded wooden spoon between their cheeks. Everybody arrived on time after that.

Charles had dinner in the dining hall that evening as Sarah was still busy sorting out the paperwork for all the medical exams she had completed. Clara Harrison came and sat next to him. "Can I have a word, Charles?"

"Of course Clara, what can I do for you?"

"I'm worried about what the governors may be saying about my work here at the school," Clara said.

"Really Clara? Why is that?"

"Well, you know that Elizabeth Crawley visited this week and Amelia said that the governors were concerned about the way I control the girls. She thinks the girls don't respect me. She also said I should talk to you."

"Well, you know what I'm going to say don't you?"

"Oh yes, you're going to tell me that I must spank the girls to get respect but there must be another way," Clara said.

"I'm sure there is Clara, but spanking a bare bottom is much more fun," Charles said laughing.

"You mean you enjoy spanking the girls?"

"Oh yes, I love it," Charles said. "And do you know what?"

"What?" Clara thought she was going to hear a new pearl of wisdom.

"Some of the girls love it too."

"Don't be ridiculous Charles. Nobody enjoys being spanked."

"If you say so Clara," Charles said. "Now, if you don't mind, I'm going to get on with my dinner."

Chapter 13 - Amy is caned

Amy Wilson was very nervous when she knocked at the housemaster's study door at four o'clock in the afternoon on Friday. She was caught spying on Mr Nicholas when he spanked the headmistress three weeks ago but this part of her punishment had been delayed, and she hated that. For three weeks she had dreaded being caned, but she knew she deserved it, and Mr Nicholas had been very good about the other parts of her punishment for that mistake. She had thought for a long time if it had been a mistake. She had overheard Mr Nicholas and Matron talking about the headmistress's visit that evening and she wondered what it was all about. Sneaking downstairs after lights-out in her nightie she couldn't really hear anything so she looked through the keyhole of the old-fashioned oak door and was amazed to see Amelia Brandon over Mr Nicholas's lap, getting her bare bottom spanked. Then she got the leather slipper and finally, Amy saw what she thought was the headmistress having an orgasm as she was bent over, with Mr Nicholas's fingers between her legs.

Amy was shocked, to say the least, and she hid when Miss Brandon left the study ten minutes later. She realised her mistake, however. She should have just run back upstairs to her own dormitory and slipped under the covers, but she waited to see what else would happen. Thinking about it now, however, she had been given the opportunity to have a few private meetings with Mr Nicholas to discuss what she was reading in her encyclopaedia and an additional meeting with Matron to talk about the things about her body that she was not sure of. This was meant to be part of her punishment but it was not a punishment at all. The next thing, however, was.

"Come in," Charles Nicholas called after he heard the knock and Amy entered. The housemaster's study was a big room decorated with Victorian furniture. There was a large oak desk in the bay window with a leather swivel chair and two matching guest chairs. The room doubled as the study during the day and also the lounge for Charles and Sarah during the evening, so it had a chesterfield settee and two matching chairs as well as various antique cupboards and occasional tables. The room also had a large open fireplace that had a coal fire burning in the winter and the settee facing it. The fire was lit at lunchtime and Mr Nicholas let it die down in the evening when they went to bed. The maid came in during the morning and set the fire for Charles to light when he had his lunch. The only thing that seemed a little out of place in the room was two armless dining chairs up against the wall on the far side. The chairs were there for one purpose, to sit on when spanking naughty girls.

"Ah, there you are Amy, on time as usual." Charles was sitting at his desk and Amy knew to come and stand beside him. Slipping his hand under her school skirt Charles cupped Amy's small bottom and patted it gently. "You're shivering Amy, are you okay?" Charles knew what the problem was. This was Amy's third appointment. The first was cancelled because Charles had to rush off to a meeting with the board of governors to present the proposal that there should be a new heating system in the school, and the second was because Amy had worked herself up so much she was ill and Matron decided she was too sick to be punished and it would have to be delayed.

There were tears in Amy's eyes as she said, "I'm scared, Sir."

"I know Amy, but you have to be punished. I'll spank you first to warm your bottom and then you will be caned. It was very naughty of you to spy on me and the headmistress and you could have been expelled you know. You're lucky that I've kept it between you and me."

"I know Sir," Amy said. "And I'm very grateful, but can we get it over with now, please?"

"Yes of course." Charles patted her bottom a couple of times and then stood up. Walking over to the far wall he picked up one of the dining chairs and positioned it in the centre of the room. "Spanking first Amy," Charles said and Amy stood next to him and bent over his lap. Flipping up her school skirt he pulled Amy's knickers down over her small bottom and started to spank her straight away. It wasn't a long spanking nor was it a hard spanking but Amy was crying when he had finished. Charles thought that was because of the anticipation of the caning to come.

"Stand up Amy," Charles said. "You had better take off that skirt, we don't want it to get in the way do we?"

Amy thought that she didn't mind at all if it got in the way but she did as she was told and soon she was naked from the waist down. Amy was the smallest girl in her class and at just five feet tall she had a small bottom as well. She had been caned once before but this time she was going to get twelve strokes and she didn't think she could take that. She had no choice, of course, so she started to bend over and touch her toes.

"No Amy, I want you to bend over the back of the settee for your caning, it will support you."

"Yes Sir," Amy said and she thought that it would be easier to stay in position if she was bent over the settee. "Thank you Sir."

Amy had to stand on her tiptoes to position her body over the back of the settee and as soon as she reached for the cushions on the far side her feet came off the floor. "Oh," she exclaimed, but she couldn't do anything about the position so she just let her feet hang.

Charles was delighted with the position she was in and he picked up the polaroid camera to record the view to show Sarah. Amy heard the click buzz of the camera and knew that her bottom had just been photographed, but that didn't bother her so much at the moment. Next, she heard the swish of the cane through the air and a second later heard the crack and then felt the sting as it landed on her bare bottom. She screamed with pain as the cane felt like it cut into her skin. It did nothing of the sort, of course. Charles was not caning her as hard as he had caned Jasmine the previous week, but Amy was not as tough as the sports mistress. The second stroke also had Amy screaming and had it not been for her position making standing impossible, she would have stood up and rubbed her bottom by now. After six strokes of the cane, Charles relented and started to rub her bottom gently feeling the ridges where he had caned her. "You have been a brave girl Amy," Charles said. "And if you like we can leave the other six strokes until next Friday."

"Oh no please Sir," Amy said through the tears. "I want to finish the punishment today, I don't want another week of waiting to be caned."

"You're a very brave girl Amy," Charles said as he started the caning again. The last six strokes were not as hard as the first six but Amy was sobbing when Charles had finished. Picking Amy's small body up he sat on one of the armchairs and held her on his knee until she stopped crying. "I've asked Matron to come in and put some cream on your bottom for you, she will be here any minute now and then I'll leave you with her. Your punishment is all over now, and I hope you have learnt your lesson about spying on other people.

"Oh yes Sir," Amy said, "I certainly have."

Chapter 14 - Clara agrees to be spanked.

Clara Harrison walked into the staffroom at four in the afternoon and slumped into one of the comfortable armchairs. The chair had seen better days and there was stuffing coming out of the arm but it was Molly Dobson's favourite chair and Clara had taken it over while Molly was away.

There was nobody in the staff room so Clara let off a little steam. "Fuck, fuck, fuck." she said.

"That's not like you, Clara," Charles said standing up from the chair he was sitting in on the far side of the room.

"Oh God," Clara said. "Sorry. I didn't think there was anybody in the room."

"No matter Clara. Can I help with anything?"

"It's the upper-sixth," Clara explained as Charles sat on the chair next to her. "They've been very well behaved for a week or two. I don't know what you said to Nicole but she has been wonderful, keeping the room in order, but she has been away for a week and they are up to their old tricks. I don't know, maybe you're right, maybe I should spank them." Charles smiled as he nodded. "But the fact is Charles, I don't know how."

"Well, I can help there. Next time you catch anybody being naughty, call me and then I'll spank them in front of you so you can see how you do it."

"I don't think that will work Charles. The word will get out that I'm not in control unless you're there."

"Well, the alternative is that I spank you just like I would the girls. You should probably know what it feels like before you do it anyway.

"What?" Clara was shocked. "I'm a grown woman."

Charles was laughing, "I'm sorry Clara, but that doesn't make any difference, I've spanked almost all the teachers here for their birthday and some of them more than once."

"Yes, I heard that Jasmine got the cane for letting the choir sing the wrong words to the school song," Clara said and she was smiling now.

Charles was smiling as well. "I had to, I had just caned two of the upper-sixth for doing the same thing."

"I heard she was showing off the cane strokes to anybody who would look in the staff room, she was proud of them," Clara said.

"It's a funny thing about being spanked, it hurts at the time but afterwards..." Charles didn't finish the sentence leaving Clara to think about his offer.

The room was silent for a few minutes as Clara was thinking and Charles went back to reading the newspaper. Eventually, Clara said, "Okay."

Charles looked up. "Okay, what?"

"Okay, I'll let you spank me, as long as I can keep my slacks on."

"Sorry, spankings are always on the bare bottom," Charles said and went back to his newspaper.

"But what about Sarah?" Clara said. "Doesn't she mind you spanking a grown woman on the bare bottom?"

"She doesn't mind, but if she did she would get a spanking on her bare bottom as well."

"Matron gets spanked as well?" Clara was shocked.

"At least once a week," Charles said. "And she likes it."

"Well I can assure you that I'll not like it, but if I have to have a spanking on my bare bottom you will have to turn away as I take down my knickers."

"I don't think you understand at all Clara," Charles said. "Once you have asked me to spank your bare bottom, and you have to ask, by the way, you will have no control over the proceedings at all. I'll be telling you what to do and you have to do it or you will get the cane as well."

Clare was beginning to tear up a little. "But I've never let a man control me like that."

"Up to you," Charles said as he lifted the paper up and pretended to read. Behind the newspaper, he was smiling to himself as he realised he was about to win the ten-pound bet he had with Amelia. "You'll never get that one over your knee," Amelia said, but it seems she may be wrong."

"Okay, I'll do it," Clara said.

Charles put the newspaper down. "If you're saying what I think you're saying you have to ask me nicely and be very clear about what will happen, I don't want any misunderstandings."

"Yes, of course," Clara said. "I want you to spank me on my bare bottom so that I can do the same to the girls in the upper-sixth when they're naughty."

"Would you like Matron in the room as a witness?

"God No!" Clara said. "I hope she never finds out."

"I've no secrets from Sarah, Clara. You should know that."

"Yes of course. Sorry. When should we do this?" Clara asked.

"Strike while the iron's hot, I always say. Or in your case, it will be; strike, and the bottom will get hot." Charles laughed at his own joke but Clara was not amused.

"Not here I hope," Clara said.

"No, we can go to my study, it's always quiet there in the afternoons."

Clara Harrison was a tall lady with short black hair and big boobs that seemed to be permanently hidden as she folded her arms all the time. She followed Charles into his study and he put the spanking chair in the centre of the room. "You don't think you're going to put me over your knee do you?" Clare said and Charles just walked towards her, put one hand on her shoulder, turned her around and spanked the tops of her legs through her thin slacks. Clare was caught off guard and didn't know what to do. "Stop, stop, you're hurting me."

"We need to get one thing straight, Clara. You have asked to be spanked like the girls and that's exactly what I'm going to do. You're here because you have asked to be here, if you don't want to be here, the door is not locked, but while you're here you will do exactly what you're told, okay?"

Clara did not look happy. "Yes," she said.

"Yes What?" Charles asked.

"Yes Sir,"

Charles sat on the chair in the centre of the room. "Come here Clara and face me," he said and she did as she was told. Charles put his hands on her hips and pulled her forward so that their knees were touching. Then he reached out and undid the button on her slacks. Clara grabbed his hands but Charles just looked up at her and she let go. He continued to loosen the top of her slacks and pull down the zip as Clara shuddered.

"Relax Clara, I'm not going to rape you," Charles said

"But nobody has ever done that before, I'm scared." Clara now sounded like a little girl.

Clara's slacks fell to the floor and Charles changed his mind and decided not to pull her knickers down yet, he would wait until she was over his knee. Turning her to his right-hand side he said "Over you go now," and he helped her over his lap. Charles was surprised to find that Clara's large bottom was covered in the most delightful pink lace knickers. They were almost see-through and he said. "These are lovely Clara, do you have a hot date tonight?"

"No, I have not," Clara said. "I wear nice underwear because I like it, now get on with the spanking, please."

Charles spanked the tops of each leg.

"Shit Charles, I thought you were going to spank my bottom."

"I haven't started to spank your bottom yet, that was for still thinking you're in control of this."

"Sorry Sir," she said again.

Taking the elastic at the top of Clara's knickers he eased them over her bottom and said. "Lift up for me please, I don't want to rip these nice knickers."

"No, you had better not," Clara said and she got another four spanks on the top of her legs.

"Okay, okay, I get it," she said as she raised herself up and Charles lowered her knickers and they fell to her ankles. "Please take them right off Charles, I don't want to rip them when I'm kicking."

"You had better not kick me, Clara," Charles said as he reached down and took her knickers right off, then as an afterthought, he slipped her flat shoes off as well.

Resting his hand on Clara's large bottom he said. "I never spank a girl quickly. Part of the punishment is the humiliation of being over my lap with my hand on her bare bottom waiting to be spanked."

"No kidding," Clara said but then she thought that it wasn't so bad. No man had touched her bottom for a very long time and she quite liked it. Then the spanking started.

"I usually start the spanking slowly and then build up the speed," Charles said.

"But you're already hurting me, Charles," Clara said.

"Well you see, that's the point," Charles said, speeding up the spanks. "Spanking is meant to be a punishment. It's meant to encourage the miscreant not to be naughty in the future."

"No Charles, this is hurting too much, you must stop now. I can't take any more."

"You'll be surprised how much you can take Clara and I'll finish the spanking when I think you're truly sorry."

"Sorry?" Clara was desperate. "Sorry for what."

"Sorry for being a pain in the arse all term. Sorry for not coming to the staff room and getting to know everybody. Sorry for the things you said about me to the governors." Charles was spanking Clara much harder now and she was crying.

"Okay," she said. "I'm sorry."

"Not good enough," Charles said and continued to spank her large bare bottom. "You have to mean it."

"I hate you Charles Nicholas, and I'll never be sorry. You wait until I report you to the governor again. You'll lose your job."

Charles stopped spanking Clara and held her in place. Putting his hand in his pocket he pulled out a portable cassette player and pressed rewind. "I had this to show my class today and I put it on record when we started to talk about spanking. Would you like me to play it"

Clara knew she was defeated. "No Charles, that will not be necessary."

Charles put his hand on Clara's bottom and the strangest thing happened. Clara liked to have his hand there. The endorphins had kicked in and the sore bottom was not so sore any longer, just tingling, and it was a pleasant tingle that seemed to go right through her body to her... She didn't want to think where the tingle was going but she wanted the spanking to start again. "I'm sorry Charles, I shouldn't have said that. Please spank me for being so naughty."

"Certainly," Charles said with a smile. He continued to spank Clara, but he knew he didn't need to spank her hard any longer. She was accepting the spanking and that was enough for now. Right Clara," he said. "Things are going to change now. I'll help you with the discipline of the Upper-Sixth but you have to come into the staff room regularly, chat to all the other staff members and watch the birthday spankings." Clara didn't reply so Charles stepped up the spanking again.

"Yes, alright," Clara said. "I'll be in the staff room with the others and I'll watch the birthday spankings."

"Good girl," Charles said as he rested his hand on her bottom. "And when your birthday comes around I'll be spanking you in front of the others."

"NO!" Clara said and Charles started spanking her again.

"Okay, I'll accept my birthday spanking." Clara was sobbing loudly now and Charles held her over his lap with his hand resting on her bottom.

Eventually, she stopped crying and he helped her up. "There you go Clara, that's a proper spanking." Clara was rubbing her bottom and didn't seem to mind that she was showing Charles the curly black hair between her legs.

"Thank you, Charles," Clara said as she retrieved her knickers and slacks. Finally turning her back on him she replaced her clothing and then sat down on one of the guest chairs and jumped up straight away. "Shit," she said laughing and Charles joined in.

"You were properly spanked today, and I would guess that's the first time you have been spanked for many years," Charles said.

"I've never been spanked before," Clara said as she sat down again gently. "But I can understand why people might like it, so is it a proper punishment?"

"Try it and see."

"Yes, I will," Clara said as she stood up. "Thank you, Charles, I know I've been a pain in the arse, and I've got a pain in the arse to prove it. I'll do better for the rest of the term, I promise."

"And if you don't, we will have a repeat performance in my study," Charles said.

"Yes Sir," Clara said as she left the room.

Chapter 15 - Upper-sixth caning

Charles was in the staff room early a few weeks later and he met Clara Harrison there. "Morning Clara, you're looking nice this morning, meeting your boyfriend?"

Clara laughed, "Thank you, Charles. Would be nice, but alas I'm on a history field trip with Amy and Nicole. Should be fun though, I'm sure you know the history of Norwich but we are going to look at the Norman castle and what's left of the city wall.

"Ah, 1066 and all that," Charles said with a smile.

'Well, 1067 but you're close enough. We actually have a Norman church in the local village and we will be exploring that this afternoon." Clara was obviously excited to be going.

"I helped Daisy on a field trip last term but we camped in fields. Yours sounds like more fun." Charles said.

"Yes, I'm not sure I would want a field trip that included fields, not my thing. But you're welcome to join us if you like." Clara said.

"No thank you, Clara, too much to do today and you will do fine with just Nicole and Amy to look after."

Clara looked at her watch. "Got to rush, bye Charles,"

Clara was gone before Charles could say goodbye and then Amelia sidled up beside him. "Clara is a changed woman Charles, did you...?

"A gentleman never tells," Charles said.

"Oh my God," Amelia said. "You did, didn't you? You spanked her. Well, whatever you did she is much improved. You know she has come up with the three strikes rule?"

"What do you mean three strikes?' Charles asked.

"She gives the girls two chances before they get caned; if they get to three, they get the cane. It's quite clever really. And I guess I have to thank you for that."

"Anything to help the running of the school Amelia, you know that."

Later that morning Charles was walking past the Upper-sixth classroom and he heard the girls singing the school song, but to the alternative words. Charles looked through the glass door and he could see that there were four of them singing, so he burst into the classroom. "What the hell do you think you're doing? I've caned two girls for singing that,"

"And a teacher?" Ella said and instantly regretted it.

"That's none of your business, Ella," Charles said. "I don't have the time now, but you will all report back here at five and you will all be caned."

"Yes Sir," They said and Charles left to go to his class.

At ten to five that afternoon Clara came back from the history field trip and found Charles in the staff room. "Hello Clara, had a good day?" he said.

"It was a wonderful day, thank you." Clara was excited and keen to tell Charles all about it.

Charles stood up. "I'm pleased to hear it, but I have to go and cane the upper sixth."

"Oh really? What have they been up to?" Clara thought that this day was getting better. Since she was spanked by Mr Nicholas three weeks ago, she had been looking forward to caning someone but hadn't had the chance. She had developed the 'three strikes and you're out' rule for the girls. Naughty once and you get a simple spanking, twice and it will be the slipper and three times and it will be the cane. "Can I help?"

"Yes, thank you, Clara, that's kind of you," Charles said, but he wondered what Clara had in mind as he picked up a thin cane from the cupboard in the staff room.

Walking to the upper-sixth classroom where the girls were meant to be caned, Clara said. "Thank you for letting me take part in this. I've spanked a couple of girls since that experience with you, but I've never caned one, or even seen one being caned. I need to watch so that I can if I need to."

"Yes," Charles said. "Especially if any of the girls get to three, you will have to follow through with your promise." Walking into the classroom they found four girls sitting patiently waiting for five o'clock. The girls stood up and said in unison. "Good evening Mr Nicholas, Good evening Mrs Harrison."

"Sit down Girls," Charles said. "Would anybody like to tell me why we are all here?" Ella put her hand up. "Stand up Ella, and tell us why we are here."

"The four of us were singing the wrong words to the school song, and we know we are not allowed to. You're here to cane us Mr Nicholas, but I've no idea why Mrs Harrison is here." All the girls laughed.

"That will get you two extra strokes Ella," Charles said, then turning to Mrs Harrison he said. "Clara, perhaps you would like to tell the girls of the upper sixth why you're here."

"Yes of course," Clara said. "As you all know, I'm new to this school and the way punishments work. Mr Nicholas has been kind enough to help me and I've spanked a couple of you. I'm here this afternoon because Mr Nicholas is going to expand my knowledge on the subject by showing me how to cane naughty girls."

"Did Mr Nicholas spank you, Mrs Harrison?" Rebecca said.

"Rebecca!" Charles said.

"It's alright Charles," Clara said. "What happens between staff members in this school is not discussed with the girls, that would not be right. But I can tell you that my birthday is coming up next month, the same day as yours Ella I think. Not the same year of course."

All the girls laughed and Clara continued, "And that remark has also got you two extra strokes, Rebecca." Clara looked at Charles and he smiled and nodded.

Charles was organising again. "I think we will start with you, Rebecca. Come to the front of the class."

"Yes Sir," Rebeca said. She wasn't going to tempt providence and be cheeky again. Eight strokes of the cane were enough.

"Knickers down, skirt up Rebbeca," Charles said and she did as she was told and she stood showing off her pussy. Rebecca was a skinny girl but an athlete so she was tough. Charles had caned her before and she could easily take a caning without crying. "Bend over Rebecca," Charles said and she put her hands flat on the floor without bending her legs. You get six plus the two extra for being cheeky, I want you to count them."

"Yes Mr Nicholas,' Rebecca said and then instantly had to call out, "One," as the cane landed centrally on her bottom. "Two," she called and then, "Three." The cane strokes were coming very fast and she missed five and had to say "Five, Six." at the same time.

Rebecca stood up and rubbed her bottom. "Don't forget you have two more to go Rebecca."

"Oh yes, Sorry Sir," Rebecca said and bent back down again.

Charles turned to Clara. Would you like to do the last two for Rebecca, she was cheeky to you."

"Thank you, Charles," Clara said as she took the cane and swung it through the air a few times. Standing to the left of Rebecca she took aim at her bottom and swung, but the stroke overreached and was ineffective.

"That one wasn't very good was it," Charles said to Clara, "we won't count that one will we Rebecca?"

"Oh no Sir," Rebecca said. "Definitely not."

"Try again Clara," Charles said. "But just aim at the left cheek because when the cane swings you instinctively stretch a little."

"Yes, okay," Clara said and she stood back and aimed at Rebecca's left cheek. The cane made a "Swish, Crack," noise and Rebecca called out "Seven,"

"Oh well done Clara, Charles said. "Much better. That was much better Rebecca, wasn't it?"

"Oh yes Sir. Much better."

"One more Clara, and I always like to aim the last stroke just below her cheeks, we call that the sit spot," Charles said.

"Oh yes, right," Clara said. "I remember." Clara aimed and brought the cane down just under Rebecca's bottom cheeks.

"Oh well done Clara," Charles said. "Perfectly done. That was perfect Rebecca. Wasn't it?"

"Oh yes, Sir," Rebecca said as she stood up and started rubbing her bottom again with tears in her eyes. "Perfect."

"Go and stand against the wall Rebecca and keep your knickers down and your skirt up," Charles said.

Leah and Jade were caned by Mr Nicholas in the same way and now there were three girls with stripes on their bottoms facing the wall. Then it was Ella's turn. "Your turn I think Clara," Charles said and handed the cane to his colleague.

"Thank you, Charles. Come along Ella, you know where you should be," Clara said, swishing the cane through the air. Ella walked to the front of the class slowly. "Don't dawdle, Ella, otherwise you will get a spanking as well."

"Standing with her knickers around her ankles and her skirt up around her waist Ella said, "Can't Mr Nicholas cane me instead." Clara didn't bother dignifying the question with an answer; she simply wrapped her left arm around Ella's body and bent her slightly. Then started to spank the tops of her legs hard and fast. "Please Miss, that hurts," Ella said. "Okay, I'm sorry, I'll take the caning from you, Miss."

Clara stopped spanking and said. "Good decision Ella, get into position." Ella had to rub her legs quickly and then bent over flicking up her skirt and failing to touch her toes. Unlike Rebecca, Ella was not sporty so she found it very difficult to reach her toes. "Just spread your legs and bend your knees Ella if you have to."

"Thank you, Miss," Ella said.

Charles was impressed with the way Clara was now handling the naughty girls. No need to worry about discipline in the classroom any longer, he thought. He was standing behind Ella and as she reached for her toes with her legs spread and knees bent Charles got a very good view of the parts of her body that she usually kept hidden. As the first cane stroke landed on Ella's bottom she called out the number but Charles could see her little anus pucker. He had never watched that happen before, having always been the one holding the cane, but he thought it was something he might explore again in the future.

When Ella got to six, she stood up but Clara was not fooled. "I'm sure you remember that the number is eight, Ella."

"Oh Mrs Harrison," Ella said as she was rubbing her sore bottom. "I've had enough."

"Nine," Clara said simply. Ella was quick to get back into position and Clara gave her three more, two of them just under her bottom where she had been spanked just a few minutes earlier. When she stood up again she was crying profusely and sent to stand beside the other girls. "That's a pretty picture," Clara said and Charles agreed.

"Just hang on here Clara, I'll be back in a minute," Charles said. "And you girls stay in position. No rubbing."

Charles hurried to the staffroom and got the Polaroid camera from his locker. Getting back into the classroom he said to Clara, "I

like to keep a record of the girls I've punished." Then the girls heard
the click/buzz of the camera as it took an instant picture. He pressed
the button again so that he had a second picture.

"Right Girls, stand like that for another ten minutes and then
you can go and study," Charles said.

Chapter 16 - Caning Mrs Harrison

Walking back to the staff room, Clara said. "That's clever Charles, I'll have to get myself one of those cameras."

"Until you do, mine is in my locker in the staffroom, help yourself. In the meantime, I took an extra pic for you." Charles said as he handed the colour photo of four girls with striped bottoms to Clara.

"Thank you, Charles," Clara said, then looked at the picture with a great deal of interest. Does caning the girls make you... You know?"

"Horny?" Charles said.

"I wasn't going to say it, but yes."

"Every time."

"Me too, does that make us bad teachers?" Clara said.

"Not at all. I've never punished a girl unless she deserved it," Charles lied.

Clara was silent for a while and then she said. "What does it feel like to be caned?"

"Only one way to find out, Clara."

"Oh no, I couldn't," Clara said.

"Okay," Charles said as they went back into the staffroom and Charles put the camera away.

It was the next day when Clara came up to Charles in the staffroom and said. "Okay."

"Okay, what?" Charles said, but he knew.

"I want you to cane me. If I'm going to cane the girls I need to know what it feels like."

Charles nodded although he thought that was nonsense. He had never been caned in his life but that doesn't stop him from caning the girls and the staff as well sometimes. "If I cane a member of the staff she would have to be naked," Charles said. He knew he was pushing his luck, but he thought it was worth a try.

"That will never happen, never mind," Clara said and she left the staff room.

"What was all that about?" Amelia said.

"Clara has yet to work out who's in charge, Amelia," Charles said smiling.

"I thought I was in charge, Charles," Amelia said.

"Not in charge of discipline Amelia, that's me."

They both laughed. Amelia had been the headmistress of the school for a few years but it was only when Charles joined at the beginning of the last term that school discipline improved. Now she was getting compliments from the governors as well so she was very happy.

"Yes Sir," Amelia said.

"Which reminds me, you're probably due a maintenance spanking soon Amelia." Charles said but Amelia looked at her watch and clapped her hands, "Classes start in five minutes, everybody," she said and there was a rumble of feet as they started to leave.

Just before Charles left the staffroom Clara came back in. "Okay, but you mustn't watch."

"I can assure you Clara that I'll be watching every move you make with a great deal of interest."

Clara was close to tears, "But nobody has seen me naked for many years."

"Then it's high time that they did Clara. Four o'clock this afternoon, my study." Charles said and he left to go to his class.

Clara was close to tears but she pulled herself together and went to her classroom. When she walked in the girls were all sitting quietly then they stood up. "Good morning Mrs Harrison," they said.

"It works," she thought to herself.

At lunch, Clara decided that she was so nervous that she couldn't eat anything so she went to her room and showered, putting on her best underwear, black slacks, grey jacket and white blouse. "Might as well look my best," Clara said to herself. "But is my best good enough?"

At five to four she was standing outside the study door at Christie House. She was about to knock when the door opened and Sarah came out. "Are you looking for Charles?' she said.

"Hello Matron, Yes, I'm to meet him here at four o'clock."

"That's funny," Sarah said, laughing. "That's the time he usually gets the girls to present themselves for a spanking. Are you here for a spanking Clara?"

"Of course not," Clara said indignantly.

"Only kidding," Sarah said. "Just make yourself comfortable, I'm sure he will be along in a minute. I have to get back, I'm still doing the medicals and they take forever."

"Yes, of course," Clara said. "Thank you."

Charles was right on time and he found Clara sitting in his favourite chair next to the fire. "Hello Clara," he said. "I see you've found the best seat in the house."

Clara jumped up. "Oh sorry," she said. "Do you want to sit here?"

"No, that's fine. Let's go over to my desk." When they were both seated, Charles in his swivel chair behind the desk and Clara on one of the guest chairs, Charles opened a drawer and pulled out a cassette recorder and pressed record. "You don't mind do you?"

"Not at all," Clara said

I just want to make sure we are absolutely clear about this, you want me to cane you so that you know what it feels like?"

"Yes, that's right."

"Okay, I'll give you six strokes with my junior cane on your bare bottom. If you have never been caned before, the senior cane will be too much for you."

"You're too kind," Clara said.

"I'm going to treat you just like the girls from the upper sixth that we caned yesterday, except you will be naked."

"Yes, about that," Clara said. "Is that absolutely necessary?" Charles just looked at her without saying anything. "Yes, right," she said. "Naked." Standing up Clara didn't quite know how to go about this. She started by undoing the clip and zip on the side of her slacks, she reasoned that Charles had already seen her with her pants down so that would not be a new experience. Keeping her knickers on she slipped off the grey jacket and then pulled her white blouse off leaving her in her knickers and bra. She wasn't wearing stockings, she had left them off because they would be too awkward to remove in front of Charles, but that still meant she had to take off her bra and knickers in front of a man for the first time in many years.

Charles did not pretend to be looking elsewhere. He was looking straight at Clara, enjoying her embarrassment. Turning her back to Charles she started to undo her bra but he said. "Oh no, face me, Clara." So she turned back to face him and let the bra straps fall down her arms, catching the bra with practised efficiency and placing it on the desk with her other clothes. Clara's 44DD breasts were now free and her nipples seemed to be growing as Charles watched. "You can turn your back to me when you lower your knickers, Clara," Charles said, so she did and her fat bottom came into view.

"That was very nice Clara," Charles said as she straightened

"I hate you, Charles Nicholas," Clara said, and at that moment she meant it.

"The door is not locked Clara, you're here because you want to be here and you can leave anytime you want to."

"Oh please lock the door Charles," Clara said. "I know I have to do this but I'm not sure I have the nerve to go through with it."

"You will do fine Clara," Charles said as he stood up and locked the study door. "Now bend over and touch your toes while I get the cane from the cupboard."

"I can't touch my toes Charles," Clara said as she bent, letting her large breasts fall free.

"Well, you know what you told Ella to do, I recommend the same position."

Clara grunted as she got into position with her legs apart and her knees bent. Walking behind Clara swishing the cane through the air, Charles looked at Clara and was disappointed that her bottom cheeks had not opened as much as Ella's, but he could see Clara's hairy pussy between her legs and he thought briefly that she may be getting excited.

"Six strokes Clara and I want you to count them and then say thank you after each stroke."

"Is that really necessary Charles?"

"Seven strokes."

"Okay, just get on with it."

"Eight strokes."

Clara was silent for a few seconds and then said. "Yes Sir."

Charles stood to the left of Clara and then landed the first stroke perfectly on the centre of her bottom. "Ow, Shit," Clara said. Charles cleared his throat. "One, thank you Sir," she said.

The second stroke landed just above the first. "Two, thank you Sir." The third landed just below the first. "Three, thank you Sir." Charles reached out and smoothed Clara's bottom and she shivered. She was going to say something but she decided against it. She had already been given two penalty strokes and she didn't want another. The next two strokes landed, one higher up and the other lower down. For the sixth stroke, Charles changed his position and landed one diagonally across the others like a five-bar gate. "Six," Clara screamed. "Thank you Sir."

Charles put down the cane and admired his handiwork. He was good at caning bottoms and this was a perfect example of the art. Gently smoothing across the welts on Clara's bottom Charles said. "That's a well-caned bottom, I'll just take a pic and you can see."

"Do you have to?" Clara said.

"You still have two more to go, do you want to make it three?"

"No Sir, Sorry Sir."

Charles collected the camera and took a couple of pictures, then he put it down and picked up the cane. "The last two will land on the same place, they will sting a little Clara, but they will come quickly and then it will be over." Charles took up his position again and landed two strokes just under Clara's hanging cheeks at the tops of her legs.

"Shit Charles," Clara said as she stood up rubbing her bottom furiously and pushing her hairy pussy in front of her. She was not worried about what Charles could see now, or the fact that her large boobs were wobbling around in front of her. She just wanted to rub away the pain.

Charles went to the cupboard to hang up the cane with the others and then picked up a tub of cream. "Just kneel on the settee and I'll put some cream on your bottom, it will help ease the pain a little."

"Thank you, Charles, but I'm sure I can do that myself," Clara said.

"I'm sure you can, but it's nicer for someone else to do that for you. Don't be so silly, get on the settee."

"Is that the way it's going to be now, I have to do as I'm told?"

Charles nodded as Clara knelt on the settee and raised her bottom in the air. Charles took some cream out of the tub and massaged Clara's bottom paying special attention to the welts that he had raised. He also put a lot of cream on the tops of her legs and she was moving with his hands obviously enjoying the attention. Soon Charles was massaging between her legs and she didn't stop him as he edged towards her pussy, "No, Charles, don't" Clara said but she pushed her bottom back encouraging him to continue. Very soon Charles was making sloshing noises between Clara's lips and she orgasmed loudly.

Clara was embarrassed and she got up and dressed. "You shouldn't have done that Charles, I'm so embarrassed. Please don't tell anybody. Oh God, what am I going to tell the Reverend Grant on Sunday?"

"Relax, Clara," Charles said. "It was just an orgasm, we all have them. At least half of the staff in this school have had at least one at my hands. It's natural and nothing to be ashamed of."

Clara was not pacified and she rushed out of the door leaving her large knickers behind on his desk.

Chapter 17 - Clara is spanked by Matron

"Listen up everybody," Amelia was talking in the staff room again. "Matron has done a fine job and finished the medicals for the girls. Not only has this saved us a lot of money, but by the sound of it, she has done a much better job than the doctors and nurses last year. I'm sure you will join me in congratulating her." There was a round of applause for Sarah. "Okay, settle down again. As many of you know she has been doing a similar medical for the staff as well and at least half of you have been through the process with her. There are just four of you left, you know who you are so I want you to present yourself at the Sanatorium for your check-up by the end of the day. There's a rota on the notice board. That's all, have a great day." Amelia walked out of the staffroom and everybody started to chat.

Clara looked at the rota and said "shit" under her breath.

"What's up Clara?" Alex Dixon was also looking at the rota and her name was last on the list at four in the afternoon.

"Oh nothing, only I'm first on the list and I have a class, can you swap with me?" Clara said.

"Sure thing," Alex said and Clara was relieved that she had put the problem off for a little longer. Charles had caned her three days earlier and there were still a few lines across her bottom. They were fading fast but maybe she could avoid the medical by leaving early.

Later that day Clara was walking out to her car to try to slip away when Sarah was coming in from the car park. "Leaving early Clara," Sarah said. "Have you forgotten that your appointment is at four and it's ten to now?"

"Yes, sorry," Clara said. "I have to get to the shops."

"Yes, me too, Clara," Sarah said, taking Clara's arm. "Come on, we will do the check-up in ten minutes and then we can go to the shops together."

"No, but..." Clara was saying but Sarah had already guided her back into the school and on their way to the sanatorium.

"What are you going shopping for Clara?" Sarah was filling in the time with conversation. She had to get the medicals finished and she wasn't going to let Clara get away without having her four o'clock appointment. When they got into the San, Sarah said. "Okay Clara, strip off down to your bra and knickers and let's have you sitting on the examination table."

Sarah did the whole medical with Clara in her underwear and she thought she might have got away with it, and then Sarah said. "Just your temperature to test, lie on the table on your tummy."

"You're not going to stick that thermometer up my bum are you?" Clara was horrified.

"Of course, Clara, it's the best way to get an accurate reading."

"But I don't like that, can't you test my temperature in my mouth?"

"Well, this thermometer has been up all the girl's bottoms and half the staff, I'm not sure you would want it in your mouth."

"Oh, okay," Clara said lying on her tummy on the table. "Just pull my knickers to one side and take my temperature if you have to."

"Don't be silly, Clara," Sarah said as she whisked Clara's knickers down. "We all have a bottom and you have nothing to hide." Looking at Clara's bottom she said, "Or do you?"

"Oh Sarah, please just pull my knickers back up and don't say another word."

"Oh dear Clara, you have been caned, and if I'm not mistaken you have been caned on your bare bottom by my husband. I recognise his trademark anywhere. The five-bar gate. Five cuts across your bottom equally spaced and then a diagonal line across them. An excellent piece of work if you don't mind me saying so. And then he gave you two at the tops of your legs as well. They must have stung."

"I'm sorry Matron," Clara said. "I just needed to know what it felt like if I was going to cane the girls."

"Don't worry about it Clara, I'm sure my husband has caned or spanked almost all the staff by now. As long as he didn't complete the job and give you an orgasm as well, I'm fine with it."

Clara was silent for a second. She didn't know how to answer that question.

"He did, didn't he?"

"I'm sorry Matron," Clara said. "I was so horny after the caning and he put some cream on my bottom and, well, I couldn't help myself. Please don't tell the headmistress, I'll never live it down."

"You horrible little slut," Sarah said. "I have a good mind to give you a taste of my wooden spoon, I expect you've heard about it."

"Yes, I have, oh please Matron, not your wooden spoon."

"Well, it's either that or I'm straight off to the headmistress to tell her you've been having an affair with my husband." Actually, Sarah knew all about the caning and the orgasm afterwards. Charles had shown her the pictures he took and described the event for Sarah's pleasure before he made love to her that evening. The following morning she told Charles that she intended to spank Clara for having an affair with her husband and he laughed.

"Okay, I'll take the punishment, as long as we can keep this to ourselves," Clara said.

"On your knees then and I'll get the wooden spoon." Sarah was in her office for a few seconds and then came back carrying the long wooden spoon they had brought back from South Africa. At two foot long it was longer than a traditional wooden spoon with a bigger face, perfect for spanking. When she came back into the surgery Clara was on her knees with her head down on the table and her bottom in the air. "That bra must be uncomfortable with your heavy breasts Clara, let me undo it for you," Sarah said, and she unhooked Clara's bra and her boobs fell free. "I'm sure that's better, now let's get on with your punishment for having an affair with my husband."

"I'm not having an affair," Clara said but as soon as the wooden spoon landed on Clara's bottom she could think of nothing else other than the sting on top of the cane marks.

Sarah gave Clara a hard spanking. Over and over again the wooden spoon landed on her bottom and she was sobbing loudly when Sarah stopped. Looking at her handiwork Sarah stood at the end of the examination table and took a picture for Charles. "You have a lovely bottom, Clara, I'll find some cream to put on it for you." Clara didn't answer so Sarah took a scoop of cream from the tub she always had in the top drawer, and rubbed it into Clara's bottom, taking special care of that place at the top of her legs where Charles had caned her.

Soon Sarah's fingers had slipped between Clara's cheeks and over her anus. "No Matron, not there," Clara said but Sarah didn't stop. Her fingers slipped lower and very soon Clara was having another orgasm at the hands of the Nicholas's

When Clara had caught her breath, she was in not so much of a hurry to get dressed and leave. "Matron?" she said. "Is this always going to happen when I get my bottom spanked?"

"Probably Clara," Sarah said.

Chapter 18 - Rebecca is spanked after the Party

The Spring term was beginning to draw to a close and the girls were looking forward to the Easter holidays. The younger girls in the school were painting eggs in their art classes and the older girls were making new outfits for the traditional Easter dance. For as long as anybody could remember, St Samantha's School for Girls had had an Easter dance, where a few selected senior boys from the local boarding school were invited to St Sam's to dance with the girls. There would be a non-alcoholic punch to drink and snacks, but the main reason for the dance was to dance.

For the teachers, this was an organisational nightmare. The dance was restricted to girls in the lower or upper sixth forms and who were over sixteen of which there were twenty-four. Twenty-four boys of similar age were selected from the local school so there would be equal numbers even though most of the boys and girls would stand in groups on opposite sides of the room for most of the evening. Putting twenty-four girls with hormones raging in the same room with twenty-four horny boys is a recipe for disaster. Add to that, soft lighting and rhythmic music and who knows what would happen.

This year however, Rebecca, the weekly boarder, brought a bottle of vodka and was able to add it to the punch without anybody knowing, so the scene was set.

Amelia Brandon, the headmistress, started the dance and welcomed the boys who all looked very respectable. Next, she complimented the girls on their outfits, all made by hand in the sewing class recently. Finally, before the dance started she told all participants where the bathrooms are and that any boy or girl found in the wrong bathroom would be severely punished. Then the music started and the dance began.

This year three of the girls, Mary Becker, Katie Owen and Nicole Asher had already picked out the boys they wanted, and approached them for a dance. The boys agreed and as the ice was broken more of the girls approached the boys. Amelia had told the staff that she didn't want to stifle the fun so there would only be one member of staff in the hall at all times, and they would take it in turns. Amelia, Daisy Andrews and Laura Taylor would rotate to make sure there was a lid kept on the activities, and Charles Nicholas would patrol the outside and the bathrooms with Jasmine Pritchard.

All was fine until the vodka started to kick in. Neither the boys nor the girls were used to alcohol, and even the teachers were not regular drinkers so a little vodka in a large bowl of punch, went a long way. The dance party was due to start at six and finish at ten in the evening but by nine Charles realised something was up. Jasmine had caught two boys hanging around the girl's bathroom and had sent them back into the hall. Charles checked the bike sheds and he found Mary Becker in there with one of the boys and while they were both fully dressed, the boy admitted that he had got to first base. Charles was not sure what that meant but he knew it wasn't good.

Going into the hall he approached Amelia who said, "It's going very well, don't you think?"

"I'm sure it is, but we should try and keep the children in here if we can, a few of them are escaping."

"Oh don't worry Charles," Amelia said. "They're just letting off a little steam." Amelia was usually the first person to stop this sort of thing, so Charles knew there was something amiss. Added to that

Amelia seemed to be a little unsteady on her feet. "Have you tried the punch, Charles? I've had three glasses, it's wonderful."

Charles took the proffered glass and tasted the punch. "Oh God," Charles said. "This has vodka in it."

"Has it?" Amelia said. "Well, it's very good."

"Yes, but not so good for the children."

"Oh don't be an old stick in the mud, Charles," Amelia said uncharacteristically. "Let them have a little fun for a change."

"I think it's time we ran out of punch Amelia, and maybe you should go to bed, I'll look after the rest of the evening."

"I'll just have another glass of this wonderful punch Charles, and then maybe you could come to bed with me, Sarah as well if you like."

"Not tonight Amelia, I'll have to look after these girls."

"Oh, you can cane them all in the morning. Come on, my bed is warm and I'm sure the girls will be okay."

Looking around the room he noticed there were less than half the girls on the dance floor, the rest were in the corners kissing. Mostly, but not all, with other boys. Charles was organising as he called Jasmine to come into the hall. "Take Amelia to bed, Jasmine"

"Oh Charles," Amelia said but her voice was getting very slurred now. "You told us that we're not allowed to do that anymore."

"Oh, I see," Jasmine said.

"Yes, the punch has been spiked," Charles said. "When you have done that, tell Daisy and Laura to come back into the hall. After that stay close to the girl's bathroom and send any boys there back into the hall. I'll manage the room for now."

Amelia and Charles had already agreed that kissing would be okay but, "No handling of the merchandise." Amelia had said and Charles agreed so he policed the room at a distance, and anybody going too far soon stopped when Charles walked towards them. Two couples tried to walk out of the hall together but Charles stopped them. Jasmine came back with Daisy but she said that Laura was not feeling well. Jasmine went back to monitoring the bathrooms leaving Daisy with Charles in the hall.

"Did you have any of the punch Daisy?" Charles said.

"Just a glass, it was very nice," Daisy said.

"It's nice because it's been spiked with vodka."

"Oh, I see," Daisy said. "So it's you and I against forty-eight horny drunks. It should be fun."

Charles laughed.

The rest of the evening went surprisingly well. One or two of the boys had to be deterred from putting their hands where they didn't belong, and most of the boys had a hand or two on the bottoms of their partners during the last dance but Charles was happy to let that go. Nobody else seemed to mind at all.

The following morning Matron had a queue of sixth formers at her surgery asking for headache pills and Amelia didn't appear at breakfast at all. Later that day Charles and Amelia were talking in the staff room. "Great party Amelia, well done," Charles said.

"Was it, I don't remember," Amelia said. "I wasn't feeling well, there must have been something in the food. I hope nobody else was sick."

"Just a few headaches this morning Amelia, the punch was spiked too much."

"What do you mean too much, and who spiked the punch," Amelia asked.

"I've no idea yet, but I'll find out, I can assure you," Charles said. Actually, he did have an idea. He thought it would be one of the weekly boarders or a day girl. If the others had vodka when they came back to school, it would be gone by now. His money was on Rebecca, knowing that a caning didn't really matter to her if she was caught. So he sent a message for Rebecca to come to his study at four in the afternoon.

At lunchtime, Sarah and Charles got together as they usually do after lunch. "What the hell happened last night at the party. I was stuck in the Sanatorium with little Pinky Turner again, but there was a stream of girls with headaches this morning."

"The Punch was spiked, Sarah," Charles said. "Amelia was out of it and I had to send her to bed."

"I bet she wanted to take you to bed with her." Sarah laughed and Charles just smiled.

"Did you...?" Sarah left the sentence unfinished and Charles knew she wasn't talking about sleeping with the headmistress. When they used to have school dances in South Africa where they were teaching, Charles used to put a half bottle of vodka in the punch just to loosen up the party.

"I did, but someone else had the same idea and added a lot more than I did," Charles said and Sarah laughed.

At four in the afternoon, Rebecca was knocking at the study door. "Come in Rebecca," Charles called and Rebecca came in but she was obviously sulking.

"Why am I here Sir?" Rebecca said. "I haven't done anything wrong,"

"Why do you think you may have done something wrong?"

"Because," Rebecca said, "When you tell people to come to your study at four o'clock it's usually for a spanking."

"Really?" Charles said. "I didn't know I was getting so predictable. Did you enjoy the party last night?" Charles changed the subject.

"Yes I did, thank you, Sir."

"And did you enjoy the punch?" Charles said and Rebecca knew that she had been caught.

"I did, thank you, Sir. But I only had one glass."

"Oh, why was that Rebecca?"

"Don't know, Sir."

"Maybe that was because you had put vodka into the punch and you didn't want to get drunk," Charles said.

"How did you know it was me, Sir?" Rebecca said.

"I didn't until right now."

"Shit," Rebecca said under her breath. "Are you going to cane me?"

"Certainly not," Charles said. "I know you don't mind being caned and you would just show the marks off to the other girls in the upper sixth. I'm not going to cane you, I'm going to put you across my knee like a little girl and spank your bottom with my hand. I know you hate that so it's a better punishment, and there will be nothing to show the girls in the morning."

Rebecca was still sulking as Charles stood up and put the spanking chair in the centre of the room. "Come here Rebecca," Charles said as he patted his knee. "Over you go."

"This is not fair Sir," Rebecca said. "Can't you just cane me as usual?"

"No Rebecca, this is a much better punishment for you," Charles said as he raised her skirt and eased her knickers over her athletic bottom. Then Charles started spanking, but it was not a hard spanking, this punishment was more to do with humiliation rather than pain, and he knew Rebecca was feeling humiliated to be treated like a little girl. The spanking didn't last long and afterwards, Rebecca was told to stand in the corner with her skirt up and her knickers around her ankles. Then she heard the click/buzz of the polaroid camera. Rebecca was still sulking as she was told to pull up her knickers and come and sit at the desk.

Charles passed an instant picture of Rebecca standing in the corner with her bottom on display. "How does that make you feel, Rebecca?" Charles asked.

"Terrible," Rebecca said but she was close to tears.

"Nobody will ever hear about the vodka in the punch at the party last night unless you tell them, and if the word gets out so will this picture. Do we understand each other?"

"Yes Sir," Rebecca said. "But to be honest, I didn't think so many people would get drunk on just a bottle of vodka."

"The problem was Rebecca," Charles said. "You were not the only person who had the idea of livening up the party with a little vodka in the punch."

"Oh, I see. Yes, that would be a problem then. Who else put vodka in the punch?" Rebecca said. Then she had an idea, "It wasn't you Sir, was it?"

"Certainly not," Charles said but he was smiling and Rebecca knew. "Off you go now and don't do it again."

"Yes Sir," Rebecca said smiling. Strangely after that encounter, Rebecca had a great deal more respect for Charles Nicholas than she had had before.

Chapter 19 - Charles Spanks a Parent again

The following day Amelia was feeling a lot better and she caught Charles in the corridor, "You're looking better this morning Amelia," Charles said.

"Yes, I'm feeling better too, Charles. I'm not sure what it was but it certainly knocked me for six yesterday, twenty-four-hour flu maybe. I remember most of the party but the end seems to be a bit of a blur."

"Yes, Jasmine put you to bed, you were obviously under the weather," Charles said. "I looked after the party until the coach came for the boys, the parents collected the day girls and the boarders went to bed giggling."

"Well done Charles, what would I do without you," Amelia said. "I have some strange memories about that night, I hope I didn't say anything to you that was inappropriate Charles."

"Nothing at all, Amelia. It must have been a dream."

"Yes, that would be it then." Amelia was relieved. "One last thing, I had a strange phone call from Mrs Lucas, you know, Sophie's mother. She wanted to complain to you about something, but I'm not sure what. I said she could come this afternoon at four, are you busy?"

"Not at all Amelia, I'll handle it," Charles said. He had spanked Synthia Lucas twice last term and he guessed she wanted a repeat performance, but he wasn't sure.

At four o'clock Synthia Lucas stormed straight into Charles's Study without knocking. "Sophie was drunk when she came home on Friday night after the party, what have you got to say for yourself?" she said sitting in the guest chair opposite Charles who was sitting at his desk.

"Who are you?" Charles said knowing exactly who was sitting in front of him.

"Synthia Lucas, Sophie's mother. I have an appointment."

"You can't be," Charles said. "Sophie's mother was a much larger lady, you look so slim and attractive."

Synthia was obviously very flattered. "Thank you very much, I've lost a lot of weight, but that's not the point. Sophie was at the party on Friday and she came home drunk as a skunk. She promised that she hadn't been drinking but I could tell she was drunk so I sent her to bed."

"So Sophie was at the party was she?" Charles said. "Well, she shouldn't have been there, it was for sixth formers only. She must have sneaked in when we weren't looking. I'll have to get her in here for the cane. And you say she had been drinking alcohol, I knew someone brought some in from home and for that she may get expelled. I'll speak to the headmistress and we will have to interview Sophie."

"No please Mr Nicholas," Synthia said. "I didn't come here to get Sophie into trouble."

"Too late for that now, someone has to be punished for bringing alcohol to the party."

"Well, it may have been my fault, Mr Nicholas," Synthia said. "She was complaining that her friend Mary was being invited to the party and she wasn't going even though she was sixteen last week. I told her that she should sneak into the party and nobody will notice."

"Some parents don't know how to bring up their children, and now she might be expelled," Charles said.

"Oh no please," Synthia said. "If you have to punish someone then it had better be me."

"It won't just be a spanking this time Synthia, it will be the cane as well."

"The cane?"

"Yes, the cane," Charles said. "Six hard strokes on top of a spanked bottom."

"Okay," Synthia said as she got up, pulled her white dress over her head, and stood in her white bra and knickers. Gone was the corset she was wearing the last time Charles had spanked her.

"Phew Synthia," Charles said. "You have really been working on your body, you look like a million dollars."

"Thank you, Charles," Synthia said.

"But that won't get you out of your punishment," Charles said as he moved the spanking chair into the centre of the room and sat down. "I think you know the position I want you in Synthia, don't you?"

"Yes Sir," Synthia said as she bent over his lap.

Charles held her close and started to spank her knickered bottom straight away. Over and over again his hand landed on Synthia's bottom and he didn't let up until she was wriggling uncomfortably. When he stopped spanking he rested his hand on her knickers and she said. "I thought you told me that spankings were always on the bare bottom, Charles."

Yes, you're right Synthia, but when you lied to me about why you were here, I thought I would not take down your knickers, you might enjoy it too much."

"But Charles, I wasn't lying," Synthia said and then Charles started to spank the tops of her legs.

"Ow, shit Charles that stings," Synthia said but that didn't stop him. "Okay, okay, I lied."

"And what's worse, you used your daughter in the lie," Charles said and spanked the tops of her legs again. "Sophie wasn't at the dance was she?"

"No, alright," Synthia said. "But she told me about the girls getting drunk."

"Nobody got drunk, Synthia," Charles lied. "They were just over-excited, that's all. It usually happens at the annual dance." Then he started to spank her legs again.

"Shit, Charles stop that will you, I came here for you to spank my bare bottom, but this spanking is no fun at all."

Charles stopped spanking and stood Synthia up. She had no idea what was happening until he went to the tall antique cupboard and unhooked a thin whippy cane.

"You are not going to use that on my bottom are you?"

"No Synthia, the tops of your legs. Now show me how you can bend over and touch your toes."

"Should I take my knickers and bra off, Charles?" Synthia said hopefully.

"No, leave them on," Charles said as he watched Synthia bend over and fail to touch her toes.

"Six strokes then, and I want you to count them."

"Yes Sir."

Charles landed six strokes just under Synthia's knickers at the tops of her legs and she found it very difficult to count them as they hurt so much. She stayed in position though, but when she counted "Six" She was sobbing.

"Stand up," Charles said. "You nearly got your daughter expelled and all because you wanted a spanking and a repeat of the fun we had last term. If you want that sort of spanking, just ask, but never, never use your daughter like that. Now get out."

"Yes Sir." Synthia Lucas said as she pulled her dress over her head and left Charles's study.

Chapter 20 - Sarah spanks Jasmine

"Where's Jasmine?" Sarah asked Charles in the Staff room just before Lunch.

"I've no idea, come to think of it, I haven't seen her for a while. Is she missing?"

"Well, she certainly has been missing. She's been missing her appointments. Four to be exact, and it can't go on. She's the last member of the staff or the girls to have a medical check and I can't finish my report until I've seen her. The report was due last week and it makes me look inefficient."

"Oh," Charles said as he went back to the report he was writing.

"Well, it's just not fair. It's not as though I've been unreasonable,"

"Of course not dear,"

"And when I make appointments I keep them."

"Yes dear."

Sarah looked at her husband. "You don't care do you?"

"No dear," Charles said and Sarah went out of the staff room in disgust. Charles went back to finishing his report.

Sarah was angry when she finally found Jasmine in the changing room next to the gym. "What are you doing in here Jasmine?"

"I was just doing something," Jasmine said obscurely. "I'll come for my medical later."

"You will do no such thing, Jasmine." Sarah grabbed Jasmine's ear and pulled her up.

"Hey?" Jasmine said. "That hurts."

"I know it does," Sarah said. "But it doesn't hurt as much as sitting in the San waiting for someone who never comes. Four Times!"

Sitting on the wooden bench in the changing room Sarah pulled Jasmine over her lap and flipped up her skirt. Jasmine had her usual white cotton knickers under her short skirt and Sarah spanked them ten times. "That's just a warm-up, when I get you back to the Sanatorium I'll be spanking you properly for missing your appointments."

"I'm sorry Matron, I just can't," Jasmine said from her position over Sarah's lap.

"What are you talking about, silly girl, of course, you can." Sarah lifted her up so that they were sitting side by side on the bench.

"No Matron, I'm embarrassed."

"I have a problem, down there." Jasmine pointed to a place between her legs.

"Oh, I see," Sarah said. "Do you think you're pregnant?"

"No, no, nothing like that. It's just a problem."

"Well, we can sort it out, but not in the changing room," Sarah said. "Follow me."

"No Matron, I can't."

"It's either the San or the headmistress's office, you choose."

"Okay Matron," Jasmine said as she stood up and followed Sarah to the Sanatorium.

Ten minutes later Sarah was laughing. "Silly girl, it's just a little infection, I'll have you fixed up in no time. Just use this cream now and three times a day and it will be gone in no time at all."

"Oh Matron, thank you," Jasmine said as she applied the cream to herself.

"That was the whole point of the check-up, to make sure things like this don't go untreated," Sarah said.

"I know Matron, but I was embarrassed."

"Not as embarrassed as you will be when you tell your friends that you were spanked with the wooden spoon by the matron for missing four appointments."

"I know, I deserve it, Matron, where do you want me?"

"On your knees on the examination table. Head on the pillow, knees apart." Jasmine was already naked from the medical so she got up on her knees and buried her head in the little pillow at the top of the table. As an Olympic tennis player and school sports mistress, Jasmine was very fit and easily got into position. Sarah also knew from experience that she could take a great deal of pain, so she was determined to spank Jasmine hard with the wooden spoon.

Sarah liked to use the cupped side of the face of the wooden spoon for the first two strokes because they leave an oval ring, one for each bottom. This is just a little thing that the person receiving the spanking would never know, but Sarah thought it was fun. After that, the spanking continued until no individual rings were evident, leaving a bright red glow on Jasmine's bottom. Eventually, Jasmine was crying and apologising for letting Sarah down and the spanking stopped.

Jasmine slowly clambered off the examination table and hugged Sarah. "I'm sorry I let you down Matron, I know you have done a wonderful job with all the medical tests and I really appreciate what you have done for me."

Sarah hugged her and patted Jasmine's sore bottom. "Okay Jasmine, get dressed and get back to the gym. Come in for another check-up next week and we will make sure the infection is cleared."

"Thank you, Matron," Jasmine said and she left.

Chapter 21 - Birthday Spankings

When Sarah woke up on the last day of the term she rolled over towards her husband in bed. "Well we have got through another term Charles," she said. "I'm looking forward to a couple of weeks without sore knees and runny noses."

"Yes, it will be nice to take a break, but it has been a good term, lots of naughty girl's bottoms to spank," Charles said as he sat up in bed.

"Is that all you think about Charles?" Sarah was laughing.

"Not at all, I think about spanking the teachers as well. I've told Amelia she can come for dinner tonight and we will have some fun afterwards."

"That will be good, you haven't spanked Amelia since the beginning of the term, have you? She will be having withdrawal symptoms." Sarah said.

"Well we can't have that, can we? And come to think about it, I haven't spanked you for a long time either."

"Oh Charles, you spanked me last week, remember?"

"A week is a long time to go without a spanking, God knows what sort of naughtiness you will get up to unless you're regularly spanked."

Sarah was laughing as she pulled her nighty over her head and bent over Charles's lap. "You had better make it a hard spanking Charles. If Amelia is coming over I'll definitely be naughty this evening."

Charles lowered Sarah's knickers and wondered at his luck. Charles and Sarah had met at the school in South Africa where they both worked for twenty years. Their relationship was slow to start but soon picked up momentum when they discovered a mutual interest in spanking. Sarah was the Matron at the school and she had to regularly spank the naughty girls. She asked for Charles's help one day when a girl needed a caning, and their relationship developed from there.

Very soon Charles threatened to spank Sarah and she said, "Promises, promises." So he bent her over his knee in the clinic and spanked her. That was all twenty years ago now but he never fails to remember those early days and how he felt when he found someone who was just as passionate about spanking as he was.

Resting his hand on Sarah's bottom he was thinking about some of the spankings and canings in St Sam's school for girls. It was a good move. Sarah wriggled to get comfortable. "Come on Charles," she said. "I'm getting cold."

"Yes, sorry," Charles said. "Let me warm you up a little." Taking the elastic of Sarah's knickers he pulled them over her large bottom and started to spank her straight away. It was not a hard spanking, just enough to warm her bottom and excite her. He was spanking each cheek in turn, just like he had done all those years ago in the clinic, and Sarah was lifting her bottom up to meet each spank. After twenty or so smacks, Charles rested his hand on Sarah's bottom massaging gently and her legs seemed to open on their own. Charles gave her another twenty spanks and when he stopped again Sarah's legs were wide open and the unmistakable aroma of her excitement filled the air. Charles's fingers slipped between her cheeks and found her wet pussy. It didn't take long. With practised efficiency, Charles brought Sarah to her climax and she stiffened and then trapped his hand between her legs as she let the excitement flood over her.

A few minutes later Sarah rolled over and kissed her husband. "I love you," she said.

"I love you too."

A little later, after breakfast, all the teachers gathered in the staff room earlier than usual. There was a buzz of anticipation in the air but the main character for the expected performance was not there. "Do you think she will turn up Charles?" Amelia said.

"Oh, I think so, Amelia. She's not the same woman who started the term."

"I know, Charles, and that's down to you I think. If Molly Dobson wasn't coming back next term I would certainly offer her the position permanently."

"She has a good job to go to and I'm sure that has something to do with your recommendation, Amelia." As Charles said that the door opened and the room went quiet. Clara Harrison walked in and everybody clapped.

"What's this all about?" Clara asked Charles but she knew.

"Somebody is about to get her birthday spanking Clara," Charles said

"Who?"

"You Clara."

"Oh my God," Clara said in mock surprise. "Is it my birthday?"

"It is," Amelia said and then she clapped her hands to get everybody's attention. "Settle down everybody. I just want to say a few words. As you all know it's Clara's birthday today, but it's also the last day she will be with us here at St Sam's so I just wanted to say how much we will all miss her. I must admit that when she arrived I was not certain, but she has certainly done a fine job here this term and she will be missed by students and teachers alike."

"Hear, hear." the teachers called.

"But as it's her birthday," Amelia continued. "I'll hand over to Charles who will perform the traditional birthday spanking, and I expect you will all want to call out the number."

"Thank you, Amelia," Charles said as he sat on the dining chair that had been placed in the centre of the room for just this purpose. Patting his lap he said. "Clara." and Clara Harrison walked towards Charles. Clara usually wore pants at school but today she looked very nice in a thin summer dress even though it was cold outside. Taking Clara's hand Charles said. "You're looking delightful today Clara."

"Thank you, Charles," Clara said. "I thought the dress would be more appropriate for this."

Clara bent over Charles's lap and he lifted up her dress to reveal her bottom covered in a beautiful pair of satin knickers, which got a lot of ohs and ahs from the rest of the teachers in the room. "Clever girl," Charles said. "But you know they have to come down for the birthday spanking."

Clara laughed. "I thought it was worth a try." The birthday spankings had become a feature of the staffroom activity and they all knew they would be subject to a spanking at some time in the year, so they started to compete with the quality of the knickers that would be displayed. Today, Clara's knickers were certainly worthy of the competition.

As Charles lifted the elastic of her knickers and bared her bottom slowly he said. "How many spanks are you getting today Clara?"

"Well, that's up to you Charles, but I'm fifty today," Clara said.

There was silence in the room. "Fifty?" Amelia said. "But that's not what you put on your application form."

"I know headmistress," Clara said from her position over Charles's knee. "But I thought I should be honest as I'm leaving today anyway." There was laughter from the room.

"Well, you had better give Clara a proper spanking for lying, Charles," Amelia said.

"I agree headmistress," Charles said and started to spank Clara slowly.

"One," The teachers in the classroom called out. "Two," all the way to forty-four. Clara was getting very uncomfortable with so many smacks but then Charles said. "The last six are for lying Clara."

"Okay," Clara said and she braced herself knowing that the last six would be harder. And they were. When the teachers said "Fifty," There was great applause and cheering but as Clara got up she had tears in her eyes.

"Phew Charles," Clara said. "Those last six were stingers." She still had her knickers around her ankles as she rubbed her bottom but she didn't care who saw her. Just then the door opened and Cook came in with a cake and lots of candles. Clara blew them out and then they all sang happy birthday.

After the room settled down and most of the teachers had gone to their classrooms, Clara was fully dressed and her makeup had been repaired. Coming over to Charles she said. "Thank you, Charles,"

"It's a pleasure, and if you ever want another spanking, I'm your man," Charles said with a smile.

"No, not for that," Clara said. "I want to thank you for showing me how to be a better teacher." Reaching up Clara kissed Charles on his cheek and then hurried out of the staff room.

What was all that about?" Amelia asked Charles.

"It was about you owing me ten pounds," Charles said, holding out his hand. At the beginning of term, Amelia had told Charles that he would never put Clara across his lap for a spanking and they had taken a ten-pound bet on it.

"Oh yes," Amelia said. "I had forgotten about that. I don't have my purse with me, I'll give it to you this evening at dinner."

A little later in the upper-sixth classroom, all the girls were talking to each other about what they would be doing in the holidays. The talk was all about boys, pop groups and discos. Then

Charles walked in and the room went silent instantly then everybody stood up and said. "Good morning Mr Nicholas."

They all knew it was Ella Hall's eighteenth birthday today and Charles knew as well but he turned to the board and wrote $111111111 \times 111111111 =$. "The first person to give me the answer to this sum gets a get-out-of-spanking free card." Charles had printed some cards just like the monopoly game cards but with a cartoon of a girl over a man's lap and the cards were highly prized.

"But Sir," Nicole said, "That's a really hard sum."

"Is it?" Charles said.

"And," Nicole continued, "Ella has her birthday spanking to come today."

"Does she?" Charles said smiling. Then the usual call started in the classroom. "Spanking, spanking, spanking."

Charles held up his hands. "Okay girls, that's enough," he said. "Come here Ella and get your birthday treat."

Ella was smiling. She knew that she could say pretty much anything at the moment, the rules were relaxed when someone was going to get a birthday spanking. "Will it be a treat, Sir," she said. "I thought it would be a spanking?"

"It will be a hard spanking as well, young lady, if you're not careful," Charles said.

"Oh I'm very careful Sir," Ella said.

The last day of term was always 'Civvies' Day where all the girls could wear their casual clothes. Charles usually found it interesting to see what each girl would wear. Some would be in jeans and a jumper, and others in smart dresses as if they were going out to a party. Their chosen clothes said a lot about their personalities. Ella was in jeans and a knitted jumper and Charles thought that was as much to do with her big boobs as her personality. She was not comfortable with her breast size and the loose jumper hid them perfectly.

Walking towards Charles she was undoing the button on her jeans and by the time Charles sat on the spanking chair in the centre of the classroom, they were around her ankles. The class broke out in laughter and Charles wondered what that was all about but when he pulled Ella over his lap he saw that she was wearing a pair of white knickers with "Spank me" in big letters painted on them. Charles was also laughing. "These are not regulation knickers Ella, are they?"

"Well, it's civvies day today so I can wear any knickers I like."

"You certainly can Ella, but I recommend you change these or you will get your bottom spanked by all the teachers."

Charles started the spanking but he left the 'spank me' knickers on while the girls called out the number. When they got to eighteen, Ella had kicked off her jeans and Charles pulled the knickers over her bottom and let them fall down to her ankles, then he reached down and took them off. "I think I'll keep these Ella," Charles said. "Go and see Matron and she will give you another pair."

"It's alright Sir, I brought two pairs," Ella said, pulling up her jeans.

As Ella was walking back to her desk Amy called out. "I've got it."

"What have you got Amy?" Charles had forgotten about the maths problem he had set.

"The sum on the board. The answer is 12345678987654321."

"Well done Amy," Charles said. "Come here and get your get-out-of-spanking card." Charles was still sitting on the spanking chair when Amy approached and he surprised her by pulling her over his knee.

"But Sir," Amy said. "Why am I getting a spanking?"

"For being too clever, Amy," Charles said as he flipped up her dress and spanked her bottom softly. Amy didn't mind at all. Since the punishment she had had for spying earlier in the term, she looked up to Charles like an old uncle and he could do anything he liked.

He stood Amy up again and then he pulled a card from his pocket. "Well done Amy," he said. "Perhaps you would like to tell the class how you did it."

"Thank you, Sir," Amy said, feeling very important. "I knew that eleven times eleven is 121, and I wondered if 111 times 111 would be the same format, and it is 12321. Then I tried 1111 x 1111 and that's 1234321, so I guessed the rest, and I was right."

"Yes, you were Amy, well done," Charles said. There was less enthusiasm in the class for clever Amy and her maths than there was for Ella's birthday spanking, but they gave her a round of applause anyway.

Back in the staff room, Charles had pinned Ella's knickers on the notice board with a note underneath saying. "New regulation school knickers for the students and staff alike."

Everybody was relaxed on the last day of term.

Chapter 22 - A Spanking for the Headmistress

That evening Amelia was in the lounge with Sarah and Charles. Amelia always found it strange to be sitting in their lounge, because it was Charles's study during the day and that's where naughty girls, and teachers sometimes, would find themselves over his knee at four in the afternoon. "Phew," she said. "That's another term over with."

Sarah laughed. "This morning Charles said that it was a lovely term, but I think he was measuring it by the number of bottoms he spanked."

Amelia laughed, "And caned as well, I think the cane came out more often this term than the last. Is that right Charles?"

"I've no idea," Charles said, but he was lying. For the last twenty years, Charles had kept a scrapbook detailing all the girls and women he had spanked. Many of them had pictures of the finished red or striped bottom to go with the description of the spanking. Charles and Sarah would often sit in the evenings in front of the fire with a glass of whisky paging through the scrapbook and reminding each other of this girl or that. When he moved to England, Charles didn't think he would get a chance to add more to the scrapbook but he was amazed when Amelia made him the school disciplinarian early in his first term, and to celebrate he bought a new scrapbook.

The pictures in the scrapbook used to be black and white which he processed in the school dark room in South Africa, but when they came to England, Charles bought Sarah and himself a new Polaroid camera each, so that they could have instant colour pictures for the scrapbook. This term Sarah and Charles had amassed thirty-two pictures to go into the scrapbook with descriptions of each punishment, and this was the highest number in many years. No wonder Charles thought it was a good year.

"But I've yet to spank your bottom since the beginning of term headmistress," Charles said as Mary Becker walked into the lounge and announced that dinner was on the table in the dining room.

"Hello Mary," Charles said. "Are you on dinner duty this evening?"

"Yes Sir," Mary said. "Well there's only Ella and I left in the school for Easter, and it's Ella's birthday so I thought I should volunteer for dinner duty."

"Thank you, Mary," Charles said. "Come on ladies, let's go through for dinner."

Back in the dormitory, Ella was eating a bag of crisps on her bed when Mary burst in. "The head is going to get a spanking this evening."

"What?" Ella said. "How do you know?"

"I heard them talking about it just before I announced that their dinner was served. Apparently, she was spanked earlier in the term as well."

"The old man is a randy old sod," Ella said. "I bet he gets an erection when he spanks us."

"I've never felt anything Ella," Mary said. "And I'm spanked more than anybody."

"That's only because everybody knows that you smoke in the bicycle sheds at lunchtime. If anybody wants a bottom to spank they just have to catch you there."

Mary was laughing. "But I like it, actually."

"Do you?" Ella was surprised. "So do I."

There was silence in the dorm for a few minutes then Mary said, "Would you like another birthday spanking?" Ella looked up and nodded. Mary straightened herself up on the bed and told Ella to push down her jeans. "I'm not going to spank you in jeans," she said. As Ella loosened the button of her jeans and pushed down the zip, Mary was surprised to see that she wasn't wearing any knickers. "No knickers? Naughty girl. You should get a spanking for that as well."

"Well, the old man took them and I didn't bother replacing them after that. These jeans have been rubbing me all day. I'm so horny I could spit."

"The phrase is 'I'm so angry I could spit,'"

"Whatever," Ella said. "Let's get this spanking over with then I can give you one." The girls giggled as Ella bent over Mary's lap.

Back in the dining room of Christie house Charles, Sarah and Amelia were just finishing the delightful meal Cook had prepared for them. Cook was going to spend Easter with her sister so this would be the last meal she cooks in the school kitchen for a couple of weeks. "So what happens here at Easter, Amelia," Charles said.

"Nothing much," Amelia said. "There are only two girls staying over for the hols and I'm off to visit my uncle in Bournemouth, so it will be just the four of you and you will have to cook for yourselves."

"I didn't realise that we would be on our own," Charles said. "Sarah and I were talking about going to London for a few days, but we can't, if there are girls here to look after."

"Is that unusual?" Sarah asked.

"Oh yes, usually we have a few more girls who stay for such a short holiday and a couple of teachers as well, but not this year."

Charles saw an opportunity to start the fun he had planned for the evening. "Well I think it was very naughty of you not to tell us, I'll have to change our plans, you will be getting a spanking for that Amelia."

"Well, I knew Charles," Sarah said.

"In that case, you will be getting a spanking as well. Stand up both of you, I'll be spanking Amelia first."

Charles pushed his chair back and pulled Amelia across his lap. She gasped as he lifted her flowered dress and he then laughed. She had taken Ella's knickers off the notice board in the staff room and was wearing them over her thin lace knickers. "What's this?" Charles said.

"Well I thought I couldn't leave them on the notice board all the holiday and I didn't know where else to put them." All three of them were laughing now and that spoiled the illusion just a little.

Trying to take back control Charles pulled the offending knickers down and then the lace ones as well before he started spanking Amelia's bottom. He wasn't spanking hard as he had other plans for Amelia's bottom later that evening, but he did bring up a pair of rosy cheeks as he stopped spanking her and massaged her bottom. "Let that be a lesson to you," he said as he patted her bottom as an indication that she should stand up. "Go and stand facing that wall Amelia while I deal with Sarah."

Sarah was quick to respond. "Why am I getting spanked, just because you don't read the memos. Anyway, I still have the marks from the spanking this morning."

"You got a spanking this morning?" Amelia said. "That's not fair Charles."

"Not to worry Amelia, there will be plenty of spanking later, I just have to spank my wife for arguing."

"I'm being spanked for arguing now am I? I thought I was being spanked for knowing something that you didn't know."

"That as well. Now get across my knee."

Sarah stretched across Charles's knee and when he pulled up her dress he laughed again. Sarah also had a pair of knickers on that said 'Spank Me'. "I certainly will," Charles said and he spanked Sarah much harder than Amelia on her knickers and then he pulled them down and spanked her on her bare bottom. When he had finished he told Sarah to stand next to Amelia with her bottom on display.

The girls were giggling and jostling each other when Charles came up behind them. I just want to take a picture of your bottoms but Amelia's bottom is not as red as Sarah's and that will look like favouritism in the picture and we can't have that can we."

"Oh no Sir," Sarah said. "We can't have that can we, Amelia?"

"Can't we?" Amelia said but then she felt Charles's leather slipper landing on her bottom. "Hey, that's sore," she said.

Charles stood back. "Just a little more," he said, and he gave her two more on each cheek. "Yes that's it, perfect," and then they both heard the click/buzz of the instant camera.

"I hope this one isn't going on the staff notice board like Ella's knickers," Amelia said.

"Of course not, it will be destroyed just like the others," Charles lied. "Now, get into the bedroom and strip, both of you, I have a new leather strap I want to try."

Running into the bedroom they continued to jostle each other and then they went quiet. Charles spent ten minutes checking all the windows and locking the doors and when he arrived in the bedroom he found them both naked and in each other's arms kissing passionately. For the second time in a day, Charles thought how lucky he was.

Two floors above them, Ella and Mary both had glowing bottoms as they kissed each other passionately. They were less experienced than the two ladies on the ground floor and they were still dressed from the waist up, although they had removed their jeans and knickers to spank each other.

"It's a bit chilly to be out of bed Mary," Ella said. "Let's get under the covers."

"Okay, Arms up," Mary said as she pulled Ella's jumper over her head.

"Leave my bra on Mary," Ella said. "My boobs are too large."

"Don't be silly Ella," Mary said as she reached behind her friend and unclipped her bra. "You have lovely boobs, and I've wanted to suck your nipples all term."

"Well okay, but only if I can do the same to you."

Very soon both girls were naked and under the covers, exploring each other's bodies.

So, at the same time in Christie house, we had the Matron and the headmistress on the ground floor and two of the students on the second floor and both couples orgasmed together, although neither of them would ever know.

The following morning Sarah walked into dormitory room seven, and found Ella and Mary in the same bed. "Morning girls," she said, making no comment about them sleeping together and throwing open the curtains. "I'm doing breakfast in the kitchen downstairs, so come to our dining room at seven-thirty and then we will discuss what we're going to be doing for the next couple of weeks."

When they got downstairs, Amelia and Charles were eating toast and Sarah walked into the dining room wearing an apron and carrying a plate of bacon and eggs. "Morning girls," Amelia said. "Did you sleep well?"

"Yes Mrs Brandon," the girls said in unison and then started to giggle.

"I'm pleased to hear it," Amelia said. "I'll be away from today so there will be just Mr Nicholas and Matron here with you two."

"Oh goodie," Mary said. "Like Mum and Dad with two children."

They all laughed. "Not exactly," Charles said. "More like Hansel and Gretel, and we will be locking you away in the dorm, while Matron and I have some fun.

"Oh, pass me the breadcrumbs," Mary said and they all laughed.

"Will we still get spanked?" Ella said.

"Of course not Ella," Charles said. "There will be no spanking at all for the entire holiday." Charles took a breath. "Unless you're naughty of course."

"Oh right," Mary said. "And who decides if we're naughty or not?"

"Who do you think, Mary?" Sarah said, glancing at her husband. "But we have a plan that you might like. Mr Nicholas and I were planning to go to London for a week to attend The Easter Music Festival at the Lyceum, would you like to come with us?"

"Would we?" Mary was very excited. "It would be fantastic."

"I've looked and I can rent a flat close to there but we will have to be a family, they don't want two teachers and two students, so Mary, you're right, it will be like Mum and Dad with two girls, and I hope they won't be naughty girls."

"No Dad," Mary said giggling.

"Not yet, Charles said.

Chapter 23 - Spanked before they left for London

"We have to go back," Sarah said half an hour after they left Saint Samantha's school on the drive to London.

"What? Don't be silly we are halfway to Ipswich. Whatever it is, we can get another one in London."

"No Charles, I have forgotten the present for Tracy, we have to go back."

Charles was angry. It had already been a difficult morning trying to get Ella and Mary to pack the clothes they would need for a week in London, and then making sure Charles's Range Rover was loaded properly. Charles was dressed in his jeans and blue checked shirt as usual for the holidays but the girls didn't know what to wear. Mary and Ella had come to breakfast nicely dressed in a skirt and blouse but when they saw Mr Nicholas dressed more casually they both changed into jeans. Sarah had on a nice flowered dress but it was cold so they were all wearing coats while they were packing the car.

"If I have to turn round the car now and go back to the school, it will add another hour to the journey, and you will be sitting on a sore bottom," Charles said to Sarah but the girls in the back seat were giggling. "And that applies to you two in the back as well if you don't stop giggling."

"But we haven't done anything Mr Nicholas," Ella said, but Mary was still giggling.

"I am sorry Charles, but I can't meet Tracy without the present I bought for her in South Africa, so we have to go back."

"Well, don't say I didn't warn you," Charles said as he pulled into a layby just outside Ipswich and turned the car around. It was thirty minutes later when Charles pulled his car into the drive of the school only to be met by the headmistress. "What are you doing back so soon?" Amelia asked.

"I forgot something," Sarah said as she got out of the car and hurried to Christie House where the housemaster's flat was situated on the ground floor.

Charles got out of the driver's side of the car and smiled at Amelia. She was standing there with her suitcase and obviously waiting for her taxi to take her to the station. "I thought you would have gone by now," Charles said, making conversation.

"No, the train isn't until later," Amelia said as she heard another car drive up. "That will be my Taxi now," she said. "Bye Charles, have a good time." Standing on her tiptoes she kissed Charles on his lips and he spanked her bottom.

"Not in front of the girls, Amelia, I have already told you," Charles said.

"Oh come on, they have both seen you spank me naked during the last holiday, and I don't think they told anybody."

"No, they are good girls, and I expect we will have to have the same rules for this holiday as well, or there will be lots of sore bottoms," Charles said, but he knew the window was open just a little so Ella and Mary would have heard him.

Amelia laughed and got into the taxi which drove off, but Charles was wondering where Sarah was. "I am going to get Matron, you two stay in the car."

"Yes Sir," Mary said.

In the housemaster's flat Sarah was hunting around for the present she had wrapped for her old school friend Tracy. She hadn't seen Tracy for the last ten years and she was looking forward to seeing her while they were in London. "What are you doing Sarah?"

Charles said as he stormed into the lounge. "I thought you knew exactly where it was."

"I think I do now, Charles," Sarah said. "I remembered packing it into my suitcase, so it is in the back of the car."

"You mean you made me drive for an extra hour to find something that we already have in the car?"

"Yes, Charles." Sarah looked down at her feet, she knew what would happen next.

"Right," Charles said as he picked up the wooden paddle that was on his desk. "I didn't think we would need this on Holiday but it seems I was wrong." He put his foot on one of the guest chairs and pulled his wife over his knee.

"Not that wooden paddle please Charles, I have to sit on my bottom all the way to London," Sarah said.

"You should have thought of that," Charles said as he flipped up Sarah's dress to display her pale pink satin knickers. Charles loved these knickers and Sarah was obviously wearing them to make him happy, but he was not at all happy so he pulled them down to display her bare bottom, and then he spanked her with the wooden paddle. The paddle was about fifteen inches long and five inches wide with a short handle carved from one piece of wood. It also had holes drilled in the business end to reduce wind resistance, which was very thoughtful of the maker, although Sarah didn't think so at the time of her spanking.

Sarah knew Charles was angry because he spanked her harder than he usually would with the paddle and she knew it would be sore all afternoon. After the regulation six spanks Sarah had tears in her eyes as Charles sent her back to the car.

When they got back to the car Charles still had the paddle in his hand as he noticed that the girls were missing. "Where the hell are they now?"

"It is coming up to lunchtime now so I guess Mary has taken her friend to the bicycle sheds."

"They will regret it if that's where they are," Charles said and he stormed off to the sheds at the back of the school. Mary Becker was the first girl that Charles had spanked at the school.

When Charles approached the bicycle sheds he could smell cigarette smoke and knew exactly what was happening so he called to the girls to come out. Mary and Ella came out looking guilty and then they noticed that Charles had the wooden paddle in his hand. "No need for excuses girls. I know what you have been up to and you know that I know. Jeans down and bend over together so that I can warm your bottoms and then we can get on with the trip."

"But Sir?" Ella said. "I don't smoke."

"No Ella, but you did get out of the car when I specifically told you to stay where you are."

Ella realised that there was no getting out of a spanking so she pushed her jeans and knickers down and bent over holding her knees right next to her friend. Charles looked at the two lovely bottoms for a few seconds before he raised the wooden paddle. He just loved spanking bottoms and while both Ella and Mary had large bottoms, they were still a delight to spank. They each got six spanks with the wooden paddle and then struggled to pull up their knickers over their sore bottoms.

"Right come on girls, let's get going."Charles hurried them along. "We are meant to be on holiday having fun."

"Yeah, right," Mary said, rubbing her sore bottom all the way to the car.

Driving away Charles was humming to himself remembering the pleasure of spanking three bottoms before the holiday had started. The others in the car were, not surprisingly, rather quiet.

Chapter 24 - A day out in London

They arrived at the address Charles was given at about four thirty in the afternoon. "Don't forget girls, we are meant to be a family. The owner didn't want to let the flat to just anybody." Charles said as they pulled into the parking space.

"Yes Daddy," the girls said in unison and then giggled.

Charles had planned to be there earlier but the caretaker of the studio flat in St John's Wood just off Finchley road was very understanding. "Mr and Mrs Nicholas, nice to meet you." The caretaker said as they got out of the lift. "Mrs Trent said that I had to look after you so let me show you around."

"It's not a large flat as you can see but big enough for you and your children for a week I'm sure." The man showed Charles into the main lounge with the kitchen off to one side and a bathroom on the other. "The master bedroom is over there," the man said, pointing to another room. "And the settee converts to a double bed for the girls."

"This is lovely," Sarah said looking out of the window. "You can see the cricket ground from here"

"Yes, but the cricket season hasn't started yet I'm afraid."

"This will do very nicely, thank you," Charles said. "What do you think girls?"

"It's very nice Daddy," Mary said and Ella giggled.

Later that evening they were all sitting on the settee watching the TV after finishing four large Pizzas. The settee was wide enough for all of them to sit comfortably. It had been a long day so Mary and Ella were already in their pyjamas feeling very relaxed. Charles and Sarah were sitting in the middle with Mary on one side and Ella on the other. They were all cuddled up and Charles was thinking that this was just like having the family that he and Sarah could never have. He liked it. He had his arm around Mary as their program finished and he patted her bottom. Come on girls, time for bed. Sarah, Mary and Ella all knew he was talking to them and there was no argument as they all stretched and clambered off the settee so that Charles could pull it out to make a bed. Surprisingly it was very easy and as Charles and Sarah went to their own room, Charles switched off the light and said, "goodnight girls."

"Goodnight Daddy," they both said and giggled again.

Over breakfast the following morning Charles was making plans. "What do you want to do today? We could go to the Tower of London, Madame Tussauds, Hamleys, or Buckingham Palace.

"What will we do in the afternoon?" Mary said.

"No Silly, I mean we can choose where you want to go. The music festival is tomorrow but today we have a choice."

"I want to go to The Tower," Ella said.

"With a bit of luck, they will lock you up," Mary responded and then Ella punched her.

"That's enough girls, or you'll both be locked up in your room," Sarah said.

"We haven't got a room," Mary pointed out.

"I would like to see the Tower," Charles said. "Let's go there this morning and then we can see after we have had some lunch.

The two girls were well-behaved as they walked around the tower of London. They loved the crown jewels display and Ella said she wanted to be a Beefeater. "Why are they called Beefeaters?" Ella asked.

"I thought you might ask that so I looked it up. Apparently, they were the king's guards for Henry the seventh in fourteen hundred and something, and they were allowed to eat the beef from the king's table."

"Did they get the Yorkshire pudding and horseradish sauce as well?" Mary asked and the girls giggled.

"I don't know why I bother," Charles said to Sarah but it was all in good fun.

They bought some sandwiches and fizzy drinks and then took a taxi to St James's park where they sat and ate their lunch. "Right girls," Charles said. "We can walk from here to Buckingham Palace and say hello to the Queen, then we can get a taxi to Hamleys if you like.

"Hamleys?" Mary said. "Oh yes, please."

The girls were not really interested in the Palace, and it was a longer walk than Charles had expected, so they were all pleased to be sitting in a taxi on their way to Hamleys. Charles and Sarah already had a private word about Hamleys. Charles wanted to keep them close, but Sarah said that they were both eighteen so they can be trusted on their own. "Well alright," Charles said. "But if they get into trouble I'll be spanking three bottoms tonight."

"Okay," Sarah said nervously.

"Okay Girls, here's the deal," Charles said as the taxi drove down Regent's Street towards Hamleys. "Matorn thinks you will be alright on your own, so you will each get five pounds to buy something for yourselves while we're away." He gave them each a five-pound note.

"Oh goodie," Mary said. "Thank you, Mr Nicholas."

"But the deal is that you're good in there and no running around. You're old enough now. And if there is any trouble I'll be spanking three bottoms tonight."

"Yes Daddy," Ella said but she was itching to get out of the taxi and run into Hamleys.

"Okay, it's a big store so we will meet you back at this entrance in say... two hours," Charles said as he was paying the taxi, but the girls were off.

After twenty minutes in Hamleys Charles and Sarah had enough so they went to sit in the cafe along the road and wait for the girls. At four thirty they were waiting outside Hamleys but the girls weren't there. At five the security guards were locking up but the girls were still not there. Charles had gone into the shop to find them but they were nowhere to be seen. "Is there still anybody in the shop?" Sarah asked the security man.

"No love," he said. "Well, there may be a few on the top floor, we will be clearing them all out now."

At five-twenty. The doors were locked and the staff started to stream out of the side entrance. Charles didn't know what to do. At five-thirty, the security man that Sarah had spoken to opened the side entrance again and walked out holding Mary and Ella by the ear. "Are these the two you're looking for?"

Charles was so angry by now that he couldn't talk. "Where have you been?" Sarah said. "We have been waiting here an hour, and we're tired and thirsty."

"I'm sorry Matron," Mary said. "We just forgot to look at our watches. And then we got stuck and..."

"Come on," Charles said as he was waving for a taxi. "We will hear all the excuses after you've had your bottoms spanked at home."

The taxi ride back to St John's Wood was very quiet. They had all had a busy day but Charles was angry and the girls were disappointed to have let the grown-ups down. Mary and Ella were whispering to each other in the taxi and when they got back to the apartment, Mary said. "We are very sorry to have let you down Mr Nicholas, and we know we will be getting a spanking before bed, but can we make up for it by cooking dinner?"

Charles looked at Sarah and she seemed to think it was a good idea. So he said. "Okay, there are steaks in the fridge and salad. There are some rolls as well so that will be simple."

"Thank you, Daddy," Mary said as they went to the kitchen giggling.

"I wonder how long that will remain funny?" Sarah said to Charles, but he just shrugged.

Dinner was surprisingly good. The steaks were just a little overdone for Charle's liking but they were very tender and the salad and crisp rolls they had purchased on the way home were fresh and tasty. After dinner was cleared away by the girls, Sarah and Charles were sitting on the settee

"Right Girls." Charles said at nine o'clock. "Spanking and then bed, go and get ready, you might as well do the same Sarah.

"But Daddy, can't we watch the next program?"

Charles moved a dining chair into the centre of the room and sat down. That was a sure sign that there would be no more discussion. Sarah went to the bedroom to get ready for bed, but Mary and Ella had nowhere to go so they just undressed in the lounge where Charles was sitting. He had seen them both naked many times before, and it didn't bother them. After taking it in turns in the bathroom, Mary, Ella and Sarah were sitting on the settee together when Charles came out of the bedroom wearing a dressing gown with his pyjamas underneath. Everybody was quiet.

"You first Mary," Charles said as he sat on the dining chair. "Take off your pyjamas and get over my knee.

"Yes, Daddy, I'm sorry." Mary said. She had called Charles, Daddy so often now, it just seemed to stick.

"Yes, you will be," Charles said as he pulled her naked body over his lap and started to spank her hard. Charles was really enjoying spanking Mary's large bottom and he probably spanked her harder than she deserved, but he wanted them all to know that he was angry with their behaviour.

Mary was crying when Charles finished spanking her bottom and he rested his hand on her large bottom. "What do you have to say for yourself?" Charles said.

"I'm really sorry Daddy." she said. "I'll try to be good for the rest of the trip."

"You see you're my girl or it will be the cane." Charles said as he helped the crying girl to her feet. "Your next Ella, get those pyjamas off."

"Do I have to take my top off Mr Nicholas?" Ella asked.

"Oh I think so Ella, You have a lovely body and I'm looking forward to spanking you naked."

"Yes Sir," Ella said as she pushed down her pyjamas and knickers and then turned to take off her top. Turning back she held her hands over her big boobs and walked towards Charles.

"Over you go Ella." Charles said, and as she reached for the floor her large boobs fell free.

"I'm sorry Mr Nicholas, my boobs are very big." Ella said.

Charles spanked her hard just once. "Never, never apologise about the size of your boobs Ella. They are really lovely and you should be proud of them. If I hear you say anything like that again it will be the cane for you every day for a month."

"Really?" Ella looked back at Charles from her position over his lap. "Do you mean you like my huge boobs?"

"Of course I like them, and so will every boy you meet when you leave school."

"Thank you Daddy," Ella said. "Can I have my spanking now? I know I deserve it."

"Certainly," Charles said and started to spank Ella's large bottom. As he was spanking her Charles felt his erection pushing at his pyjamas and he realised that it was probably a mistake to change before the spanking started. He spanked Ella hard just like Mary and she was crying as he held her bottom. "And what do you have to say for yourself?" he asked.

Ella was wriggling around on Charles's lap when she said, "I'm sorry Daddy, for making you wait. But I love you for being nice about my boobs." When she got off his lap she kissed him on his cheek and ran to the settee to sit with the others.

"One more bottom to spank I think," Charles said looking at his wife.

"Not in front of the children Charles please." Sarah said but he just looked at her and she knew what that meant. Standing up, Sarah pulled her nightie over her head and didn't cover herself. She wanted Ella to know that she was proud of her body even if her boobs were a little larger than they used to be and she had put on more weight than she wanted over the last few years. Bending to slip down her knickers, her boobs wobbled delightfully, and the other three could see that her nipples were erect.

Charles guided his wife over his lap and started to spank her straight away. All three of the girls knew that Charles was spanking Sarah harder and for longer than he had spanked Ella and Mary, and she had tears running down her face when she got up, although she was not actually crying.

"Right Girls," Charles said. "I'm sure you can manage the bed on your own by now." Then he held Sarah back as they both watched two naked eighteen year olds bending over to pull out the bed. It was a glorious site and luckily Charles had his polaroid camera to record the activity.

Later Sarah was lying next to her husband. "It was a wonderful day, Charles." Sarah said. "I loved every minute of it, especially watching you spank the girls, and then spank me in front of them. I'm horny as hell now, please make love to me."

At the same time Mary and Ella were lying in bed naked playing with each other's nipples. "Did you hear what Daddy said about me, Mary?" Ella said. "He said I have lovely boobs. Do you think he is in love with me?"

"Don't be silly Ella. He was just being nice."

"You don't know, I felt his erection poking at my tummy when he spanked me. That must mean that he is in love with me."

"I don't think so Ella," Mary said. "I felt it too." but Mary was lying.

There were no more spankings on the trip and they all arrived back at the school looking forward to the following term, but Ella was still desperately in love with the only Housemaster at St Samantha's school for girls.

The End

By

Paula Mann

paula@spankingbooks.com

xxx

Ask Paula to write a personal book for you

We're now taking on commissions. If you've got a particular book in mind, let me know, and I'll consider writing it for you. There are certain advantages to having a book written especially for you:

1. I'll not be restricted by Amazon's rules with regards to ages, activities, content, or book covers.

2. I can include the names of people you would like me to write about.

3. I can even use your descriptions of the people in the book and the places where the action happens to make it more personal.

4. Mann Publishing will still own the copyright, so you will not be able to republish the book in any format.

If I write a book for you, it will be in my usual format of about 10,000 words, but I could make it shorter or longer; that would be up to you. It could go on to be a series of books, if you like.

Your investment for a 10,000 word book is US$100.

Just email me with the details of the book you want me to write, and I'll let you know. paula@spankingbooks.com

Subscribe to our website to get a free spanking book every month, along with free chapters from our new books. https://www.spankingbooks.com/

Don't miss out!

Visit the website below and you can sign up to receive emails whenever Paula Mann publishes a new book. There's no charge and no obligation.

https://books2read.com/r/B-A-RWZY-TYORC

BOOKS 2 READ

Connecting independent readers to independent writers.

Also by Paula Mann

Spanked in the Office - The Complete Story
Spanking the Babysitter
Spanking the Girls School Sports Teams
Secret Santa - Spanking Dreams
A housemaster in a Girls' School

Watch for more at https://www.spankingbooks.com/.

About the Author

Paula Mann is a young sixty-year-old and is always looking for interesting subjects to write about. She has been writing business books for over thirty years and now exclusively writes erotic romance novels, just for fun. "Business books are boring," she says and then giggles. "I like to write for both men and women, variety is the spice of my life."

Paula is unattached and likes it that way, leaving plenty of time to write and play online.

Read more at https://www.spankingbooks.com/.

www.ingramcontent.com/pod-product-compliance
Ingram Content Group UK Ltd.
Pitfield, Milton Keynes, MK11 3LW, UK
UKHW040619190225
4658UKWH00012B/99